Louis could barely ⟨…⟩ **I see this crown and** ⟨…⟩ **for the evening? Meet your princess cousin, as it were?"**

Hussam nodded and the servant withdrew the sheet on the life-size canvas.

Louis nearly gasped, but not because of the magnificent jewel set upon a crown on top of her head. It was because hers was the same beautiful face he'd been sketching for weeks. The wide-set eyes. The dark auburn curls. The heart-shaped face.

The one Louis hadn't stopped thinking about.

Princess Mervat was the young lady he'd met at the Louvre!

Author Note

Mervat and Louis's is a love story, but it is one inspired by the contention around cultural artifacts. Who decides what is or is not worthy of being categorized as one? How has this decision-making process historically marginalized certain populations, rendering them as "uncultured"? This is a novel with a lush palace setting, but Mervat is a conscientious princess who deeply feels the disparity between classes. She wants to open a museum so all will have access to the artifacts only held at court (like the fictional Cleopatra Cerulean!), but she is also a mild-mannered woman, awkward. Until Louis, she is a lonely one, too, friendless in her mission. It seems to me that the stories of such people, those "behind the curtains" of cultural endeavors, are rarely told. In researching the novel, I was surprised to learn that Verdi's *Aida* was commissioned by an Egyptian khedive and first performed in Cairo—but Verdi himself didn't consider that as the opera's debut, giving that distinction to its European production in Milan months later. Having Mervat be there was exciting because it allowed me to suggest that the genealogical explorations of which she is so passionate are exercises that can, even today, inspire us to reflect on the complexities, appropriations and sometimes downright misinterpretations of artifacts. If we can better understand and are aware of their origins, we can tell stories about them in ways that might, even a little, reclaim them for people who were previously (and unjustly) considered uncultured.

A Viscount for the Egyptian Princess

HEBA HELMY

HARLEQUIN
HISTORICAL

HARLEQUIN®
HISTORICAL™

Recycling programs for this product may not exist in your area.

ISBN-13: 978-1-335-59615-4

A Viscount for the Egyptian Princess

Harlequin Enterprises ULC
22 Adelaide St. West, 41st Floor
Toronto, Ontario M5H 4E3, Canada
www.Harlequin.com

Printed in U.S.A.

Egyptian born and Canadian raised, **Heba Helmy** holds an MA in English literature and a PhD in language and literacies (both from the University of Toronto). She is a former high school teacher and current part-time university professor. Her academic practice focuses on culturally sustaining narratives— and her creative one is all about storytelling that centers love. She lives far too much in her own head, but you might find her online at hebahelmy.com.

Books by Heba Helmy

Harlequin Historical

The Earl's Egyptian Heiress

Look out for more books from Heba Helmy coming soon.

Visit the Author Profile page at Harlequin.com.

For M and A,
the finest daughters a mother could have

Prologue

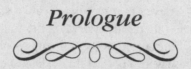

The Louvre,
April 1873

Mervat Abbas told herself that one did not come to the grandest museum in the whole of Europe—after a very covert operation to escape the not very watchful eye of her mother—to listen to a talk about antiquities found in one's home country. Yet, she found her feet, in the simple slippers she'd brought from Egypt and smartly hidden beneath the ruffles of the only non–haute couture dress acquired for her during this trip, doing just that...following the viscount who'd told her of the event only moments ago.

Mervat had been standing before *Psyche Revived by Cupid's Kiss*, notebook in hand, when said viscount had sidled next to her. She'd been solemnly transcribing details of the sculpture in her accumulated pastiche of languages—the Arabic of her father, the Turkish of her mother, the English and French of her tutoring—when the scent of his cologne wafted over her.

Her body stilled like an unsure rabbit realising it was not alone. Then, frustrated with her own timidity, Mervat closed her eyes to draw a steely breath. What if her *anne* had woken from her nap to notice her daughter missing and sent one of their guards to find her?

She swivelled, slowly opening her eyes.

A foreigner.

The deep-set eyes that met hers were a startling blue. They were richer than Nile waters on the sunniest day, his golden lashes failing to dim them in any absolute way. But his brows—those were a perfect frame, long and just the right thickness. They were a golden brown, a shade darker than his wavy blond hair and his sparse moustache and beard. Tall and thin but with broad shoulders, he was dressed casually in dark chequered trousers and a simple but well-tailored white chemise.

He was, quite possibly, the handsomest man Mervat had ever seen.

'Mademoiselle is a writer.' He spoke in French, looking down on her with a smile that was, Mervat decided by the visceral flutter in her chest, a most charming one. He waved the notebook in his hand. *'Moi aussi.'*

A formal note in his tone alerted her to the fact he might not be French, and since it was not the language she was most comfortable in, she chanced to answer him in English. 'Not a writer, I am afraid. I am more of a stenographer, not in any formal capacity, only in that it satisfies my interests in the genealogy of museum artifacts.'

He nodded knowingly, but then frowned sheepishly. Meeting her English, he said, 'I haven't a notion as to what that might entail.'

Mervat explained, 'I like to discover the layers of an item's history. Puzzle it out. Hold it up to the light and look at it from all its angles so it tells me its secrets. I trace an artifact's life backward, how it has been perceived in the past and how it came to be where it is now. Then, I try and consider what knowledge it can gift to people for the future.'

Mervat didn't need much encouragement when it came to talking about her passion and perceived the interested look on the Englishman's face as her cue to continue. 'Take, for instance, this very sculpture. Depending on one's ideology, *Psyche Revived by Cupid's Kiss* is either about the perils of a woman's curiosity or how a great love can conquer the darkest of times. Yet, there is much more to this piece! It was completed by the Italian Antonio Canova, a man who started working with marble at the age of ten. Though his father had died when his mother remarried, he was raised by his paternal grandfather, a stonemason who taught him the trade. Under the tutelage and mentorship of other greats, Antonio attended the finest art academy in Venice and won accolades that would lead him to Rome. Beyond Florence, those two cities were central to the Renaissance period. This piece was first commissioned by a Welsh baron, one John Campbell, in 1787. But—' here, Mervat held up a finger '—he never received it.'

'No?'

'Baron Campbell was a proud collector with fine aristocratic tastes, but he often spent more than his allowance permitted. Perhaps because he could not pay, the baron gave too much leeway with regard to a deadline for the finishing of the sculpture. There *are* letters from Antonio to the baron, ones laden with excuses and apologies for the delay despite his gratitude for the patronage. Nevertheless, when it was finally completed, Antonio sold it to Joachim Murat, the brother-in-law of Napoleon himself rather than give it to the baron. Why? If I had to guess, it was the treacherous political games which are wont to happen in royal courts that turned Antonio Canova into a traitor to a man his letters prove that he admired.

'Then, of course, if we consider that the sculpture emerges from the mythology around Cupid, the Roman god of love and desire...'

Mervat bit her lip. She could talk incessantly of her interests with anybody willing to listen—and any who would listen *were* rare—but Cupid was naked before them, his hand cupped to Psyche's breast. To prattle on about an emotional moment between lovers to a complete stranger of the opposite sex would be in poor taste.

Yet, for his part, the stranger didn't seem to notice.

'Brilliant! Where does it say all this?' He circled the sculpture, but she knew he would only find a small plaque with the sculptor's name and the date on which *Psyche Revived by Cupid's Kiss* had come into the Louvre's possession.

'It is from my research. Hence, the *genealogy* of artifacts.' Mervat spread her hands wide as if she could gather it all in her arms: the history of the Louvre palace as a whole and this room in which they stood. This was the Salle des Cariatides, with four sombre statues of the caryatids holding up the musician's gallery like women forced into hard labour then turned to stone only to be gazed upon or ignored by gawkers. 'I came here to observe a few pieces in the flesh which I had already studied in the pages of books. This is one of those pieces.'

He tossed her a quizzical look and lightly teased, 'No *Mona Lisa* for you?'

Mervat smiled through the thumping in her belly, as if the startled rabbit she'd felt like before now happily hopped there, unencumbered. She managed to toss back, 'There is a bit *too* much mystery around her for my tastes. Is that unreadable gaze of hers a smile or a frown?'

The man chuckled in an easy manner, making it seem like they were more friends than strangers who had met only moments ago.

'Would it be terrible for me to admit,' he questioned with a slight grimace, 'that I only happened here on chance? Lost on my way to the Egyptian Pavilion, I saw a lone lady so clearly in awe I had to see for myself what captured her ardent attention. My grandfather taught me never to let an opportunity pass one by.'

'Lucky you then. I would have been in the library, but it has not reopened since the fire of 1871.'

'Are you at the Louvre alone then, Miss…?'

Mervat stepped back, her senses finally registering what a 'stranger' could entail in a shadowy, lone corner. *Without* the guards assigned them from the embassy.

But he, immediately sensing his faux pas, held up a hand. 'Please do not feel obliged to share your name. It is only that I have been in Paris for weeks and have yet to cross an English lady. If your chaperone is near or an…um, *husband*, then I should very much be inclined to introduce myself.'

He bowed graciously, a gesture overflowing with charm. 'Louis Wesley, Viscount of Allenborough, at your service.'

A gentleman, then.

Mervat's cousin had spent his school days at Eton, said the friends he made there were good fun, a mostly honourable sort. Still, she could not disclose to the viscount her name or title for it might get back to her mother and those tasked with protecting the Egyptian royal family outside of the country. Besides, if her brown eyes and olive skin were not indicative of the fact that she was not an English lady, then she saw no reason to correct him.

'It is a pleasure to meet you, Lord Wesley,' she said, surprised at how much she meant it. Mervat didn't have many friends and she couldn't think of any who would genuinely listen to her as he had just done. 'I am in France on a shopping trip with my mother who, alas, would rather attend to fashion houses than entertain my…interests.'

That, at least, was the truth. She wouldn't tell him her *anne* had spent most of Mervat's twenty years ignoring her daughter for court intrigues or that while she had hoped this excursion to Paris would be a way to make up for lost time, she now believed her mother had an ulterior motive for suggesting it in the first place. A motive which Mervat had yet to deduce.

She pointed to the notebook in his hand. 'You haven't told me what you write in yours.'

He folded his arm behind his back, almost shyly. 'Nothing as detailed or smart as yours. Scribblings of what I see, hear, smell. Sketches sometimes. A collection of my memories, as they happen.'

He stopped abruptly, as if embarrassed to share too much despite it being only a little and especially considering how long Mervat had spoken about the sculpture.

He cleared his throat before speaking again. 'Which reminds me that I have come to the Louvre to attend a talk by the famed Orientalist Mr Richard Henries. He will speak about his time in the Middle East, and in keeping with the mystery around the *Mona Lisa*, he will speak of a jewel or crown or some such thing he's recently come to be aware of. It is called the Cleopatra Cerulean. Have you heard of it?'

Mervat pictured the crown in her mother's rooms back home. She'd never thought to trace the rare jewel at its centre, the one she herself would inherit on her own wedding day.

Rather than lie, she lowered her gaze demurely. 'I should like to learn more about it.'

'I am certain even a famed Orientalist cannot provide

genealogies to meet your standards, but you are most welcome to join me.'

Lord Wesley spoke unironically, as if he were truly impressed by her and she felt a surge of warmth, a confidence she'd rarely had occasion to feel.

And that was how Mervat Abbas first found herself following and then sitting next to a handsome viscount she was certain to never see again, listening in on a talk about an antiquity she definitely knew to be located in her home country.

Chapter One

May 1873,
Cairo

Louis

The Nile riverboat quivered beneath Viscount Louis Wesley as he disembarked onto the harbour deck. He relished the scene before him, revelling in the moment, beholding the particulars so he might recall and make note of them later.

Dusk. In the wide burnished apricot sky, the sun bowed low. Pillars from mosques or castles, some stately and latticed, others domed and lustrous, rose high and were blanketed in its glow. Everywhere, palm trees swayed gently, their immense leaves like floating keys of a pianoforte. And there, in the far distance, three otherworldly triangles.

'The pyramids,' Louis heaved.

'Lord Wesley, *marhaba*! Welcome to Egypt.' Louis had been addressed by a fellow, one of three who marched towards him. They wore maroon suits, matching fez hats and the brightest of white gloves. They moved as if they'd been plucked from a royal parade but, as the one who had spoken explained, they were servants from the khedive's palace. 'Prince Hussam eagerly awaits your arrival.'

Louis hadn't expected his old friend to show such care, when, as far as he knew, he was the only one of their mates from Eton to accept Hussam's invitation. Everyone had mostly gone their separate ways after they had left school seven years ago.

The prince's letter mentioned that his father had built a new royal palace, Sesostris, and was looking to inaugurate it with a marriage ceremony. Hussam's.

There should be a wedding before summer's end.

Although his friend hadn't sounded absolutely sure in his letter, Louis had done his own research and knew that Hussam's father, the khedive of Egypt, hoped to bring his country into the modern era and what better way than with an occasion witnessed by other royal dignitaries from across Europe? The khedive was eager Egypt should separate itself from the Ottoman Empire which had long regulated political powers here. With the Turks gone, the chasm of influence left in their wake would be fought over by the French and English.

Louis could potentially secure a diplomatic position with the latter. Why shouldn't he be an ideal candidate for the British Embassy in Cairo? He was, after all, a nobleman *and* friends with the prince.

What most people wouldn't know was that he was also a twenty-seven-year-old man with few career prospects and only a meagre allowance from the Allenborough estate. And although his father was also doing his best to modernise, looking into purchasing new farming equipment and attracting tenants with more forward-thinking ideas, one seemed to need money to make money.

Plus, his younger half siblings had needs. Futures they had to be set up for. Louis could not afford to spend the summer visiting Egypt and waiting for a wedding to happen, *but* he had determined to turn this visit into a permanent, well-paying post, and he was hoping Hussam would help him in this endeavour.

'I am most eager to see him, as well.'

Louis watched the khedive's servants transport his luggage from the riverboat and hoist it onto a hidden compartment atop the handsomest of carriages, led by two beautiful black stallions.

'Is that all, sir?'

''Tis.' The chest and two suitcases were in fact all Louis had had with him in Paris when the letter from Hussam had arrived. As he'd read it, he could almost hear the ghost of his grandfather encouraging him to Egypt post-haste.

It may be a chance to make something of yourself, Louis! A boon for our family name beyond the symbolism in the title, a fortune to help your father, and for your brothers a model of enterprise.

It *had* arrived at an interesting time. Louis had come from the Louvre talk on hitherto undiscovered jewels like Cleopatra's Cerulean, which had stirred his imagination enough, but, paradoxically, also given him a reason to *not* want to leave Paris so soon. He hadn't discovered the name of the captivating young woman he'd met at the *Psyche Revived by Cupid's Kiss* sculpture—she'd rushed off as soon as Mr Henries's talk concluded—but he had returned each day until his ship sailed, hoping to see her again. Learn more about her. But alas, it was not to be.

Louis should have forgotten about her. She shouldn't have materialised in his mind so often since that fateful day. Her hair, dark auburn curls piled high but loose on her head, so as not to get in the way of her intelligent brow. Her slightly hooded eyes were set far apart, her lips an ashy rose against the olive hue of her tan, her chin, a dainty thing. Hers was a face in the shape of a heart—and it had stolen into his in the most alarmingly sudden of ways.

Louis had sketched the mystery woman—even nicknaming her 'a *Mona Lisa*' in his notebook—described her features and the wonder he'd felt when she spoke, how it had lingered with him. How he wished she wouldn't have stopped talking about the genealogy of the sculpture. How he would have liked to hear her ideas about anything and everything she had ever studied. A museum guide like no other.

He heaved a frustrated sigh. It had been weeks and miles of distance. He had no hope of ever seeing the girl again and yet he could not stop thinking of her.

Were his grandfather alive, he'd have rebuked Louis. He'd have made use of one of his oft-repeated life mottos: *'Opportunity's reason should always supersede folly's longings.'*

His grandfather had spoken from the hard lessons he'd learned, ones that Louis's father had had to face, as well. Both men had married hastily because they had fallen in love.

Louis would not fall in love before marriage lest he be tempted away from a suitable arrangement that would monetarily benefit the estate. He would work to make himself worthy of the right woman, treat his wife with the respect she deserved, but he would fall in love with her only *after* he married her. It was the only way to avoid the mistakes of his father and grandfather.

Louis had to put Allenborough first. Its future prospects. His would be an arranged marriage that would benefit the estate, plain and simple. Falling in love before marrying would distract him from that goal and Louis was determined to avoid it at all costs.

'Why the melancholy look, my friend?' came a boisterous voice from inside the carriage. A man peeked out of the velvet curtain covering its window, his black eyes merry, his grin a soundless laugh. 'This is Misr, Umm al-Donya! Egypt, Mother of the World. And mothers hate their visitors to be sad.'

Prince Hussam vaulted from the carriage and shook Louis's hand while simultaneously hugging him in greeting. 'Surprise! I was telling my mother, my actual one, not the country, that if no other of my Eton mates comes but Louis Wesley, then we will finally have a *celebration* on our hands. He was the life and blood of us all!'

People were bound to change and grow up from their formative years, but Louis had indeed been the socialite of their group. It was a skill he'd had to hone in order to keep his pride intact amongst those who were wealthier than he and his family were. Through it, he'd collected many acquaintances but maintained lasting and authentic friendships with only a few.

Hussam was one of those few.

'As I recall, *you* were the one who would avoid studying at any cost, devising one mischievous idea after another. Ideas that would inevitably result in all of us being dragged into the headmaster's office for a proper scolding.'

Hussam chuckled. 'Such fun! Remember what I used to say—freedom in England...'

'Until I become khedive of Egypt and am forced to behave,' Louis finished for him.

'Not yet the khedive and yet made to behave, regardless. But we will have our fun, sprinkle it with a smidgen of debauchery, perhaps?' Hussam sobered. 'And how is your father? Your siblings? I wanted to come for your grandfather's funeral, but I heard of it too late.'

'We received your card, the flowers, thank you.'

'What title does that afford you now? I never understood the British peerage rules whilst studying in England and cannot claim to know how they work now.' Hussam had a way of turning sombre subjects into lessons—a trick he employed on those occasions they were called to the headmaster's office—but Louis was grateful for it now.

'Ours is a tad complicated. Great-grandfather was an earl who lost much in poor speculations. My grandfather was forced to take up a navy post and it was his commodore title he preferred above his earldom. He married for love, rather than a rich heiress—hoped my father would do differently but could not begrudge him when he, twice, did the same. When grandfather passed, my father became Earl of Allenborough and I, the viscount.' Louis shrugged. 'I'm not sure that explains it better. Mind you, with a young father and four half siblings who're all but children, it is, as my grandfather liked to remind me whilst he was alive, only a title. One that comes with much less monetary value than that of other gentlemen.'

Hussam clapped Louis's back and happily exclaimed, 'Then prepare yourself for the debauchery of a lifetime, my friend. Gluttonous meals, decadently furnished rooms. Parties that they *sometimes* let the harem out for. You'll be my guest and stay as long as you desire or until the politics of court life wear you down.'

Louis recalled his friend's generosity in England. Here, in his home country, Hussam was sure to spare no expense. 'I am ever the diplomat and perhaps will need your help in securing a position, but I do not want to take advantage of our relationship.'

'You wish to extend your time in Cairo?' Hussam's excitement was palpable.

'If there was a post with a high enough salary at the British Embassy? Yes, indeed.'

'You should take the consul's job, the man is an acrimonious bore.'

Louis figured there was much time to talk about it later;

he wanted to hear about his friend's possible wedding. Before he could ask, one of the servants cleared his throat and spoke some words in Arabic to Hussam, pointing as he did to the sconces being lit along the harbour and the crowds gathering along the river promenade.

When he wasn't sketching the young lady he'd met at the Louvre, Louis had picked up a little Arabic from listening to others on the ship crossing the Mediterranean. He gathered now that the servant was telling Hussam it wasn't safe to linger out in the open.

His friend confirmed his understanding, leaning in to whisper, 'Usually, commoners see us amongst them and rejoice but there are those in Egypt who dislike the royal family's ways, rumble about us being out of touch with their poverty. My father's guards want us to be more cautious.'

They were ushered up the carriage steps and into the lush interior of its body. A lantern secured above the door burned gently, illuminating the space, one nearly as nice as a sitting room. Cushions embroidered with gold thread were heaped onto seats of rich black velvet. He smelled lingering tobacco smoke mingled with an oud-like musk.

After Louis and Hussam were seated and the door shut, the tail end of the carriage heaved low. A knock on the carriage body set the horses trotting.

'The servants ride on the back?' he asked.

'In case of the aforementioned threat. They keep their swords or pistols or whatever weapons there. I keep telling them not only does it ruin the demeanour of the carriage, but it alerts the populace that someone they might consider targeting is inside. I do not mind drawing attention when I want it, but know how to avoid it when needed. They, unfortunately, listen only to my father who is…a complicated man. On the one hand, the khedive likes to maintain a traditional iron fist of power—on the other, he admires pomp, circumstance and the wealth that comes with the modern.'

Hussam bent to pull a basket from beneath his seat, producing a silver flask from inside, which he offered to Louis before retrieving a replica for himself. 'Slake your thirst.'

Louis took a swig, expected something hard and whisky-like considering the vessel. Instead, it was champagne bubbling on his tongue.

Hussam grinned. 'Like old times, but different too.'

'We used to down cheap wine that tasted more like tar!'

'I miss it.'

Louis watched his friend. 'You were adamant you would never marry, so when I received your letter, it was surprising. Tell me about this bride of yours who has, if not changed you, at least managed to have you send out "prepare for a wedding by summer's end" invitations.'

'Mervat? She's a sweet enough girl. My cousin.'

Louis must have looked surprised because Hussam added, 'Distant.'

English men married their cousins, it wasn't so much an oddity—but for the prince *héritier* of Egypt, a man Louis thought he knew?

'You used to talk of *passione*,' he said, stressing the Italian pronunciation, 'wanting to burn for the lady you'd make wife.'

Hussam used both thumbs to brush down the sides of his already groomed moustache. 'The khedive demanded I change. Mervat and I are not in love—I suspect ours will only be a marriage of convenience, meant to secure the line of succession. Perhaps it will have to be a cover for other women who might, as you say, help fulfil my desire for *passione*.'

Sympathy flared for a young woman Louis had never met. 'And your cousin? Will the princess Mervat also be permitted whatever passions she might fancy?'

Hussam was a good-natured fellow, had a charm about him that rivalled Louis's own, but the look he gave him just then barely contained his disapproval. 'Mervat is as a sister to me and a most decent sort of girl. And, we have a court harem which upholds protocols. Such behaviour from its women would not be tolerated, even if Mervat were so inclined, which I know she is not.'

The call of a particularly loud peddler caught his attention and Hussam drew the curtain. Across the road, the fellow stood alongside an open cart askew with clay pots of different shapes.

'Ya khedive, ya khedive!' The peddler shouted something more in Arabic that Louis couldn't make out, but he felt one of the servants leaping off their carriage and heard him shouting back.

The driver clucked, the leather reins snapped and the horses quickened their pace. But if they—or the peddler—were in any danger, Hussam decided he would not watch. He dropped the curtain and continued as if nothing had happened. 'Although, Mervat has lived much of her life away from court. I don't know if she is adjusting well to it. I will be sure to ask tomorrow, at the luncheon gathering. We will have it to honour your arrival.'

'I shall look forward to meeting her.'

Hussam nodded, then got this far-off look on his face. Louis couldn't be sure because it was dark, but when his friend sighed, loudly, he heard the weariness in it. 'In truth, there is another woman I would have been pleased to marry were it permitted. Nadine is beautiful and rich but, alas, she is not of noble blood.'

'Oh.' Louis did not know what it was to be in love with one woman, yet alone betrothed to another one who was not her. From what he'd witnessed of his own father's life with his stepmother, Louis believed that love-match marriages were inferior, childish even, compared to arranged ones which improved the stability and management of an estate's needs. While the Countess of Allenborough seemed tickled when his father caught her waist in a spontaneous waltz or gifted her with a bouquet of wildflowers, she was often frazzled with the duties of motherhood and the work of stretching paltry sums to maintain a household.

But Hussam would not want to hear that considering *his* dilemma. 'If there is anything I might do to help,' Louis offered instead, 'you must let me know.'

Hussam clapped his hands on his knees, forcing away his dismal mood. 'Never mind me! All sons should obey their fathers, even if they are not kings of Egypt.'

The rest of the journey passed quickly with reminiscings on adventures they'd had at Eton. Louis knew they were near their destination when the carriage slowed, the ground beneath them going from pebbled road to one as smooth as cold butter and the noises of Cairo's bustle shifted to the song of crickets. They passed wrought iron gates and the soldiers who manned them saluted.

The ambrosial scent of guava fruit trees perfumed the air, and while Louis admired the grove off to their left, it was the brand-new Sesostris Palace that demanded all the attention. As they descended the carriage, the palace stretched before him, as formidable as any he'd previously seen. Slightly less stately than Buckingham or Versailles, but no less magnificent, in width and breadth. Illuminated by a myriad of candles and lanterns, the details blurred in their glow, but Louis felt sure an exploration of those would be exhilarating.

He and Hussam took the wide steps to the main doors, large enough for an elephant to pass, while servants buzzed around them in their desire to make themselves, well, of service.

The man who'd spoken to Louis at the riverboat seemed

to be the only one who knew English and Hussam instructed the fellow, whom he called 'Faisal,' to be vigilant in ensuring that 'the viscount's needs are met.'

'Are more people now fluent in French?' Louis asked.

'A few, but it is mostly Turkish, in addition to the native Arabic. I keep telling my father that he should mandate English. It will be the language of the future.'

'As it was in the past.'

Hussam quipped, 'Some empires never let up.'

Although the grandness of the foyer was even more breathtaking, Louis felt a touch of fatigue, exhaustion from his Continental journey finally catching up to him and preventing him from appreciating it properly. He determined that tomorrow he would capture it all in his notebook, after a good rest.

'The family should be gathered to greet you!' Hussam said contritely. 'They never take my orders seriously.'

'I am humbled enough by *your* welcome, Prince Hussam.'

'Let us do away with titles, Louis.' He held up a finger, 'Although I will not permit you calling me *Hussy* per my nickname at Eton before I learned the meaning of the word.'

'It was a creative play on the name. I cannot recall who first thought it.'

Hussam rolled his eyes. 'The cad, George. I'm reminded of him constantly by my favourite aunt who has called me by it since I was a wee lad, not knowing the British meaning. I don't have the heart to correct her, but you will know her by my mortification upon answering her "Hussy this" and "Hussy that."'

Louis laughed with his friend. He couldn't help but stifle a yawn soon thereafter.

'You must be tired. Would you like to be shown to your quarters? I can have a tray sent up.'

'That would be much appreciated.'

When Hussam rang the bell on the nearby wall, they were waited on by another servant. Louis could barely keep track of how many had passed them already, but it was the English-speaking one he wished for.

Faisal finally came through a side door, lugging a wrapped canvas as tall as he was. 'Apologies, my prince, the artist commissioned for Princess Mervat's portrait says his painting is mostly completed but wants a closer look at her mother's crown. According to the painter, he was "busy painting as she chattered", and only afterwards did he know he should have paid more attention to the jewel at its centre. Called it the "Cleopatra Cerulean."'

'Never mind that now, first you must ensure the viscount is settled in his rooms,' Hussam said.

For his part, Louis had heard mention of the jewel and was reinvigorated. From the talk he'd attended in Paris, he learned that the crown was thought to have been passed down through a Turkish sultana line and was currently in Egypt, but he hadn't thought it could be here, at court.

Louis could barely contain his curiosity, 'May I see this crown and painting before I retire for the evening? Meet your princess cousin, as it were?'

Hussam nodded and the servant withdrew the sheet on the life-sized canvas.

Louis nearly gasped, but not because he was awestruck by the magnificent jewel set upon a crown on top of her head. It was because hers was the same beautiful face he'd been sketching for weeks. The wide-set eyes. The dark auburn curls. The heart-shaped face.

The one Louis hadn't stopped thinking about.

Princess Mervat was the young lady he'd met at the Louvre!

Chapter Two

Mervat

'I will not marry him! Please, Anne, try and see it from my side.' As much as Mervat insisted she should have a choice in the matter of who she was going to spend her life with, her mother was as determined to ignore her.

There was nothing new about that.

For much of her twenty years, Mervat's father's home had been away from court and she'd lived there to tend to him, each of them pursing their own interests with minimal staff, leading a quiet, companionable existence. And while her parents were not divorced, her mother had chosen to live at court in the centre of Cairo. With the completion of the new Sesostris Palace, Mervat believed her mother would finally leave the khedive's harem and come home to her and Baba.

She'd been wrong.

When she'd received the invitation to join her mother in Paris, then to stay with her at court, Mervat agreed, thinking it would be a chance to get close to her mother and, *maybe*, convince her to finally leave.

Yet any attempts to engage her on Mervat's part were met with judgement rather than acceptance. How many times had she borne Anne's barbs over the things she cared most about?

'Why do you prattle like a scholar enamoured of useless trivialities? You are like a child who trails sand in the desert, believing each grain leads to an oasis. But it's only sand and it leads to nothing. Nobody listens.'

And how many times had Mervat endured Anne's calls to change who she was?

'A princess should care for fashions and jewels. Looking beautiful. Let others tend to your leisure, entertain you. You behave more like a maid.'

Yet, guilt riddled Mervat. She wanted to be on better terms with her mother, desperately desired they should have a relationship. There were things she would have liked to talk to her about, family stories she would have liked to hear. She had so many questions to ask about Anne's childhood in Turkey.

What sort of genealogist knew more about artifacts than about where she came from? But when Mervat reached out to her mother about this or that subject, she was ignored or met with excuses. She'd imagined the trip to Paris to be one where mother and daughter strengthened their relationship with excellent food, strolls along the promenades and visits to historical sites.

It had been merely a fashion house extravaganza.

The only exciting part of the Paris trip was when Mervat had sneaked out to the Louvre and had the chance meeting with the very charming Viscount Louis Wesley of Allenborough.

If only she could tell her mother about him and how being in his company had stirred feelings in her she'd never felt before. The flutter in her belly then. The one that returned each time she thought about what they might have done near the *Psyche Revived by Cupid's Kiss* if they hadn't been strangers.

Mervat had been eager to discuss what she'd learned at the talk on the Cleopatra Cerulean with her mother as soon as she returned from the Louvre. She'd imagined that with her mother's love for jewels and Mervat's for the history of artifacts, it could be a research project they worked on together. Instead, she'd had the worst news of her life.

'The khedive has decided. You are betrothed to Prince Hussam!'

It was a betrothal Mervat had never wanted, never agreed to. Her father was the khedive's cousin, and while many thought he should have inherited the title when his father died, Mervat's grandfather had appointed his brother's son rather than his own. Not many knew that it was her father's decision to abdicate a political life. Or that Hussam's father, the current khedive, had long lived under the shadow of hers. Her father would never challenge him, nor did she have any brothers, but, according to her mother, 'Who was to say Mervat's son wouldn't someday lay claim to the throne? If your son is also Hussam's son, then the khedive can relax.'

Back in Paris, Mervat had immediately refused, but Anne only stared at her, a look of knowing suspicion in her eyes. 'Where have you been?'

Mervat couldn't tell her about the viscount she'd met, and that the thought she should marry Hussam somehow particularly disagreeable now she had. She would likely never see Lord Wesley again, though she may want to. And it wasn't just because he was handsome. He'd listened to her, not grown bored with her chattering. He'd been charming during the talk too; asking questions of Mr Henries which he'd wondered if she thought them befitting of a genealogist. When she teased that he had the makings of one, he sat taller in his chair and claimed that he wished to 'impress a certain young lady who is most impressive in her depth of knowledge.'

Had Louis gone back to the Louvre to look for her?

'Don't forget rouge!' Anne rubbed the concoction into

Mervat's cheeks. 'If they resemble apples, you look healthy, ripe for bearing sons.'

The movement brought her back to the present and away from the spectre of Lord Wesley.

'Anne,' she reproved, feeling her cheeks warm so much they probably didn't need rouge.

Her mother chuckled. 'You will be the delight of the khedive's luncheon.'

Anne lifted her by the shoulders to have Mervat look into the full-length mirror next to the armoire. It was wide enough to capture both their figures from the top of their auburn hair to the tips of their bejewelled sandals. Her mother's hair was peppered with powder to cover the grey, and she wore a tiara and veil, while Mervat's was braided with ribbon and lay loose and thick across her back.

The gown was a pale blue lace over silk with a cinched waist and draping wide sleeves. And though it was elegant, Mervat couldn't imagine actually eating in it without being worried she would spoil it. Nor did the exasperation over the possible engagement to her cousin make her feel light.

Mervat might look pretty enough, but she felt like a rain cloud, heavily burdened. She met her mother's gaze in the mirror and repeated, 'I cannot marry Hussam.'

And her mother repeated what she'd been saying since Paris, 'You and the prince are friends. It is more than most royals have, my sweet *kiz*.'

Her mother turned away from their reflection and squeezed her shoulder. 'In this dress, you will pull Hussam's gaze away from any others. He will love you one day. Passionately.'

'Others?' Mervat heard the indignancy on her behalf in her mother's words and knew the source of it. 'You mean Nadine? She seems nice, Anne.'

'Be wary of her! She thinks because she has green eyes and

yellow hair that she is the most beautiful girl in Egypt, when she is nothing but a low-born trader's daughter. She's always wandering out of the harem, pretending she is unfamiliar with its rules.' She wagged a finger. 'You cannot allow Hussam to spend time with her. You must make him desire *you* alone. Want to be with you. To do this, you should show him you will welcome *any* of his advances. Nadine does it with immense skill.'

'I do not think of Hussam in *that* way at all.'

'Zuk!' her mother scolded, 'enough of this gibberish. You have no say in the manner, Mervat. Unless Hussam says otherwise, you *will* marry him and he, at least, is smart enough to know his duty, what will make his father happy. And lest you think the khedive plays games, know that if your father wasn't such a lover of his solitude, he'd have been dead by now. This marriage is the khedive's way of ensuring Abbas's line never threatens his own. You will do what the king of Egypt tells you to do.'

With that little speech, her mother marched out of her room, commanding her with a final entreaty. 'Be gracious at luncheon, the prince is hosting a gathering for his London friend. You may practice your language skills but please do not talk too much!'

Mervat watched her go, considering the opening she'd received.

Unless Hussam says otherwise.

Did her cousin have to be the one to refuse their betrothal? And though she wasn't close enough to Nadine to know if there was love shared between them, Mervat could definitely learn more about her relationship with Hussam. She'd speak to them the first chance she had.

As Mervat made her way down the curved staircase to the parlour, she held tight to the railing, but her dress sleeves made it slippery and she stumbled. Although the two servants who rushed to her were trying to be helpful, their offer of aid further flustered her.

'I am accustomed to a home on one floor,' she rushed to explain.

'Me too,' answered the older one, but he was given a sharp look of reprimand by the other, younger one. It was likely that the younger was higher in rank amongst servants.

Mervat utterly disliked life at court and this was why. There was the obvious separation between the members of the royal family and those who waited on them, but to see such a hierarchy amongst the servants themselves, with no regard for societal norms outside of the palace? Outside the palace, people treated elders with respect. And if the khedive were a proper leader who truly wanted Egypt to prosper rather than being worried about the lines of his succession, he should fix things in his home before he could hope to do it on the outside.

Mervat took the arm offered by the older servant.

'Shukran, amu.' He wasn't her uncle but the marker of respect felt right. 'Whereabouts is your home?'

His chest puffed. 'Tanta.'

'Oh, Tanta is said to have the best *halawet el-moulid*. My favourite dessert.'

He was tugged away by the younger servant before Mervat could thank him for his help or ask his name. It was because a quartet of women from the harem were passing through the foyer and only the most trusted and senior of male servants could engage with them outside of it. Mervat, however, held her ground when she spotted Nadine amongst them.

Women came to the harem in different ways. Mervat had a familial connection but did not normally live here and Nadine was only visiting at the behest of her father, a wealthy industrialist from upper Egypt come to learn court ways.

With their mutual temporary status at Sesostris and similar ages, they might have known each other better, but Nadine seemed to prefer spending time in the hammam with others, rather than in the harem library with Mervat.

When Mervat called her over, she was taken aback by the look of trepidation in Nadine's face as she separated herself from the others. She curtsied low. 'Princess.'

Mervat saw no need for preamble; her mother would reprimand her for being too late. So, she whispered, 'Are you in love with my cousin?'

Nadine's voice wavered as she answered, 'I hear he is to be your husband as the khedive demands. And Hussam must listen to his father, he understands tradition and duty. I will not come between the two of you.'

She did love him!

Mervat offered Nadine a reassuring smile. 'It is I who wishes not to come between you and my cousin. Know that I mean to end this farce of a possible engagement which has yet to be confirmed. Will you help me?'

Nadine sniffled hopefully. 'How?'

'Come into the luncheon with me, people should see we are friends. We will find Hussam, look for a chance to talk to him together. Between the three of us, we can come up with a plan, I am sure.'

'Not all the harem was invited,' Nadine protested though it looked like she was in agreement and wanted to be Mervat's friend. 'The khedive would not like it.'

'Sadly, neither would my mother, yet we must find a way to make them *listen* to us.'

'*Y'Allah*, then.' Nadine locked arms with her. The two entered the drawing room at the precise moment a harp player finished his song so that the scraping of the opening door drew the guests' attention to them.

A servant rushed over to offer them a tray of jade flutes filled with French champagne.

'No, *shukran*.' Mervat avoided alcohol firstly because she was Muslim and believed it to be *haram*, but also because even though it was prohibited in the whole of the country, at court it was allowed. Anne told her it was to welcome foreign dignitaries and guests. Yet, even when there were none, the khedive kept the drink flowing and many partook.

Yet another example of the court's hypocrisy.

When Nadine followed suit and refused the drink, as well, Mervat felt a rush of protectiveness over her, one that grew when she caught sight of her mother. Anne's face barely masked her contempt as she made her way towards them.

'Courage,' she whispered to Nadine. 'Anne is only upset because she thinks your beauty makes me look plain.'

Nadine's nose wrinkled, indignant on Mervat's behalf, 'She couldn't be more wrong! I have jealously watched you, tried to understand how your beauty works.'

'Oh? And what have you determined?'

'That the true mark of it is imprinted and then grows after you've left a room. Your face is unforgettable, its effect like *sihr*.'

It was an odd description that leant on flattery, but it made Mervat think of the Viscount. Had her face lingered in Louis Wesley's mind since their meeting in Paris?

And then, like the magic Nadine referred to, *he* was there.

Standing next to Hussam, who'd cut off her mother's path.

Mervat knew her mouth must be agape, that she should school her reaction, but the racing of her heart at seeing him incapacitated her senses. The vibrations that rocked through her being were born of disbelief, and yet, it was surely him.

How was Viscount Louis Wesley in Cairo?

Chapter Three

Louis

He knew she would be there.

Louis had trained his gaze long and hard on the very tall double doors until his neck cricked and he feared he'd be haunted by the scroll pattern embellishing their frames. Yet, when the princess Mervat actually walked through them, he realised how little his expectation had prepared him. His chest tightened; his breathing strained. He'd thought about her for weeks, relived their moments together in defiance of his belief they were some sort of fever dream. Once on the crossing over and disturbed by rough waters, Louis had woken from a nightmare in which her silhouette stood frozen before *Psyche Revived by Cupid's Kiss*, a sculpture herself, for he could not turn her attention towards him.

Then to find out that his young mystery woman was the would-be fiancée of his friend! Despite his arduous journey, Louis had barely slept last night for worrying about it. More disturbing was the way Hussam felt about the marriage. Did Mervat know that her cousin would treat her like a sister, that he was in love with someone else? And what if, as wife to the crown prince of Egypt and subject to the dictates of the harem, the princess would be required to suppress her pursuits, the genealogies she was passionate about?

Faced with her person in the flesh, by the now-open doors of the Sesostris's grand drawing room, the emotions hit Louis at once. She was a princess. He was a man with a title, yes, but a paltry inheritance. Their nationalities and traditions differed, they were entirely ill suited…but he had experienced enough of her that even if she were not a princess and only a random young lady at a museum, he knew she deserved to be cherished.

Mervat…

Louis had practised saying her name, written it beneath the sketches he'd done of her in his notebook. And here she was, statuesque yet *alive* before him, rendering his sketches as subpar forgeries.

'It is a pleasure, Lord Wesley,' she spoke, alerting him that Hussam had already made the introductions. The timbre of her soft voice wavered and, examining her face more closely, he thought she might be nervous. Did Louis flatter himself with the familiarity he perceived in her smile, as secretive as it was gracious?

From it too, Louis understood that Mervat hoped he would not expose their previous acquaintance.

'The pleasure is entirely mine, Princess Mervat.'

He would have liked to take the gloved hand she put across her chest in greeting to his lips or ask her for a waltz. But this was not a ballroom in England. And she was not a single woman with an empty dance card.

Indeed, it was a testament to the modernisation in court to have the women of the palace harem attend functions with foreign men, proof that the khedive, according to European newspapers, was pulling away from Ottoman norms.

Louis contented himself with mimicking Mervat's gesture,

putting his own hand to his chest. He dipped slightly so their eyes were locked on each other.

'How are you enjoying your stay thus far?' The kindness and brilliance that seeped from her lovely voice was at once as disorienting and grounding as he recalled.

'It has been pleasant, a wondrous surprise.' Louis wasn't sure what he even meant to say, but she smiled graciously, seeming to understand regardless.

He would have liked to stay like that for longer, his eyes on hers, feeling there was only them in the room, but he pulled his gaze reluctantly away when Hussam greeted an older woman who'd joined their party. 'Gulnur Hanem.'

She wore a subtly embroidered kaftan but it was in the richest shade of green silk, shimmering with wealth. Her hair was parted severely down the middle to anchor a lavish silver tiara that looked as if it would weigh down the thickest of skulls, but she bore it as if it were a feather.

'Meet Hussam's friend from England,' Mervat said in English after she'd spoken to the woman in her language. She'd used the word *anne*, which Louis understood to be the Turkish word for *mother*. He didn't think the two looked much alike but he supposed the resemblance was in their colouring.

He couldn't believe he'd ever thought Mervat an Englishwoman with her dark brown eyes and olive skin. He'd been so impressed with her knowledge when they first met and now that he was listening closer to the nuances in her accent, he understood it was one in which the syllables were enunciated rather than one which signalled a place of upbringing.

But her mother was not interested in greeting him and as Louis tried to make sense of the tension in the air, he understood it was geared towards the woman who'd accompanied her daughter.

'Nadine *is* my guest,' Mervat claimed it in a number of

languages as the young woman backed away at something her mother said. She was the one Hussam had told him about.

And he wasn't even trying to hide how besotted he was by the girl standing next to the woman he was supposed to marry. Louis nudged his friend but Mervat was pulling Nadine away, protectively.

Louis watched them go to the musical corner of the room. The harp player had moved to the piano and was readying himself to play it. Louis wished to follow, talk to her about Paris, but now was not the time for Hussam was being admonished by Mervat's mother. At last, the older woman left them with a huff and no acknowledgement of Louis's presence in the least.

Hussam said, 'Do you see why I must be in love with Nadine?'

Louis wondered why anyone would risk hurting a betrothed in such a way. Especially someone like the princess Mervat. 'Your cousin was very cordial. Would she know?'

'Mervat is a smart girl.' Hussam frowned. 'She must have realised Nadine's presence would upset Gulnur Hanem. Mervat's mother has always aspired to rise at court, but my father has only allowed her to remain in order to keep her away from her husband."

Louis's face must have registered his confusion for Hussam gave his arm a friendly shake. 'I warned you about court politics, no? In short, Mervat's father has a claim on my father's throne.' He gestured around the room. 'In fact, most here would agree it is a stronger one. But her father is a recluse who completely shuns politics.'

A hush fell over the crowd of gathered diplomats and dignitaries. Next to him, Hussam straightened and Louis was inclined to do the same because the khedive had made his appearance.

'Friends, family. I greet you all.'

He spoke the simple words in a few languages before going silent. He was a shorter man, stout, with a thick handlebar moustache over pursed lips and matching brows that shrouded shrewd eyes. He wore a burgundy red fez cap like many of the other men in the room, but that is where the similarities ended. His black suit coat was decorated with badges. A chain of medallions crossed his chest, and beneath it a bright red sash met a ceremonial sword that dragged on his left side. To his right stood a blankly smiling woman who was dressed very much like Gulnur Hanem. They might have been sisters but Louis knew that it was the khedive and Mervat's father who were the cousins. Hussam had told Louis that his mother, though not his father's only wife, was his first official one and mother of his eldest son. According to the Ottomans, therefore, she was deemed most important in the harem and would be the one to emerge from it in order to accompany the khedive at public occasions.

Hussam pointed out the British consul before leaving Louis with the excuse, 'My parents will expect me at their side now, but I will introduce you later. In the meantime, turn on that charm of yours to mingle before luncheon is served.'

Louis could not resist sneaking an admiring look towards Mervat first. Against the opulent room's shades of green, from the emerald motif in the oriental rugs to the chartreuse of the velvet draperies and armchairs, Mervat was a vision of grace in blue, her aura drawing Louis like a bee to hydrangea. She was a pool he should like to linger near.

As he watched, her mother dragged her away from Nadine and towards Hussam and his parents.

If seeing her come through the door had made him forget that she was his mystery Louvre woman, here was a reminder that Mervat might one day marry his good friend.

So, Louis turned and forced his steps towards the man Hussam had pointed out.

The British consul, Sir Stuart Williams, was an older surly fellow who, according to the papers Louis had read on route here, was said to not be on stellar terms with the khedive, unlike his younger, more charming French counterpart, who was a veritable court fixture.

'Sir Stuart—' he stuck out his hand '—it is an honour to make your acquaintance. I am—'

'Viscount Louis Wesley, the first of Hussam's Eton friends to visit Egypt upon his invitation. If I am correct, it is because you had nothing better with which to occupy yourself.'

Louis's tersest smile had been honed for men like this. 'I would have made the time for him. My grandfather, the late Earl of Allenborough, would often quote *Hamlet*'s Polonious to teach me that "Those friends thou hast, and their adoption tried/Grapple them unto thy soul with hoops of steel".'

Sir Stuart finally shook the hand Louis hadn't pulled away. There was nothing quite like quoting the bard to stuffy old Englishmen to prove you were worthy of a moment of their time.

He begrudgingly said, 'Then Hussam is fortunate to have you.'

'I am surprised you know me.'

He stared at Louis for a long beat before answering. 'It is my business to know everything that impacts British interests in Egypt. To be quite frank, I am disappointed that more of Hussam's friends have not come over the years. He is the future of the country and though his father remains in power, the more ways the English are connected to the family, the better.'

Diplomats were usually more *diplomatic* but the consul's forwardness suited Louis's goals. Because they were on the margins of the room and relatively alone, he decided to speak boldly. 'In all honestly, sir, I have another motive for being here. Prince Hussam is aware, of course, but I might as well tell you, as well, that I seek a post, one that will allow me to serve Her Majesty's interests in Egypt. I would value your advice, mentorship if you were so inclined.'

He felt the consul's hard stare for a long moment, before the man rudely answered, 'There are scores of intrepid upstarts or second sons of noble fathers who seek a position with our office. You cannot fathom how many similar requests I entertain in any given month. You must prove yourself beyond a passing friendship. Had you a family name that held any esteem outside of England, perhaps—but in lieu of that, what can you offer that no one else can?'

Louis swallowed the insult to his family name, making the flint in his tone clear before presenting his case. 'My grandfather was a commander in the Anglo-Afghan war—he was a celebrated hero, but he had one regret. That the koh-i-noor was within his grasp before anyone knew its significance. I have learned of a similar, hitherto unknown jewel with an interesting background, one right here in Egypt.'

Sir Stuart quirked an eyebrow, 'You mean to steal it?'

'No, certainly not!' Mervat wasn't near, but Louis was afraid she'd hear and misunderstand his intention. According to her painter, she had spoken about the Cleopatra Cerulean. Maybe he could talk to her further, enlist her help in…what exactly? He wasn't sure, but he would very much like to find out.

'I mean to prove its worth as a national treasure, endear us, the British, to our allies, the Egyptians.'

Sir Stuart flagged down a servant, replaced his empty glass of wine with a full one. 'Egyptomania is a popular trend but, dare I say, a passing one. Tourists come smitten with this or that pharaoh's tomb and the riches or curses contained therein. Even if you did find this jewel, what comes after? I was a military man like your grandfather, but unlike romantic stories of regret, my time was spent learning to value sustained, ongoing demonstrations of worth. What *talents* do you possess, Louis? May I call you by your Christian name?'

What a deplorable man this Sir Stuart was, condensing and dismissing the experiences of his grandfather. Louis had a mind to walk away; he didn't think he could ever work with such a fellow. Then it struck him that he wouldn't have to work with him *if* he took his job. Hadn't that been Hussam's suggestion? First, Louis had to find a way in.

He said, 'I write.'

The man scoffed. 'Novels? That is the purveyance of the Austens and the Shakespeares. It is no use to diplomats and politicians, merely a gentleman's leisure. A post in the embassy would pay well, an allowance akin to a king's ransom here in Egypt. Plus, it will likely garner enough acclaim to engender goodwill and credit in England. The sort that would be admired in the House of Lords or amongst rich families looking to make suitable matches for their offspring.'

It was almost as if the consul knew exactly what Louis needed for Allenborough.

'Not fiction,' he answered, his mind racing. 'If I may be blunt, sir, I learned of you and what some call "your failures" in Egypt, from the papers before my arrival. What if I could tell other stories about the country and the English presence in it?'

For a long moment, Sir Stuart looked between Louis and where the French ambassador stood next to the khedive, laughing.

'Show me what you can do. Perhaps then, I will consider your suit.'

Chapter Four

Mervat

Viscount Louis Wesley was here and sitting across from her.

The singular thought came to her during the soup course—a creamy artichoke—that she would seek the recipe for because she was sure her father would love it and they only knew how to boil the vegetable and eat the hearts in a salad.

Viscount Louis Wesley was here and sitting across from her.

The thought persisted during the main course—crispy stuffed pigeons and buttery potato medallions—which she, already satiated from the soup, left mostly untouched. Mervat tried to tell the servant who collected her plate that it shouldn't be tossed and that there were families strapped for food not very far from there. 'Maybe take leftovers to the mosque on Fahad Road? They distribute it the same day to those in need.'

Viscount Louis Wesley was here and sitting across from her.

Mervat was still contemplating the thought during dessert—white cake with apricot preserves which she enjoyed because she never turned down sweets and believed they should be the first course of any meal.

She was accustomed to quicker, simpler fare in Baba's cottage. Often, she cooked for them herself, simple dinners for two, eaten standing next to the stove or sink, more sustenance to sustain her reading and research and Baba's gardening than anything else.

The table in this dining hall was a long one, formal seating for at least fifty, narrow enough that if Louis reached over and she did, their hands would easily meet. Or, if he stretched out his leg and she did the same, their toes would touch. For fear she might act on it, Mervat keep her feet knitted together under her chair and her hands in her lap as much as possible.

With the servants scurrying around them, the collecting and exchanging of plates, and her mother at her side, she had little opportunity to speak to Louis but plenty to watch him discreetly.

He was a slow eater, gentlemanly in his habits, savouring the flavours as if he were trying to think of the perfect words to describe them. She remembered his notebook at the Louvre, how he mentioned capturing memories there.

Mervat caught him looking at her too. Each time, she felt the leap in her chest, the flush in her cheeks. And then he would smile at her. As if they shared a secret.

Louis was handsomer than she remembered. He'd only arrived yesterday, but he must have caught the sun on his crossing over because he was golden, the tan bringing out the chisel in his cheeks, the deep-set nature of his eyes, the luminance of his hair. He wore a camel-coloured shirt and a loose collar that exposed his Adam's apple. With each swallow, it bulged in a way that brought a lump to Mervat's own throat.

Then she came to the horrible realisation that Hussam might have mentioned to Louis that he and Mervat were supposed to marry. But an engagement wasn't official, and she'd certainly not known the prospect of it when she'd first met Louis.

Not that she'd been meaning to flirt with him in Paris!

Mervat wriggled in her seat. She had to get Louis alone. Explain it to him.

The khedive stood at the head of the table and announced, 'A salute.'

People lifted their champagne glasses all around but she merely pressed her lips together. The British had an idiom, *a fish out water*, and Mervat, despite being amongst her own people, felt it on her skin as materially as the silk of her gown.

The khedive spoke niceties in Arabic and Turkish, but when he switched to English, he talked about the table setting, how it had come from China via the Suez Canal, the boon it was for global trade. Many in attendance likely wouldn't care, but Anne whispered, 'You will translate for me later.'

Mervat nodded happily, she relished any chance to use a skill to please her mother.

'We celebrate my son's friend come from England today, as well,' the khedive continued. 'Viscount Wesley, welcome.'

'I am most grateful for it, Your Highness.' Louis rose and spoke with an air of confidence, his manner captivating.

Definitely not a fish out of water, Mervat thought. He seemed like he already belonged here.

'I am utterly enamoured with Egypt's beauty and look forward to knowing *her* better.'

Had he meant to single Mervat out with the words? As his eyes circled the table, politely acknowledging the chorus of welcomes, did they linger on hers for longer?

'The viscount's arrival marks the start of a wonderful summer at the finished grand palace of Sesostris,' the khedive said, switching back to Turkish. 'We—' he lifted a pointed brow in Anne's direction before patting Hussam's shoulder '—mean to conclude it with a special occasion.'

Her cousin's grimace gave Mervat hope. She'd witnessed his reaction to Nadine earlier. Hussam would be an ally in her quest to have any notion of their marriage forgotten by their parents. He had to be.

Soon after, the khedive and his wife left and the guests dwindled, but when her mother pulled her aside for the requested translation, Mervat lost sight of Louis.

'Don't be *takoz*,' Anne said with a scowl, the Turkish for dim-witted. 'Nadine was sent back to the harem because she had no invite to the luncheon, and we are a court of traditions. Your naivety marks you as one to be taken advantage of, and that girl is the type who would move against you. Heed me, Mervat. I know these things.'

Anne didn't wait for a response before marching off with nary an explanation for why she wished to hear about the khedive's Suez Canal remarks. Mervat didn't care about politics or gossip. She'd come to court to spend time with her mother, develop their relationship after a lifetime of separation.

Mervat whispered, 'Please know too that Hussam will never be my husband.'

She found her cousin shaking hands with a departing Frenchman near the palace's main doors. He asked, 'What did you mean by bringing Nadine?'

'You love each other, and we need to prevent this farce of an engagement.'

Hussam frowned. 'You do not wish to marry me?'

'Your ego isn't that large you need be surprised. We are not in love and I have no wish to end up like my parents or yours for that matter. Living together or apart, per the dictates of the khedive. You used to feel the same.'

A servant approached and said the khedive was requesting the prince's presence.

'Wait for me in the study. My father's meetings don't take long.' Hussam pointed her towards a part of the palace she'd yet to familiarise herself with. Sesostris could have been a city on its own. A daunting one she'd hadn't yet explored. Thankfully, Mervat found the study doors open.

The built-in shelves were sparse now but could house a large collection of books. To his credit, the khedive did encourage the literacy of the women under his care so there was a library in the harem, but it too was not well stocked. And because of its proximity to the hammam and the gossip there, here might be a better place for Mervat. Emptier. But as she rounded the last bend in her exploration, she realised she wasn't alone.

Louis sat in an armchair, legs crossed, lost in his notebook, frantically writing.

What memories of today was he seizing upon?

She sucked in a breath, stared at his long fingers wrapped around the pencil. His bowed head, the waves of golden hair on his brow.

She cleared her throat gently so as not to startle him. It was a move she'd needed to hone with her father. When Baba was in his garden, he'd be as lost in his task and sudden noises would upset him. Louis, however, was nonplussed and it took a few subsequent—and louder—attempts to get his attention.

He scrambled to his feet when he caught sight of her. He set aside his notebook and then swooped to catch the pencil as it fell. His flexed biceps and forearms in that position, looking up to her, put every nerve in Mervat's body to attention.

'Princess,' he said in that lower position before lifting himself to tower over her. They'd not been this close at the Louvre. She'd not realized then as she now perceived that he was a whole head taller than she. Why did the sensation of it thrill her so?

'Viscount Wesley, please call me Mervat. I am unaccustomed to titles and am the plainest of Egyptians, having lived outside of court all my life.'

'I would not allow for you being the "plainest" by any stretch.' His right brow quirked, revealing the tiniest of scars at the tip of it, near the bridge of his perfectly straight nose. She clenched her fingers, fought the urge to reach her hand up and finger it. 'But I am honoured to comply with your wish, if you will call me Louis.'

It felt too intimate to do, but she nodded despite the knocking of her knees.

'I am sorry to interrupt you now and to have put you on the spot earlier by having to deny our previous meeting. I am sorry too for that meeting. Not disclosing who I was, my name. I would have returned—had even hoped to meet you again at the Louvre and explain who I was—but we were called back to Egypt soon after. You've met my mother now and can see she's not the easiest of people to get along with. Oh, and I am sorry too for her behaviour at luncheon, but that had nothing to do with you. She was mad at me for...'

Mervat was talking too much, per usual. People interrupted her when she forgot herself, but as he had at their first meeting, Louis was content to let her ramble. She stomped her foot and offered a final, 'Sorry.'

'No apology needed, but it is accepted. Honestly, Princess, er, *Mervat*, I was pleased you remembered me but also put out to learn you are engaged to my dearest friend.'

He held her gaze for a long moment while she tried not to gasp in response to the musicality of her name coming from his lips. She opened her mouth to say something, a denial of some sort, but it took a beat too long to find the words and he filled the silence.

'All these weeks contemplating a beautiful young lady I'd met at the Louvre, only to learn she was not free.'

Louis had been 'contemplating' her? He thought her beautiful? Mervat's heart thumped as he stepped back.

'My behaviour that day, the flirting. If I had known you were a princess, set to marry Hussam no less...'

So *he* had been flirting with her?

'Hussam and I are not going to marry, and I did not know it was a possibility then.'

She watched as he raked his graceful hand through his golden hair.

'The khedive desires it, no?'

Mervat wanted to detect hope in the question, in the deepening of his blue eyes, but if anything, he looked more guarded. It frustrated her. If she could not convince Louis, how was she to convince Anne? 'Even so, Hussam and I will not marry.'

'Cousin!'

Hussam's voice boomed behind them, an—dare she suppose it—unwelcome intrusion. 'It is a good thing Louis is my mate, otherwise I see that my brotherly advice of keeping your bold-faced honesty with strangers to a minimum has not been remembered.'

Despite his playfully wagging finger in her direction and big grin, Louis sidestepped Mervat, putting his body between her and Hussam. It seemed like a protective move to make but she might be reading more into it than was there.

But then he said, 'The princess's honesty is refreshing and her instincts are sharp, for she knows I can be trusted. You need not take your cousin to task, Hussam.' The pitch of his voice had hardened, but he smiled softly when he looked back at her.

He *was* being protective. Perhaps it was just the way of all English gentlemen.

'I could never take Mervat to task. She is my favourite cousin.' Hussam brushed past them to slump into the chair Louis had vacated. He strummed the arm rest. 'Only, the meeting I came from now? My father says he has grand plans for the Midsummer Festival, but that our marriage ceremony will be *the* event to inaugurate the world to the new Sesostris, a new Egypt. Modern, free from the dictates of a closed-off harem and old Ottoman traditions. I don't know how we can stop a marriage between me and Mervat from happening.'

Mervat mustered, 'My father abdicated his rights. I can go back home, promise to remain there or stay out of his way until the khedive forgets my existence as he did Baba's.'

Hussam scoffed. 'You think he's ever forgotten your father? Abbas is a noose around his neck which might tighten at any moment. Maybe not in his generation or even mine, but the khedive desires to secure his line like the great pharaohs once did. Cousin, you only know him from afar, but one day with him when his mask is off and you would see his narcist, selfish leanings. His cruelty when challenged.

'And your mother has been working on your behalf, Mervat. Playing into his fears, convincing him our marriage is the only way to put them to bed. She turns every bit of gossip or political game to her advantage. The khedive decides to woo the world, modernise? Lo and behold Gulnur Hanem touts Mervat's language skills, her ability to speak to the commonest of folk, her smart ideas.'

Hussam chuckled wryly, gestured to Louis. 'Apparently, Mervat's self-directed education is better than the one we got at Eton!'

Mervat felt Louis watching her and it buoyed her despite the surprising news that Anne had been working for her benefit, misguided as she was. And, to have abandoned her for most of her childhood whilst she did? It tore at Mervat's heart.

All that time mother and daughter could have spent together had been wasted.

'She will not heed my refusals,' Mervat said. 'It has to come from you, Hussam. Anne said as much. You have to take the stand—tell them you love another.'

She threw a furtive glance at Louis, but Hussam dismissed her worry. 'There are no secrets between Louis and me. He knows about Nadine.'

He switched to Arabic and grinned, wriggling a finger in scolding. '*Uff* on you, Mervat, for bringing her, making me ignore her.'

Mervat teased, 'You call that *ignoring*, cousin?'

'I should excuse myself,' Louis interrupted. 'This seems like a private conversation.'

'Stay,' both Mervat and Hussam said at the same time. She might have been embarrassed by her strong reaction to the chance of him leaving, but if Louis noticed, Hussam did not.

'We require your counsel, knowledge of how an Englishman might traverse such a situation,' he said. 'My father has been taken by the British most of all, or at least the money they're offering. I suspect that bit about the Suez Canal was for your consul's benefit.'

'All right.' Louis dragged two chairs from a nearby table that housed an exquisite black and white marble chess set more for decor than actual playing. He placed them opposite Hussam offering Mervat the first, before settling into the second.

'You previously implied that marriages of convenience are the way of the harem. That they would allow for…pursuing passions elsewhere.' Louis looked sorry to disclose Hussam's confidence, but Mervat read it as a sensitive consideration of her feelings. 'And forgive any ignorance or misconceptions I may have, but I only wonder if you were to tell the khedive that you care for Miss Nadine, what's to stop him from saying you could keep her alongside a wife of his choosing?'

'Or as a second wife even?' Mervat added.

Hussam furiously rubbed his eyes. 'Nadine is not some poor maid happy to have any attention from a prince. Her father is one of the richest men in Egypt. He brought her to the harem to learn the mannerisms of the upper class and plans it so her time here will land her a powerful husband. It doesn't have to be me. Any prince would do. Nadine's father will not allow her to be a side wife or a dalliance. But, even if he did, my father expects that the first marriage in Sesostris will completely embrace the ideal of one wife, one chance for happiness. As I say, the khedive has been pulling away from Ottoman influence and wants to show the British that our Egyptian values are like yours and unlike Turkey's.'

Mervat swallowed back the acrid taste of artichoke, the luncheon soup heavier than she'd thought. 'Then, let's go with my earlier suggestion. I go home, refuse to return? Defiantly object to the marriage.'

'That might be an English way, actually. The defiance of customs, thumbing our noses at convention,' Louis said, backing her idea.

Hussam looked between them, his eyes widening. 'What if you two were to pave a path to this so called "defiant" love. *That* might shift the khedive's mind.'

Had her cousin perceived Mervat's attraction to Louis?

'Us?' Louis asked.

'You would not actually fall in love and have to marry— it would be a ruse, enough to cause a ruckus at court so it seems like I was a cuckold if I married Mervat despite it. It would buy me time to work on establishing Nadine as a viable option. The four of us would go about the city. Spend time together.'

'You cannot compromise the princess's reputation,' Louis objected.

'Nor can you drag the viscount into our family disputes,'

Mervat added. 'What if by defying the khedive, he is kicked out of the country or worse?'

Hussam considered their objections, first speaking to Louis. 'It will not be a relationship to hurt Mervat's long-term prospects—she is a princess sure to have her pick of any suitable Egyptian or Turkish men. The former are, generally speaking, quite accommodating and not very jealous, and the latter are far enough away they will not have heard of any bad reputation.'

Then, he addressed Mervat. 'As for Louis, I have something that will make it worth his while.' Hussam leaned forward, put his hands on his friend's knees. 'At the debriefing now, my father mentioned he likes your manner. I told him you wish for a position in the British Embassy.'

Mervat held her breath. Louis wanted to stay in Egypt.

For his part, he seemed put out when he answered, 'I spoke to the consul myself.'

Hussam asked, 'Did he ask what talents you possess?'

'How did you know?'

'He likes people to do somersaults to gain his favour. If he didn't have sway over finances coming from England, my father would have ousted him from Egypt long ago. Did you tell him you write?'

'I did.'

'And his answer, I'd wager, was to tell you to show him your worth before he'd consider your suit?' Hussam grinned, seeing the truth of it in Louis's face. 'I told you he was a prig, but the truth is that I had a similar thought. Remember how you used to write letters to the headmaster at Eton? Apologies with earnest summaries of what we had done so that he wouldn't suspend us after our *adventures*.'

'How do you know they were earnest?' Louis asked with a chuckle.

'True, we never read them, but I once overheard the headmaster saying how they made him feel young, like he was one of the lads, right there with us.'

Louis shrugged, turning to Mervat with a self-deprecating smile.

'They must have been excellent,' she said, a yearning to read his writing taking her by surprise, 'to ensure my mischievous cousin would be spared punishment.'

'You see how well Mervat knows me! And when my father was dictating to me as if he were my headmaster just now, I thought, *Louis can save us*. His writing. You write about your time here at Sesostris. Our friendship. Cairo. Whatever suits your fancy. My father offered to put you in contact with an important editor at the *Telegraph*.'

Louis exclaimed, 'I would relish the chance!'

Exhilaration churned in Mervat's chest. The prospect of him staying here. Near her. But there was danger in it too, as Hussam next pointed out. 'Look at this man. How handsome he is! You mustn't worry, Mervat. No woman would be blamed for falling in love with him.'

Mervat's cheeks warmed; she hoped neither of the men would notice if she were blushing.

'We would need an excuse for you two to spend time together.' Hussam winked. 'Nadine and I can follow as chaperones. The four of us can be a quartet of "defiant love". Perhaps you can suggest one of your artifact projects, Mervat?'

'The Cleopatra Cerulean.' As soon as she'd thought it, she'd realised she'd said it aloud.

'Louis, isn't that the crown you mentioned, a talk you attended before coming here?'

'It is.' Was that a bit of flush Mervat detected in Louis's cheeks, as well? It did not seem that he'd spoken to Hussam about their meeting at the Louvre. If her cousin had told him about his feelings for Nadine, wouldn't it also follow that Louis would tell him about a mystery woman he'd been contemplating?

'It was destined!' Hussam clapped his hands. 'We are Muslim, right, Mervat? We believe Allah brings people and circumstances together for a reason. Or many reasons.'

That day in the Louvre *had* brought them together, and while the plan of Hussam's might not be a right enough reason, Mervat was being pulled into it. And despite her reservations that centred on how upset Anne would be, the chance to work with Louis on a project when she'd only ever worked alone was tempting. Of course, like her projects, it too would come to an end. He was a viscount who might want a post in Egypt, but noble foreigners who worked here would ever remain so, their connections to their countries of origin, their homes, strong.

As it should be, she thought.

Hussam urged, 'It would only be a few weeks, until we can guarantee there'll be no marriage. What do you say—are we all agreed on this plan?'

'Nadine? Should we not ask her?'

'Nadine's answer to any of my questions will always be yes.'

Mervat would've teased Hussam's overconfidence were the weight of his stare not set upon her. But it was Louis, patient, looking away to let her consider without pressure from his side that convinced her.

'I am agreed.'

Chapter Five

Louis

The servant unfastened corded ropes to draw open the study's curtains and let in the bright Cairo sun. Beyond the wide window's polished glass loomed rows of rose bushes. Magenta in colour, their thorns were noticeable, unpruned, riddled with pricks.

They'd prove a sharp fence, a deterrent to any who'd try to breach the palace.

Though they were merely flowers and Sesostris had layers of defences at the ready, Louis recorded the thought in his journal, nonetheless. He inhaled and noted too that the scent they gave off was akin to dried honey and unripe, unpeeled oranges. Soft, barely there.

Now that the khedive's office had put Louis in touch with the *Telegraph*, he would need to gather any and all contemplations in order to write the stories his new by-line required. He'd already sent over his first piece about the palace luncheon—everything from the opulent meal menu to the melodies played in the drawing room and the intimate but politically powerful guest list.

Nothing about an engagement or Mervat. Louis wasn't sure exactly why, but he wanted to keep the princess out of the realm of public opinion. She seemed as though she'd want privacy.

'Do you happen to know the genus name? I have not come across the variety in England.' Louis pointed to the roses, but the servant blankly shook his head.

He didn't speak English and only gave him the Arabic word for flowers. *'War'd.'*

Mervat could probably tell him the entire history of the variety. How it came to Egypt. What particular conditions gave it such a bold colour. Who first planted it in the royal garden and why this particular one in lieu of any other.

Louis wrote the title *A Genealogy of the Roses* with a flourish. He permitted himself a private chuckle before trying to banish the very distracting image of the princess—and the directions her mind might take his own.

It had been a few days since he'd agreed to act the tempter to the more tempting Mervat, but they had yet to put any plan into action. Maybe it was for the best. It was a risky proposition on all counts. In truth, he'd only agreed because Mervat had. He had done it for her since it was unlikely Hussam would withhold his help in Louis's quest to secure a diplomatic post nor would his friend lose out on being with a woman he wanted. And it sounded like Nadine would give him that.

But perhaps Mervat had come to her senses and changed her mind about marrying her cousin. He was a prince after all and would be the khedive one day. Maybe even the king of Egypt, were the country to banish Ottoman influence entirely. Where would that leave Louis, who, while he was a British viscount, was currently only working as an essayist in the hopes he would someday attain a diplomatic post?

'Always be hungry,' his grandfather used to say. *'The sweet or the spicy can each prompt the desire for more food,*

but the bitter blunts the tongue and kills an appetite. In life too, bitterness is a useless emotion and you should not wallow in it.'

Even as Louis did his best to deny *who* he most hungered for at present and decided *she* was entirely comprised of all things sweet, he came to feel her presence in the room.

He inhaled deeply before tilting his face towards Mervat.

'I didn't want to disturb you,' she said, her voice low.

She wore the same frock he'd first seen her in at the Louvre; he experienced a moment of disorientation. Louis stood to bow. 'Only scribbling.'

She carried an ornate box and, beneath it, a newspaper. The first she set on the table next to where he'd abandoned his notebook, the latter she waved in front of his face before folding her legs beneath her dress and relaxing into the opposite end of the Chesterfield he'd vacated.

'Scribbling?' She waved the paper as though it were a fan. 'What then is this, dropped off a short while ago with a note to peruse page five, the bit headlined *Dispatches from Cairo.*'

Excitement pulsed through Louis. 'The *Telegraph* published it already?'

She patted the place next to her. When he sat, he felt it that the Chesterfield was not made for two unmarried people sitting far enough apart to be proper. His knee touched hers and he could practically feel the heat between them. He immediately took the paper she offered and slid as far away as he could.

Louis skimmed the piece, finding it hard to focus on anything other than Mervat's steady breathing as she watched him read. The compliment that came as soon as he'd finished.

'Your writing is incredible,' she said. 'Transportive. I drifted on the riverboat with you, heard the harp song, savoured the meal we'd taken again. You have a way with words, Viscount Wesley.'

'Only Louis,' he reminded her, his heart squeezing at her praise. He would have called her by her name, but the servant who'd opened the curtain still stood by the window and Mervat noticed him at the same time Louis remembered he hadn't dismissed him.

The way her face lit up kindly as she waved to him and the subsequent short conversation in Arabic they had fascinated Louis. The older man's face had gone from stony indifference towards him to complete cheeriness with her.

When he bowed on his way out of the study, Mervat rushed to lift the servant straight. *'La, ya Amu Taha, min fadlak. Ana zay bintak.'*

Louis had picked up enough Arabic to recognise the words for *uncle* and *daughter*.

'You're related?' He asked when she'd resumed her seat and the servant had gone.

'It is a marker of respect. If he's close to a father's age, we call them *uncle*. I now know his name. It's Taha. Amu Taha. And he's from Tanta.' She grinned shyly, pleased with the alliteration while Louis perceived how his happiness rose to meet hers.

Everything sweet. Nothing bitter about Mervat.

'He seems to appreciate you.'

She frowned, looked at Louis intently before asking, 'Do you think it was rude on my part to tell him he could leave us? It's only that I didn't want us talking in English and him feeling left out of the conversation.'

Louis could have made a witty remark about how her vigilance opposed that of other nobles who would not spare servants a second thought. Instead, he found himself admitting, 'We've never had many at Allenborough so my experience is limited. Ours is a poor estate and those few who do help out are tenants with nowhere better to go.'

Louis had always hidden his family's poverty from others. At Eton, it was easy to do—the lads often convened in the homes of others, there were many to choose from. And afterwards, the charm he'd honed and the connections he had made there granted him access and invitations into all the best events in London. It was only after his grandfather had died last year that Louis started to tire of them. He had no one to come home to and share this or that opportunity with—opportunities that didn't amount to anything really, though they had kept his grandfather entertained. Hopeful.

'My grandfather left the main house at one point to ease the burden on my stepmother. Took to the empty rectory cottage and I would often sleep there with him. Just the two of us. Doing for ourselves.' Louis shook his head abjectly. 'I don't recall ever telling anyone that.'

Mervat interlaced her fingers, fiddled with them in her lap. Louis might have craved her touch, but if she said or did anything out of pity for him, he would regret his honesty. Besides which, talk of Allenborough underscored why he could not be distracted by wanting it in the first. His mission here was to improve the estate's prospects, not romance Hussam's cousin!

Mervat replied, 'That is like me and my father who live mostly alone. We have only one guard by order of the khedive and a housekeeper who has been with Baba since he was a boy. Fateema is older now and finds any excuse to not make the trek to our house, though hers is only down the road.' She chuckled, then sighed. 'I miss them.'

'You do not prefer court life?'

'I was happy to be called here, to get the chance to spend time with my mother. But now I have been for a while, no, not at all. The hypocrisy, the life lived inside these walls that has little awareness of those struggling beyond it…it disheartens me.'

She looked at the *Telegraph*. 'Do not mind me—I do not mean to skew your perceptions.'

'Not at all. You must always speak your mind with me, Princess. Er… Mervat.' Louis did feel differently. This court was a place of wonder for him. Exploration. Each beautiful corner celebrated prestige and power. Unlike Allenborough, Sesostris was a place that would always attract money, always have enough to provide a livelihood for people. It could not solve all the suffering outside its walls, but it could be gainful employment for some, like her Amu Taha.

Louis did not know if Mervat sensed his opposing mind, but she changed course. 'You mentioned a stepmother. May I ask what happened to *your* mother?'

'She died giving birth. To me.'

The look on Mervat's face brought a lump to his throat. Not pity, but hurt. For him. A man she barely knew. And while he had the feeling that she would have directed such sincere empathy to anyone, it felt *nice* to be the object of it in that moment. It put him on alert too. How could such a soft heart withstand any harmful fallout of Hussam's plan?

'I have no recollection of her,' Louis hastened to add, if only to console the sensitive young woman sitting next to him. 'How does one miss what one has never known? My father suffered, certainly. He loved her deeply and tried his best to be there for me. He believed he'd never remarry but met the new Lady Wesley after I'd gone to Eton. The siblings started coming on like the best of floods.' He smiled, 'My father was making up for lost time.'

'How many?'

'Four, at last count.'

Louis happily named them for Mervat. 'They are an utter joy—one cannot be melancholy around them. We climb trees together, I tutor the eldest in Latin and attend the grandest tea parties with my youngest sister's peg dolls.' He laughed, 'But there is quite the age gap between us. They nearly call me *Amu*, as well. And not as kindly, mind you.'

'You cannot be that old,' she teased. 'Hussam is twenty-five so you must be about the same?'

'Well, four children under the age of eleven tend to make one feel so. Maybe too I feel older because of the time spent caring for my ailing grandfather. He didn't want my brothers and sisters to watch his decline, but I was happy to be there—in the aforementioned rectory's cottage. Quietly noting his words, wisdoms.'

'Leave no opportunity unseized,' she quoted shyly.

Louis had mentioned it at the Louvre.

His hand hovered over where hers were still latched in her lap. He dared not lower them, however, no matter how undeniable the sentiment simmering in him was. Mervat was not his to touch. There could never be anything between them. Yet, when their gazes latched on to one another, he thought she might be feeling something similar.

'You remember,' he said.

'Yes.'

She was too close. The beauty in those wide eyes. The heart shape of her face. The lips.

It was ridiculous how badly he wished to touch them. It didn't even have to be a kiss. The pad of his thumb would suit.

She twisted awkwardly and pointed to the jewellery box. 'I took it without asking so we should probably...'

Louis cleared his throat and then retrieved it for her. The octagon shape was covered in a deep flaxen velvet and laced with stars of blue marbled gemstone.

'Lapis lazuli,' Mervat said, 'which you would know.'

He longed for one of her glorious discourses. 'Do I? Please, I'd like to hear you tell.'

She lifted a disbelieving brow but did not refuse him. 'For centuries it has been a literal mark of civilisations. The blue pigment was extracted from gemstones to make paints used in scripts long before the printing press was popularised in Europe. We find evidence of it in handwritten Bibles and decorative pages of the Quran of the medieval era. Before that, the Vikings used the gemstones in their jewellery as did the ancient Egyptians. My favourite story of lapis lazuli and perhaps the first recorded example of its existence comes from the *Epic of Gilgamesh*, eighteen hundred years before Christ.

'In it, King Gilgamesh returns home to Uruk, his home city, after a long battle to find a chariot there. The chariot is made of lapis lazuli and piled with gold and jewels. It is a gift from Ishtar, goddess of love and war, who wishes him to be her husband.'

Louis trilled, 'I certainty did not know that. What happened? Did he agree?'

'Alas, he refused. Gilgamesh said he was far beneath a goddess and would not know what to give in return to someone who had everything.'

Louis couldn't help but feel sorry for King Gilgamesh.

'Ishtar, so enraged at his refusal sent him a bull made of lapis lazuli, which he then had to slay in order to save his life.'

'She was a fiery one, yes?'

'Women should not be scorned.' Mervat laughed and the sound of it was like a silk blanket spreading in his very soul.

Louis brought his knees together, reminding himself once again that she was all but promised to his friend and he had his own goals to focus on.

'What I do know of lapis lazuli,' Louis confided, 'is that it is mined in the caves of Afghanistan. A mountainous region known as Bactria, hard to navigate because the tribes who live there have an intense dislike for foreigners.'

'Really? I did not know that.'

'Then I am happy to be of use. I know it because my grandfather was there. He served during the Anglo-Afghan War.'

'He must have had stories of the time.'

Louis found himself confiding in her about his grandfather's experience in Afghanistan, and the biggest regret of his life. 'The koh-i-noor was within his grasp, a diamond sitting in a box not too different than the one in your lap, I imagine. There was danger and he had to depart quickly, but it would eventually go on to be the most treasured of the Queen's crown jewels. In his mind, he thought if only he'd recognised its future status then, his life would have been different. Hence his life motto which you recalled.' Louis used the word he would evermore associate with Mervat, 'Does that fit a *genealogy*?'

'I don't think your grandfather should have regretted walking away from it. Some things, lives particularly, are more precious than jewels. He had to return to his family. The people he loved. You, born a few years after.'

Louis had never thought of it that way and he was in awe of her wisdom for her young age. When Mervat looked at him with a heft of emotion, his own vision seemed to blur. How was it both comforting to talk with her and yet so difficult?

Beside Louis's focus needing to be on Allenborough, this was the khedive's court, and he was a powerful man who believed Mervat would marry his son.

Theirs was only supposed to be a ruse of defiant love.

Speaking of which… 'Hussam hasn't put our plan into motion yet?'

She seemed caught off guard by Louis's change of subject. 'No.'

He stood. 'Only I was thinking it would be dangerous for a gentleman to be caught alone with a lady. He might be forced into a duel or a quick marriage.'

'Alone? You mean in a…compromising position?'

It was an innocent question, but Louis couldn't help but imagine a compromising position or two he'd put Mervat in. 'Not necessarily. Even just alone.'

'As we are now?'

Louis didn't know if she was teasing him, but he had to trust she was. The alternative felt more dangerous. 'Yes. In England, unmarried young ladies must be accompanied by a chaperone when out in society. A male relative or elderly aunt, for example. I was wondering if Hussam's plan, where he is your chaperone and Nadine has none would even get past the palace gates?'

'I don't know how it is in England, or honestly, even how it is completely with Egyptians. But I have seen boys and girls talking in the streets or the marketplace. Unmarried ladies wash laundry in the Nile, knowing they are being watched by the unmarried men near Baba's house. We attended a wedding celebration the street over for a couple who took their watching further. They are poorer, certainly, and things in the harem are very different. My mother would know more of its rules.' Mervat sighed. 'I suppose if Anne knew I was here in the men's study, *alone* with you, she would not like it.'

Her sad expression tore at him and he recalled how abrupt her mother had seemed at the luncheon. 'Forgive me, but why must you let her likes dictate your life?'

'You are a man and do not know.'

He shook his head. 'Hussam is the same as you. I am an Englishman and do very well know the value of arranged marriages, I believe in them wholeheartedly, against the experience of the men in my family. My great-grandfather and grandfather both married for love, my father did it twice, and Allenborough suffered for it. Hussam is a prince who needn't marry for advantage. He could stand up to his father and demand to marry Nadine without the hassle of a plan meant to convince the khedive to see it his way.'

'Perhaps it is that Egyptians care more about our parents' good opinion whilst the English favour society's.'

If Mervat were making an astute observation, it was one that roused Louis's ire.

'After we come of age, parents should be under our sway. They should want us to be happy and successful in society,' he countered.

'Parents are our elders. Their demands are how they demonstrate their care. And because they are nearest to us, their opinions should matter most.'

'Enough to marry a man you do not love, to spend a lifetime with him?' Louis heard the frustration in his voice, though he wasn't sure from whence it stemmed. He raked a hand through his hair, told himself to calm his exasperation. Mervat did not deserve him—or anyone—yelling at her.

Feeling the tension perhaps, she waited a moment before continuing, 'I only mean to say that it is the ideal. My father makes few demands on me and my mother had never tried to sway me on any matter before I came to court. I hate that she and I are not in agreement over Hussam, but you are right. I cannot make such a life decision based only on what she wants for me.' She offered him a placating smile. 'In any case, it is because of my cousin's plan that I mostly sought you out today.'

'You wish to forgo it?' As soon as he asked, Louis hoped she would say yes. From what he knew of her, a fake relationship conflicted with what she believed in. 'You are authentic, honest. It is not in your nature to be disingenuous.'

'Thank you,' she acknowledged. 'In truth I have tried desperately to convince my mother that I do not want to marry Hussam and were the khedive to ask, I would tell him the same. But it has been hopeless. Maybe by agreeing to my cousin's plan, we can both ensure that our parents will accept our refusal. Does that make sense?'

Louis nodded.

'Moreover,' she said, 'I agreed to his plan so we can learn more about this.'

She lifted the jewellery box lid, exposing the magnificent crown beneath. Its tiara base was burnished gold, glorified with triangular pieces that could have been silver or diamonds. It was hard to tell which, for while they themselves might have been precious, they bowed beneath the glory of the blue gem at the crown peak. It looked like it might have been carved from the night sky itself, its facets an infinity of stars, blinding in their shimmer.

'The Cleopatra Cerulean,' Louis breathed. 'Incredible.'

'What do you remember of what Mr Henries said about it at the Louvre?'

He grinned. 'Not much. You'll excuse me for my preoccupation with the lovely young lady who'd accompanied me there.'

Her cheeks pinked. 'Your charm comes too naturally.'

'That was not charm, only truth.'

'Then thankfully, *I* was paying attention. Mr Henries said his best guess is that the jewel was originally mined in a cave in the Nile Delta, found by Alexander the Great himself and gifted to his sister who also happened to be named Cleopatra, not the more famous last queen of the Macedonian dynasty in Egypt. His sister Cleopatra never left their home. Mr Henries said that when the Ottomans excavated sites in Greece during *their* occupation of the country, they found and took this jewel. That was also when they found the infamous Parthenon marbles, purchased by Lord Elgin who was later accused by Lord Byron, of looting them.'

'The poet?'

'Yes. Because of his status and popularity, he was influential enough that an enquiry into the marbles was ordered. Although Lord Elgin was absolved, the marbles were then put into the British Museum trust. A lesson in how power might be wielded towards good.'

'I did not know that either.' Louis blew out an impressed breath. 'Your depth of knowledge is most admirable.'

She shrugged. 'With each of my research projects, it dawns on me that museums are ways everyone can enjoy a nation's cultural legacies. This crown, once we find out its complete story, will only go back to be stored in my mother's armoire. A shame, truly.'

'But if you were to marry Hussam, it would come to you?'

'Since that is not going to happen and when she realises it will not, Anne is likely to never let me see the crown again. Anyhow, we aren't talking about the marbles now! Let us get back to Mr Henries. He mentioned that there was an Egyptian during the find who took advantage of the Ottomans' generosity and claimed the crown was in the name of Cleopatra and so should belong here. Mr Henries said Lord Elgin and the other British there did not counter this unnamed nobleman because they didn't wish to risk political tensions between our countries.

'But that understanding seems wrong. When I asked my mother, she said it's a symbolic gift from Turkish nobles to

Egyptian brides or the other way around, Egyptian nobles to Turkish brides—a way to solidify relations between the two countries. When Anne first wore it, she believed my father would be khedive one day. But her explanation doesn't make any more sense and when I probed, she refused to clarify.'

Mervat finally took a breath. 'I apologise for talking too much. It is a horrible habit.'

'Please, don't apologise for it, not to me. I like listening to you.'

'When I begin to ramble, most people tune me out. Not you. I cannot tell when I have lost you.'

'You could not lose me,' Louis said, then quickly added, 'I am not much of a history aficionado, yet find myself transfixed by your knowledge. It saddens me when you stop.'

Her brow crinkled with a laugh. 'How are you not a history aficionado? We met in a museum.'

'I appreciate experiences, the *senses* of things enthral me. The *feel* of them.'

The words rolled from his tongue too sensually; he'd spoken too liberally.

And their bodies were too close.

Louis had leaned forward to examine the tiara and hadn't yet straightened.

From his vantage, the flicks of black in Mervat's eyes darkened against the amber there. She bit her lower lip ever so slightly and Louis thought of Lord Byron, whom she'd mentioned. Were he him, he could pen a poem about how the ridges of her upper front teeth were jagged, sharp things pricking into the lush defences of her lower lip. Thorns on a hedge of roses of a genus variety he desperately longed to know, one which had been planted beyond a glass.

Out of Louis's reach.

Chapter Six

Mervat

She lowered the jewellery box lid.

'I am most eager to learn more about the Cleopatra Cerulean. It's why I risked my mother's ire to show you. She clings to it like it is her anchor at court, bring it out for only the most important of occasions. When she told me I was to sit for the painting and had me wear it—'

'Wait,' Louis interrupted. He searched her face. 'Did you willingly sit for a portrait knowing it was for Hussam? Would that not be akin to demonstrating your consent to the marriage?'

Mervat had not known Hussam had anything to do with the portrait. But the flash of suspicion in Louis's eyes unnerved her. Did he believe her to be lying or hypocritical?

Maybe he could not understand that while she had defied her mother in certain things and would still in some matters, Mervat hated to do so. She wished Anne would see her side, listen to her, get to know her daughter and who she was before coming to court. And in Mervat's quest to improve their relationship, she *would* agree to the things her mother asked if they didn't affect the trajectory of her life too much.

The fact of it was that Anne had said that there was a

similar portrait of her at the same age in Turkey and she had wished to begin a tradition.

'One day, your daughter's portrait will hang next to ours.'

And Mervat desperately desired to be a part of Anne's traditions. Rather than explain it all to Louis, she looked down at her lap and said, 'My mother's approval is important to me.'

Louis bolted from his chair, putting space between them. Pacing around her for a minute before coldly saying, 'We need to establish rules for this farce. Parameters.'

She bristled. 'What do you mean?'

'As you yourself have already noted, you are a princess and can, if the worst happens in this defiance plot, escape to your father's palace. Even conversing here alone with me cannot damage your reputation. I, on the other hand and despite Hussam's best efforts to secure me a post here, could be forced back to England, seen as a cad there. Never taken seriously, my chances for a respectable vocation dashed.'

'You make me sound like a temperamental royal. I promise you, Louis, if you saw my father's house you would not count me as a princess or it as a palace.'

He stopped and took a deep breath. 'I did not mean to offend you, Mervat. Forgive me.'

She tilted her head, tucking a strand of hair behind her ear. 'You suggest I should not care for my mother's approval, may I suggest *you* should not care for society's. You have a talent, Louis, your words, these dispatches are—'

'Are but a gentleman's hobby,' he finished for her. 'Allenborough needs more from me. I require a good, well-paying position, a means to increase its monies, help it prosper. My younger siblings need me to be a model, education funds for the boys because that pot ran out on me, and dowries for the girls, otherwise they have little chance in good society.'

Mervat had not realised the risk to him, his siblings.

Though she could not claim to know British norms, his plea now enlightened her. 'I will speak to Hussam, tell him we need to find another way. I cannot let you or your family suffer at our expense.'

The words seemed a balm to whatever anger had been simmering in Louis. When he resumed his seat and gifted her with a wide grin, the lines crinkling handsomely in his cheeks, Mervat fought the urge to cry with relief.

'Nor do I want you to suffer.' He pointed to the jewelled box. 'If Hussam wants the rest of Egypt to think we are lovers then after you have broken off any chance of a marriage with him, will you let it be known our relationship was based solely on the Cleopatra Cerulean?'

'How would that absolve you?' she wondered.

'If I was working on learning more about it, the pursuit would be seen as honourable. In service of the Queen, who appreciates romantic escapades that concern crown jewels.'

Mervat fought a wave of disappointment. 'That is your intent? I know you and Hussam are working towards the embassy post, but I truly thought you were interested to learn of its genealogy, like me.'

'I won't lie and say my grandfather's experience with the koh-i-noor has not impacted me. I *am* interested and want a post but the purpose of said post or in lieu of it has always been about securing a future for my family, prestige for our title.' He paused before adding, 'A wife, for myself, perhaps.'

'You wish to marry.' Mervat made an extra effort to steady her voice for she was not sure why the prospect should bother her so much.

'A viscount who has brought England's attention to a jewel like the Cleopatra Cerulean and secured a diplomatic appointment because of it would render me an eligible suitor, a good match even. Not to a princess, to be sure. I could never hope for that, but a lady of some means could be arranged. A family of my own.'

He watched her carefully as he spoke and the image of him, away from Egypt—and her—passed through her mind. Louis, chasing golden-haired children like him in a wide green field in the English countryside. A woman watching them, one who wasn't Mervat.

She shook her head, banished the picture. 'My hope is that when we find out all we can about the jewel, we might donate it to a museum. There aren't many grand ones in Egypt but perhaps this will be the piece to make one so. I had put in a project idea with the khedive's office when I first came to court, seeking to occupy myself with it whilst here, but I have yet to hear back. Certainly, my mother would not agree to part with it for that, but it is supposed to come to me *eventually.*'

Mervat would not bring up the matter of her marriage again; they'd talked about that enough.

'Both our intentions are in the open, then,' he said. 'A central rule is established. Namely, honesty about our intentions for the Cleopatra Cerulean Crown. You want it in a museum. I, to tell the world of its existence.'

Mervat was still fretting over the potential harm to Allenborough, Louis's siblings. 'What if I were to give an interview after all is said and done. Would that help you?'

His eyes widened. 'An interview? As in, an official one?'

'If it comes to it, yes.' She spread her arms as if she were reading an imaginary headline and altered her voice. *'Princess Mervat Abbas of Egypt breaks her silence. "'Twas only a farce. I never loved the viscount. He lacks charm and is definitely not handsome enough to tempt me."'*

He threw her a playful pout before sobering. 'Your mother might not allow it.'

'I will not allow your reputation to be harmed, Louis. I promise.'

He nodded, closed his eyes for an instant before opening them again. Meeting her gaze. 'Thank you.'

When he reached over her for his notebook, his closeness, the aroma of him—a fresh, faint blend Mervat could not name the smells of even if her life depended on it—made her feel like she was walking barefoot on hot sand.

'Pardon me,' Louis heaved in a way that made her question if he experienced the same thing she had at their proximity.

There can be nothing between us!

It was one thing to refuse a proposal from her cousin, quite another to entertain one from a foreigner, someone with a different religion than her own. Even if Baba allowed a break from family traditions, her mother would never. And though princesses or other Egyptian ladies might dally with men—whether for fun or in hope of securing a marriage commitment—Mervat did not know how to play such games.

Besides, given what Louis had said about his life back home, the future of his estate, she knew she was an unsuitable match. He would want an English bride who would hold the viscountess title. Someone who looked the part, knew the customs. A woman with a dowry like his sisters would possess. Young Egyptian ladies did not typically come with dowries, they were given dowries. And she had her own traditions and customs to uphold.

Mervat had to be more in control of her emotions when in Louis's company! It would have to be *her* personal rule for this farce of Hussam's.

It would help if he stopped looking at me like that.

'I do not mean to stare,' Louis said, as if reading Mervat's thought. 'It is only…has anyone ever told you your face is shaped like a heart?'

Why would he say such a thing? Was it merely an observation? Or was that glimmer in his eyes indicative of more? Did he appreciate the shape of her face? Find her pretty?

She could not trust herself with a response or even think of one that wouldn't give voice to her questions, so Mervat held her breath until he'd turned to his notes and his neat script began to fill a page in his notebook. When he was done, Louis faced forward and she too, promptly and primly, straightened.

That was how Amu Taha from Tanta found them when he entered carrying a serving tray of tea and news that Hussam was back.

'Shukran.' After he had left, Mervat realised it might be a warning. The older, wiser man was afraid she'd be caught with her cousin's friend alone, proving Louis's earlier argument. Perhaps Egyptian society wasn't so different from the British.

It meant Hussam's plan had merit.

'He meant to warn me that my cousin is back, and he might not like to find me with you,' Mervat explained while pouring them each a cup of tea. She tried not to stare as Louis blew gently at the rim. His puckered lips were full, a natural crimson in hue. She sipped her own tea too soon. The strong, heavily sweetened blend scorched her tongue.

'You're upset, having to put Amu Taha in that position,' Louis observed and she loved the cute way he spoke the name in Arabic. 'You disdain court life yet most would envy what you have achieved. Wealth, prestige—and the loyalty of a discrete servant.'

She heard in his words the appreciation he had for it, perhaps even the desire to remain at Sesostris. A warning blared in Mervat. No matter how impossible it might be to form a real attachment with Louis, on this there could be no compromise, ever. Even if he did not have his own estate he needed to return to in England and were he to stay at court here, in Egypt, Mervat could not be with a man who wanted to live somewhere she did not. She'd suffered the physical separation of her parents even though they were in the same country and would never subject her future children to such a fate. When she married, *if* she married, Mervat and her husband would have to have a clear agreement beforehand on where they would spend their lives.

'Well, are you two not the epitome of clandestine meetings?' Hussam greeted them loudly, then commanded a servant to drag a chair closer to where they sat. He dropped into it like it was a canopy bed and waved the fellow off before speaking in a lower tone.

'Sorry for yelling but how else to get gossip mills milling?' He reached for a *ka'ak* ring from the tea tray and spun it around his finger before putting it back and winking. 'Miss me?'

'Where have you been?' she asked.

'Hand delivering the khedive's invites across Egypt for the midsummer festivities. Hinting at a wedding before summer's end,' Hussam answered.

'Why, if you do not plan on having one?' Louis said with a huff before Mervat could.

'Courtesies, mate. My father maintains strong ties with nobles, so none challenge him.'

'As you're about to do.'

'As *we* are about to do.' Hussam cocked an eyebrow. 'Besides, I had an ulterior motive.'

'You saw Nadine's father,' Mervat said, realisation dawning. 'Did you ask for her hand?'

'Not yet, but we had a good talk in which I was led to

believe he would welcome it. In the meantime, I mentioned my cousin wanted to take Nadine under her wing. My very smart cousin with fluency in multiple languages and acumen in the scholarly pursuits of history, archaeology, et cetera, et cetera.' He turned to Louis and cocked a brow. 'I am extremely proud of Mervat.'

She gave him a mock kick and tried not to overthink Louis's admiring glance in her direction, 'As you should be.'

'I have also taken the liberty of arranging our first outing. My dears, Project Defiant Love begins now!' Hussam's self-satisfied smug adjourned their meeting and had Mervat feeling proud to be a part of her cousin's plan.

Chapter Seven

Louis

As he and Hussam trotted through Cairo in an open carriage, Louis absorbed the details absentmindedly. The road changed temperamentally, some parts bricked or cobblestoned, others paved smooth with a dried dirt. The width of it was surprising as was the cornucopia of homes lining their path which somehow looked as if they could have been built on either a sandy desert floor or tilled green land. There were multifloored complexes, modern flats with shutters and verandas crowded with lines of drying laundry or oriental carpets bathing in the sun. Peppered between them were older villa-type dwellings with exposed wooden additions or cornice facades. Scattered trees acted as shade for the odd fruit or vegetable seller, their trunks serving as places to park mules and carriages.

'Where are we meeting the young ladies?' Louis *tried* to claw back his excitement. Though they had established their honest intentions for their farce of a relationship, he kept coming back to how exciting it had been to be with Mervat in the study. Alone. The way she'd looked at him that made Louis feel like maybe her admiration was not false. That the admiration that was burning inside of him for her wasn't one-sided.

He knew there could be nothing between them, they were worlds and life goals apart truly…yet he kept coming back to Mervat's insistence that she would not let his reputation be harmed despite what her mother would want, which had truly touched him since she clearly desired her *anne*'s approval most ardently.

On the other hand, Mervat might have done the same for the servant Amu Taha.

The thought was a blatant reminder of *his* own lowly status in comparison to her.

Did Louis truly only want her to care for him in the same way she did Amu Taha? It should be enough for him to be respected by a woman with such a good heart. He tried to remind himself that theirs was a risky plan and if they succeeded without her being harmed and with their friendship intact, then it would be a win on all counts.

'Mervat thought the Al-Azhar Library would be best,' Hussam replied. 'The Khedival National Library in the former palace endeavours to be the largest collection in the country but with the move to Sesostris, some of its holdings are in archives difficult to get to. Besides which, my father's men may still be there and we don't want them to know of our venture.' Hussam winked. 'You and my cousin work on your little project while her friend Nadine and I wait, very bored, and having to entertain ourselves for all to see.'

Louis felt hopeful for his friend, but said, 'I wonder about Princess Mervat's father. Surely, he would not approve of his daughter gallivanting about town. Would the khedive see that as an additional challenge?'

'Your diplomatic mind is developing.' Hussam whistled with approval. 'Abbas *is* direct competition blood-wise, but in no other way. Recall how they had us read the occasional American writer at Eton? Thoreau. A pond or life in the for-

est or some such was the title? Well, Mervat's father could
have written it himself. He is strange. Lets her do whatever
she pleases because he did whatever he pleased. Leaves his
wife at court for nearly two decades without nary a visit. He
must have a deep philosophy, a raison d'être for doing what
he does, not that he shares it with anyone. Unlike his daughter, Abbas is a man of very few words.'

Louis frowned. 'It must trouble her.'

'If it does, she has never let on. Mervat is a dutiful daughter.' Hussam pointed to the al-Azhar complex as they came
upon it. It was like a scene in a painting, the dip in the road
made for the perfect angle to catch the breadth of its ancient
brick, the rise of its minarets and crouched domes domineer-
ing in a watery blue sky with wisps of white cloud on the
horizon.

As soon as the carriage passed its gates, they were met by
a flurry of people. A line of sheikhs and religious scholars
wearing pristine white kaftans and loose robe *abayas* stood
to greet them. They spoke in a rich Arabic that sounded quite
different from what Louis had heard in the palace. Curiously,
he found it easier to make out a few of their words, the enun-
ciation of letters was more pronounced, the pace with which
they spoke slower.

When he remarked as much to Hussam, his friend said
it was because the court had been Turkish for so long and it
melded with local dialects in ways that weren't always clear.
'This is where people come to learn the purest of Arabic.
Arabi fus'ha, it is called.'

Most in the line were abundantly welcoming towards the
prince, but more cautious with Louis. One even glared at him
openly and referred to him as *ajnabi miseehi*. The Christian
foreigner.

With each introduction, Hussam shook a sheikh's hand

than patted his own to his chest. When they were finally done, he explained, 'I said we're waiting for my cousin, come to see a librarian she knows and has worked with before. They've gone to fetch the librarian to verify because they can't believe a princess of Egypt was here and they weren't aware of her status.'

'What of him, with the frowning face?' Louis knobbed his head towards the one.

'He thought he was doing me a favour, implying that all foreigners are spies. When I said you were my dear friend, he offered to teach you Islam so our relationship could be made *halal*.'

Louis understood what the opposite of *halal* was. *Haram*. 'He thinks our friendship should be forbidden?'

'Al-Azhar is a religious university held in esteem because of its long history in Egypt but it collects all sorts of people. Some hold extreme and troublesome ideas. There are hypocrites here too.' He pointed to where the line of men had stood. 'They say they are independent of politics but why the special welcome if not a chance for the khedive's favour through me?'

Louis would have said more, but he perceived the change in the air by the rising hairs on his arms.

Mervat.

He turned towards the courtyard entrance, his body primed to be enthralled by her presence, take in whatever new gown she was wearing, then have to tear away his gaze. But she was covered in a black cloak from head to toe, and a bejewelled veil was pulled across the lower half of her face, only her eyes, doe-like and lined with a thick layer of black kohl, were exposed.

Louis might have thought her garb was for religious reasons but next to her, Nadine wore what she might have at

Sesostris, the top of her hair covered with a plain hijab scarf pulled over her braids, her face completely bare.

Though Louis found the discrepancy strange, he was the only one who seemed to. Nevertheless, there was a bit of a kerfuffle he did not quite understand and, led by the fellow who'd insulted Louis, most of the men who'd greeted him and Hussam were now shaking their heads at Mervat. Louis wished he could come to her defence, but it was Hussam who finally stood between them and called his cousin *sadiqa*. Truthful. Had they been accusing her of lying?

'Mr Ali,' was the name repeated in Mervat's response to their continuous questions, until the studious fellow who answered to it appeared.

Mr Ali's face widened with recognition when Mervat spoke to him and he kindly greeted the princess, whilst not paying attention whatsoever to the prince or him. This action garnered Louis's respect and Hussam expressed his displeasure at the other men. His short tirade caused them to disperse, freeing Mr Ali to lead them to their destination.

Hussam was wedged between Louis and Mervat. Nadine flanked the other side of their foursome as they crossed the courtyard.

'Mr Ali is the librarian and he told them he knew my voice but they wanted an explanation as to why I, a frequent visitor, usually come alone, not in my princess garb.' Mervat looked across Hussam to explain for Louis.

She was always so thoughtful; she knew he would have felt at a loss without any translation.

'They asked to see my face but Hussam said it was an insult to women of the harem. I reminded them that my last project was looking at the archives around the initial plans for the Suez Canal and the French sculptor, a man named Bartholdi, who tried to sell them the commission of a statue inspired by the *Colossus of Rhodes*. It would be a ninety-foot woman in Egyptian peasant robes, holding a massive torch, like a lighthouse to guide ships into the harbour. He called it *Egypt Bringing Light to Asia*. Alas, Bartholdi was denied, but I suspect the world has not heard the last from him on this idea.'

'I know you wouldn't have minded showing your face Mervat,' Hussam said, skipping over her artifact story, 'but that man insulted Louis earlier and I wanted to teach them a lesson.'

'Obliged, mate,' Louis said.

Hussam grinned, 'Just don't turn out to be a spy.'

'You have my word.'

Mervat hung back a bit and Louis followed suit so that Hussam's quicker pace put him and her in step. Beneath her veil he could tell she was smiling at him.

'I should have already bid you a good morning, Viscount,' she said.

'And to you, *sabah el kheir*, Princess.' He lowered his voice a notch, 'You seem to have a discerning attraction to sculptures—past and future.'

'Most discerning.'

Before he could work out if they were flirting with one another, Hussam fell back to his place, once again blocking Louis's view of Mervat.

Rather than be disappointed at the loss, he distracted himself by marvelling at the way the sky reflected the marble expanse at their feet, pooling ahead to look as he imagined an oasis in the desert might. They passed a group of young boys sitting in a circle, cross-legged, each with his own Quran opened on a small tablet. Their recitation was individual, but their collective harmony reminded Louis of a choir rehearsal. Older students passed them too, some not Egyptian at all; they looked as if they could be from China or India. Many sought introductions or gawked at Hussam while their minders kept looking back to apologise or shrug as if they'd no clue as to how anyone knew who he was. Yet, it was clear that this was an announced visit and the entirety of the al-Azhar population knew exactly who they were and had been anticipating them.

When the courtyard ended and they turned into the library, Hussam stopped to make an announcement to those gathered there. He didn't translate, but Louis inferred that he demanded the area be cleared for the *ameera*, or princess, and that only the aid of the librarian would be required.

They scrambled to do as the prince asked, ushering everyone outside. Mervat's stance seemed both apologetic for and embarrassed by her cousin's order.

When the door was shut and only Mr. Ali remained, Hussam waved them off. 'Start your project. And take all the time you need.'

Nadine followed him to a small table for two in a shadowy corner whilst Mervat lowered her veil. Louis tried not to stare at her beautiful face beneath it, but it was hard just then. Of course, he knew what she looked like, but this was a side of her he hadn't seen. He wasn't sure why it intrigued him so except to think that maybe her genealogy talk had influenced him. If artifacts had multiple sides, surely people had nuances as well. And he found he wanted to ascertain Mervat's, even as he reminded himself that he should be anything but interested.

She introduced him to the librarian. 'Mr Ali, meet Viscount Louis Wesley, a palace friend and writer with a British newspaper.'

He shook hands with the fellow, a dark-skinned middle-aged man with thick glasses and a too-close shave.

Mervat continued, 'He is helping gather information about a jewel and crown, called the Cleopatra Cerulean. It might have been found in Greece by the Ottomans, but we know nothing beyond that.'

Mr Ali understood the English but answered in a heavy accent, 'Anything for help Miss Mervat.' He corrected himself, 'Princess Mervat. Sorry not knowing it you in *milaya*. You come before as common girl?'

'*M'aalish*, Mr Ali. I did not mean to lie to you in the past but a common daughter of Egypt is how I wish to be seen always and I am only staying at court temporarily.' Mervat grimaced modestly, then graciously transitioned back to their project, 'Perhaps we start with records of finds in Greece, anything that pertains to treasures originating or connected in some way to Egypt?' She looked at Louis for approval.

He agreed, 'Sounds good to me.'

Mr Ali said he would fetch what he could find in the stacks, before pointing them to wait at a wide mahogany desk with a pair of oil lamps and a matching number of rickety chairs. Louis held one for Mervat. While she took a beat gathering her garments, he couldn't help but breathe her in, closing his eyes to decipher the notes.

The roasted Turkish coffee blend caught in the fibres of her cloak.

The orange segments she'd have eaten at breakfast.

White jasmine soap from her bath.

The perfumed water scenting her flesh.

He opened his eyes with a start to find her looking up at him from her seated position. Louis nearly tripped getting into the chair opposite for he was much too tall for it. Or, he was afraid Mervat had seen into his imagination and knew precisely where it had been.

Further proof of it was in her question. 'Is it odd to see me covered like this?'

'Women should wear what they wish.' Louis spoke quickly, to stomp on what nearly sprang from his lips.

I should like to see you utterly uncovered.

Mervat lowered her chin and gifted him one of her small smiles. It was a movement he was starting to recognise as uniquely hers. The tilt that stressed the heart shape of her face, the intense look in her eyes that made it seem she would only ever be focused on who was before her right then and there.

'It is a tradition of the highest ranking in the harem. When women leave it, they should be covered completely. In other Muslim countries, women dress so but not so much in Egypt. Here the full veil is a marker of status and though the khedive moves to modernise, my mother is a traditionalist.'

Louis would not get into a tiff with her about her mother again. 'Well, the English certainly have their traditions.'

Mervat looked around nostalgically. 'The people here are not used to me in it. I used to come often. Al-Azhar isn't so far from my father's home. They dedicate the afternoons for women scholars and students. The library is never this empty.'

Louis was surprised. 'Women study here? I only just read in the paper you so kindly brought to me the other day that Oxford is considering admitting its first female student to much fuss from the masses. Not that I agree with the masses. I should one day like my sisters to be as educated as my brothers.'

Mervat spoke proudly, 'Al-Azhar has been graduating *shaykhas* nearly since its inception, jealous perhaps that the first university dedicated to women's education began in Fez, Morocco, in the year 859.'

'Incredible. One of the imams offered Hussam and me a tour earlier but I've a feeling it would be better guided by you.'

Mervat sighed. 'It is one of my favourite places in all of Egypt. The sun obscured the magnificence of the courtyard when we entered, but at dusk, the intricacies reveal themselves. The latticed borders on the domes are like little pyramids in design.' She chuckled. 'You would find better words to describe it. Maybe if we're here long enough I can show you.'

'Or another time?' Louis surprised himself with how much he wanted there to be.

'Ramadan is especially beautiful.'

'You fast it then?' He knew of the holy month, but mostly it was from Hussam who had considerable trouble with it back at Eton.

Mervat nodded. 'Since I was ten years old. It is the best month in Cairo, the city beats with the heart of it. The decorations, the spirit of kindness and generosity. Some nights Baba and I come to the mosque here, pray the *taraweeh* with hundreds of others. He loves it too. Other times in the year, he would avoid crowds of people but that changes in Ramadan. He becomes a different person. Is yours a churchgoing family?'

It was a reminder of the differences between them.

'There weren't enough funds at Allenborough for a proper rectory so ours was a more "distanced" experience. Oh, but we Wesleys certainly celebrate the big ones like Christmas and my stepmother loves to make Easter special for my siblings.' He flattened his palm on the table, found it surprisingly smooth and cold. 'It wasn't until Eton that I learnt other faiths existed. It was Hussam actually and another of our friends—a Jewish lad from Austria—who taught me the connections between our Abrahamic traditions.'

It occurred to Louis that while people thought Mervat was a talker, she was an even better listener.

A short while later, she asked, 'I've told you that this is my favourite place in Egypt, tell me about yours in England.'

Louis struggled to think of a place as grand or historic as here, one from the many he'd been granted entry to because of his title or the friends he was with, but it was the grassy, unexpansive moors of Allenborough that came to mind.

'There is a brook at home. I used to run the length of it as a boy pretending it was an ocean. Its little fish were enormous whales, its mossy rocks an oyster reef brimming with pearls and its bed of sand ready to be panned for gold.' He lifted his fingers from the table and wriggled them. 'Rather absurd, I know.'

He'd never told anyone of his childhood game and he found he was eager to read her reaction. Mervat's brow furrowed, the lines there prominent, but then like a bird, they fled and were gone. 'Not absurd at all.'

She looked as if she meant to say more, but Mr Ali returned then. He carried a wooden crate filled with scrolls and a few ledgers. Some contained notes in Turkish, others in Arabic. Thankfully, Mervat knew how to read both while Louis poured over the few English or French records. They were scant and proved worthless so he turned to sort whatever she and Mr Ali set aside. Anything they found interesting, Mervat translated to Louis and he noted it in his journal.

They found one instance of a crown that sounded similar—but there was no talk of a jewel in it, nor did it reference Cleopatra at all, only the design of a knot that sounded like it could hold the cerulean gem. They would have forgone the mention altogether had Mervat not recalled that Isis's symbol was a knot and Cleopatra was believed to be a reincarnation of the ancient Egyptian goddess. That information was from the Turkish lead excavation in Greece where the Parthenon marbles were collected. They found another bill of sale that had no connection to it but was rather close in timing, for one precious blue stone to a Turkish pasha with multiple holdings in Egyptian businesses. The stone was named the 'Nile Blue'.

'These don't match up with Mr Henries's talk at the Louvre at all,' Mervat said, puzzled.

'I can write to him,' Louis suggested, 'politely enquire as to his sources.'

'That would be wonderful!'

Mervat's enthusiasm swelled in his own breast, but it was an altogether conflicting emotion for Louis. *Why* did he so ardently yearn to please her?

'There is nothing of how the Cleopatra Cerulean came to be a marker of the relationship between Egyptian royal grooms and their Turkish brides. That is how my mother speaks of it,' Mervat said after they'd exhausted the container and Mr Ali had left.

'Perhaps we should interview her?'

'She does not care to explore its genealogy with me. After the Louvre, I implored her by saying it could be a mother-daughter venture but...'

Mervat sighed and he followed her gaze as it trailed a nearby pillar then climbed to the very high ceiling, exploring the rafters and calligraphic script painted there. Her fingertips rapped the table as she got lost in her thoughts. Then she leapt from her seat and led him to another part of the library, towards a large cabinet with glass panes and a number of drawers. She knew which one she wanted, rustling through it to pluck a scroll from within. She cleared a nearby table and asked Louis to anchor its sides with his hands as she spread it wide.

'It's the family tree of all nobles with connections to the Ottoman Empire.'

She found a magnifying glass from another drawer. She squinted, reading names aloud as she traversed one side of it closely. Mervat stopped at one.

'There. Anne's sister. My aunt Feride. She visited us once. I was called to court to meet her. I was young, no more than ten but remember her being terribly grumpy. She came with a container of items from their familial house in Turkey and my father was called to collect it. Baba never went to court but he did to collect that container.'

Mervat's gaze widened as it met Louis's. 'We need to go to my father's house.'

Chapter Eight

Mervat

As soon as Hussam heard, Mervat regretted suggesting it. Baba was not accustomed to guests, and to bring them all without warning would not be fair to him.

'It's perfect,' Hussam said. They stood before the palace carriage she and Nadine had come in, the open carriage he and Louis had travelled in a bit ahead. 'Controversial enough to irk the khedive, but even he would know that I could not well forbid my betrothed from visiting her father. Of course, I will not be able to come. And Nadine would want to respect her harem host. We will take the leisurely route back home.'

'Making both of you look good and the princess and me look—' Louis started.

'Very involved in one of her projects,' Hussam mused. 'As I said, it's perfect.'

'Please do not refer to me as your "betrothed", cousin,' Mervat corrected in Arabic, an eye towards Nadine. The girl stood like a roped lamb between them, wordless. On the way over from Sesostris, Nadine has said she'd never visited a place of higher learning, that a tutor her father once hired even suggested she should depend on her beauty and wealth to make her way in the world rather than her brain because that would get her nowhere.

Hussam was inconsiderate, unthinking.

He should have agreed to a tour for Nadine's sake. Asked her where she'd like to go now.

As Louis respected her.

Even if he had his own motivations for researching the Cleopatra Cerulean, at least he'd been honest with Mervat about them. And she quite appreciated his note-taking earlier. The way he'd supported her ideas. She'd not have remembered the encounter with her aunt if she'd not been talking about family with him.

Hussam apologised to them in advance for his aggression. Then he called the carriage driver to ready himself and wagged a finger at Mervat. Raising his voice, he nearly shouted, 'You will not speak to Amca Abbas on matters of court.'

Louis bristled and when Hussam noticed, he angled his head so none but them could see his wink. 'You are a gallant gentleman but he *is* a rival for the throne.'

Nevertheless, Mervat couldn't stand Baba being drawn into their ploy. 'My father has no desire for the throne, he'd throw himself in the Nile rather than take it.'

'That's the only reason keeping my father from tossing *him* into it.' Hussam jutted his chin to the youngest servant who'd accompanied them, 'You! Find my cousin a *hantoor*!'

Then, with a sweep of his jacket, he waved away the open carriage he and Louis had come in and installed Nadine into the carriage Mervat and she had come in, leaving her and Louis alone with the unfortunate servant. The boy was barely grown and looked quite distraught.

'My father's house is near and we don't need a *hantoor*.'

'Please let me do as I was asked. The prince trusts me, it is an honour.'

She nodded and pointed to a *hantoor* passing by on the other side of the street. While they waited for the servant to flag it down, Louis said, 'Hussam is too accomplished at acting. I'm sorry you had to experience that.'

His care for her reaction endeared and embarrassed her a little. Hussam had called Louis *gallant* and she agreed that it seemed to come to him instinctively.

After he was sure the hantoor was coming to them, the servant ran to catch up with the palace carriages, not sparing them another glance.

The *hantoor* driver was an older man with sunburned, leathery skin from too much work, his *galabaya* wrinkled and greasy. When she told him that he too could go on because her father's house was nearby, he spoke humbly in a Sa'eedi accent, 'Permit me to take you, for these streets are not safe for women of the harem.' He gestured towards Louis. 'And foreigners can be swindled.'

'The end of Mouez Road, then.'

'That is fine, but I do not think my horse can make it back to the palace.'

'Never mind that. My father has a driver and carriage who will take us back.'

'Very good.' He gestured for them to board. 'Careful, it is a high step.'

Louis held out his hand to her as Mervat climbed. She might not have needed it, but in the extra layer she was wearing and the rickety nature of the two-person carriage, she took it.

Or maybe she only wanted to feel what it was like, to have her hand held in his.

And did he keep hold of it longer than he otherwise would have?

Louis had probably offered his support to any number of women's hands before—but Mervat had never been touched in such an intimate way. Her stomach flipped, her chest restricted. She was as disappointed when he finally let go as she was worried she might have combusted if he'd held on for any longer.

They rode in an amiable silence, she let the sounds of the city lull her as Louis took to writing down his observations. The closer they got, the more nervous she was about introducing him to Baba.

'If we'd walked, we'd have arrived already,' she whispered, 'this horse strolls at his own pace, as a tourist might.'

'He's like me,' Louis joked, then hastened to add, 'though I hope not in odour.'

He turned to look at her with a lopsided grin, one which made Mervat ridiculously happy for a minute. And then came the thought that she'd miss it when it was gone from her life.

'Since we have been talking about favourites,' she said, 'can you guess what my favourite smell in the whole world is?'

'Flowers.'

She shook her head. 'No. They belong in the fresh air.'

'Honeyed sweets.'

'If I am very hungry, perhaps. Otherwise, wrong again.'

'The crisp wind on the moors, on one of the last of autumn's days.'

He swallowed as he said it, the light mood between them heavier somehow. He was talking of his home, a place she would never visit. 'I cannot claim to know it.'

They fell to silence again. And she'd forgotten her initial question when, at the end of their *hantoor* ride and the gates of her house appeared, Louis turned suddenly and said, 'Clay.'

His gaze was intense, anticipating. Mervat recalled comparing his blue eyes to the Nile when she'd first met him but perhaps their shade was more akin to the brook's waters in Allenborough.

'Yes, that is my favourite. I cannot sculpt, but the earth, the mud, is a clean, pure smell—one I have lived with all my life. To me, clay is the perfume of possibilities.'

Baba did not rise from his seat in the garden when his only child, whom he had not seen for weeks, came to greet him. Not because he was upset with Mervat or busy at work—it was her father's way. He worked hard to keep his moods on an even keel.

Anne had once told Mervat that when they were first married, she thought Baba's lack of words and emotion was due to shyness, and though she might have found it endearing at the start, it became the largest point of contention between them. After she'd given birth to Mervat, she'd chosen to stay at court and the khedive had allowed it, everyone suspected, so that she'd not give birth to a son who might have threatened his reign.

Mervat used to believe that if Baba had been smoother, more charming, Anne would have stayed with them. When she experienced her first menstrual cycle at thirteen and knew she could not talk to him about it, Mervat had yelled, 'Why did you drive Anne away?'

He'd been emotional at her unhappiness, cried that he hadn't wanted to make his own wife unhappy and now his daughter was. It had taken months after that for them to get back to the equilibrium in their relationship. Him, not saying anything but allowing Mervat to fill their silences. Perhaps it was why she didn't know when to stop talking with others now.

She crouched, took both his hands in her own and pressed

a kiss to his knuckles, rough with his garden work. '*Salam alaykum*, Baba, I missed you.'

'The seeds you sent from France.' He pointed to a patch to their left.

'Lavender. It is fragrant, a pretty purple. They put it in soaps.' She didn't tell him that the woman in the apothecary said the herb was thought to help with weary spirits.

'We will see if what grows there can have a life here,' her father mused.

'Under your thumb, they'd grow in desert sands.' She smiled. 'Baba, I want you to meet Louis, he is a friend of cousin Hussam's.' She said it in Arabic first, then in English. Her father grunted and shook his head, refusing the introduction. When Mervat looked up at Louis apologetically, his expression was one of understanding.

He crouched too, his knee scraping against hers, making her feel weak in both.

'*Ahlan, Amu. Ana sa'eed ala almuqabala.*' Louis laboured to express his pleasure at meeting her father in Arabic, but Mervat couldn't recall a sentence that had ever touched her so.

Baba frowned, searched his daughter's face before asking, 'He called me *amu*. Are you going to marry him?'

She hoped Louis didn't understand that part. 'He is only helping me with a project.'

She stood, avoiding Louis while he did the same because she had the feeling he *had* understood. 'Where is Fateema today?'

Baba shrugged. 'Her grandson has a rash.'

'And Mustafa?' The khedive's guard hadn't been at the gate. And worryingly, neither had the carriage that was meant to return her and Louis back to the palace.

'Has not been here since you left.'

That's strange. She had not seen him at Sesostris either.

She looked closer at her father, noticed how the hollows in his cheeks had grown deeper. When Fateema wasn't here, Mustafa would be the one to remind Baba to leave his garden, take his meals.

'We haven't eaten lunch,' she said. 'I will make something for all of us. Do you have food?'

'Look in the house.' Baba waved them towards it.

It was a humble one, built so as to not draw attention of neighbours. Whitewashed concrete and in a plain rectangular shape, it was not the sort Louis could write about in one of his pieces, but it was her home and she wanted him to like it.

She said as much when she ushered him inside. He spun slowly, appraising—the old table where they took their meals, the shabby sofa that sat low to the ground but held a multitude of colourful cushions, the paintings on the wall of Quranic verses because Fateema insisted they were the only way to ward off the evil eye.

'It is utterly charming,' Louis said.

And it was something, coming from him, the most charming man Mervat had ever known.

Chapter Nine

Louis

He was still thinking about the way Mervat casually picked at the dirt beneath her father's fingertips, how she seemed so much more at ease here with her *baba* than in the palace, where the tautness was apparent in her posture, whenever her mother was in proximity.

And what a place this was in comparison to Sesostris. Mervat's home was more garden than it was house. The windows were plentiful, each looking out at a tree or a patch of green and this contributed to the feel of the interior, rendering it more of a leisurely resting spot. A refuge. The solid pieces of furniture were necessities, lived in, somewhat unfashionable but pleasantly as cottage furniture was wont to be. It was comfortable way in which Mervat moved through the space that most, well…*moved* him. It beautified the place, heightened its amiableness in a way Louis could sense, even if he could not entirely put it into words.

'Make yourself at home while I look for something suitable to wear,' she said.

Louis nodded but did not sit, sure it was inappropriate he should be alone with her inside.

When she emerged from what he assumed was her bedroom, Mervat had exchanged the harem cloak and veil for a loose burgundy kaftan with tiny yellow hearts embroidered throughout. She shook out her hair, not realising the effect it was having on Louis. It was down to her hips, the dark curls gloriously shiny. It shocked him how badly he longed to touch it, but thankfully in few flicks of her wrists she'd gathered it into a high bun and secured it with a bandana, none the wiser.

Probably for the best.

With her dressed like that and in close quarters, the gap between them seemed to narrow. He should not be considering her in any way beyond Hussam's plan for them because when it came to an end, as it must, he did not want to be sorry that it had.

It was hard to remember here, however.

Here, she wasn't a princess out of the viscount's reach. He wasn't a viscount with responsibilities at home that he had to prioritise.

Here, she was Mervat and he, Louis.

Her father rushed in then, a scant grey tabby clutched close. He spoke to his daughter excitedly while Mervat watched as the cat pawed, eager to jump out of his arms and into hers. Even as the cat settled there, he wasn't content and moved to Louis. Mervat's laugh was unabashed joy. Had he ever heard her laugh? He was sure he hadn't for he'd not easily forget the sound of the blithe music it made.

The thin, bony cat settled in his arms and both Mervat and her father petted it there.

'Apparently Baba hasn't seen Mishmish since I left, but if it was me that he missed then why did he come to you?'

'Mishmish is his name?' Louis asked, much too aware of her nearness.

'It means *apricot*. I don't know if anyone ever named him—it's what Baba and I call him.'

Her father fetched a saucer of milk. Mervat lowered her nose to sniff and wrinkled it in the cutest way. 'He'll get sick from that. Water only, Baba, and we'll give him from our lunch.'

Abbas nodded in understanding, though she'd only spoken half the words in Arabic.

'He understands English?' Louis whispered.

'Yes. French, Turkish, even some Spanish. He was the one who taught me, but sometimes even I forget how educated he was as a khedive in training.'

When her father returned and had barely set down the water, Mishmish leapt from Louis's embrace and lapped.

'Atshan, miskeen,' her father mumbled.

'Likely hungry too,' Mervat declared.

'You're welcome to our house,' her father said to Louis in English, gesturing for him to sit.

Mervat grinned. 'Baba doesn't crack open the vault of languages he has for just anyone. He must like you.'

Louis put a hand on his chest, grateful for the cat who'd allowed him to make a connection with *her* father. 'I'm honoured, sir. *Shukran.'*

'Baba, we're here to look for a box. There is a project I am working on and Mr Wesley is writing about. It is a box from Turkey. Anne's sister brought it when I was young.'

Except Abbas was no longer paying them any attention. He sat on the floor cross-legged, focused entirely on the cat. Mervat brought him a cushion. 'We will talk after eating.'

Louis followed her into the back of the house, past the bedrooms with their closed doors, and into a kitchen with the most basic of necessities.

Mervat took an inventory of the ice box, pulled together ingredients: brown-shelled eggs, ripe red tomatoes, long green onions, and arugula. The latter she fanned in the air so Louis could smell their peppery freshness. 'From Baba's garden.'

She lit two burners: on the first she emptied a bowl of beans into a pot and on the other, she placed dampened bread to be heated.

'Let me help.' Louis disliked feeling useless, merely standing there and watching her work. His stepmother would shoo him away from the kitchen in the Allenborough manor, saying it wasn't where a gentleman belonged. Yet, between the time he'd spent with his grandfather and in Paris after he died, Louis had learned his way around a kitchen. Even perfected a few dishes.

'I can cook with my daughter.' Mervat's father had come to stand in the doorway.

'Let the viscount get his hands dirty, Baba, you try to remember what happened to that box from Turkey!'

Abbas left as quickly as he'd appeared.

'I have to be persistent with him, push him a bit sometimes,' Mervat explained, intimately lowering her voice in a way that would lead any man to distraction. She continued, obliviously, 'Thank you, too, for your grace. Most people don't seem to understand Baba and he only likes those who animals approve of.'

'I suspect Mishmish only considers me a new food source.'

'Animals have good instincts. And we Egyptians love cats. They are very smart creatures.' Mervat held Louis's gaze for a beat, looked like she might have said something more but then turned to fetch a knife. 'Can you dice tomatoes?'

He joked, 'You might regret giving me this task if your father dices better.'

She lifted a brow. 'He's terrible at it.'

Mervat worked around Louis as he began, adding ingredients to her pan or reaching for spices from the shelf over his head.

'Smells good,' he commented.

'It will be nothing like palace food.'

When she took the tomatoes, the back of Mervat's hand brushed Louis's wrist and she kept it there for a beat longer than she probably should have, perhaps waiting for something. Did he imagine the tension between them being like a too-taut violin string? He couldn't help but sigh when their touch ended. A sigh that was much too loud.

'Sorry,' she apologised.

'Mervat,' he heaved her name like a prayer. There was a heaviness in his tone that alerted him. He wondered if she'd heard it or felt it too when she turned to face him, her lids lowered so that her thick lashes were nearly touching her upper cheeks. He bent instinctively to watch how she caught the side of her lower lip between her front teeth.

Louis forced his feet to step back. Whatever this was, it wasn't proper. *And* it would lead to nowhere since a real courtship between them was not possible. 'Forgive me.'

She bobbed her head, but didn't meet his gaze as she turned back to the meal. With a large wooden spoon, she tasted the beans and then added a large spoon of a fragrant spice, earthy. 'Cumin. Completely necessary for *ful medames*.'

She emptied the contents into a large platter, then drizzled a golden olive oil in a pretty pattern that pooled even as they watched it in silence.

What was she thinking?

Mervat made to set the table and called for her father to join them. She then asked Louis, 'Would you prefer a utensil or to eat like a local?'

'When in Egypt, do as an Egyptian,' Abbas answered for him.

'As you say, sir,' Louis agreed.

They sat around the table and the three sopped directly from the platter, using bites of bread to scoop up the *ful* and vegetables.

'It's delicious,' Louis complimented. *'Tislam al ayadi.'*

It was a phrase he'd heard on the ship from Paris that wished peace and blessings on the hands of the chef who'd made the a favourable meal.

'*Ful* is most common dish in the country,' Abbas said, 'but it is never served at court, right Mervat?'

'Amu Taha says it is made in the kitchens for them daily at Sesostris. He's one of the servants who's been kind to me,' she said to her father. 'He says he will bring *halawet el-moulid* the next time he visits his family in Tanta.'

She explained to Louis, 'It is a crunchy candy made with sesame seeds and split peas only available near Eid days in Cairo, but because they are experts in it in Tanta, you can purchase it throughout the year.'

Mervat kissed her own fingertips to emphasise how delicious the sweets were, but Louis had to look away, frustrated with his inability *not* to be affected by her every gesture.

How was it that they'd shared a most filling meal and yet he could still know hunger? The sudden need to catch those fingers between his own lips?

It was getting to be very inconvenient. And hard to remember that they were merely part of Hussam's plan.

Defiant love be damned!

Louis was beginning to feel rather weary of the whole endeavour.

Abbas seemed to not want to hear anything about the palace so he went back to the platter at hand. 'Only Mervat cracks the eggs on top, frying them in the sauce. Others boil them on the side. Hers is the best way.'

'I learned how from you, Baba.' Mervat's expression softened. 'When Anne used to visit us and then leave, I would cry. One of the first times, I was young, but you made this to cheer me, remember? You said we were free to try whatever we wanted, nobody could tell us what we should or should not do. That we could even mix the eggs with the *ful* now.'

Her father didn't talk for a long time after that. When he did, he surprised both Mervat and Louis. 'I have the box your aunt brought from Turkey.'

Chapter Ten

Mervat

Baba had retired to his room for his regular scheduled afternoon nap and was already snoring gently. Mishmish had eaten their leftovers and found his own quiet corner to do the same. It was past *Asr* and outside was the time of day when it felt too dark to do anything that required the sun's brightness but not yet dark enough to light the lanterns.

And just then, it was a very dangerous place and moment to be alone with Louis. Sitting on the floor of Mervat's house, their backs pressed against either side of the sofa seating, a chest of *mentos* from Turkey between them alongside a plate of very ripe, very sweet guavas.

Which they were both eating with abandon. The fruit's soft flesh was contrasted with the hard crunch of its edible seeds. Mervat wiped the juicy dribble from the side of her mouth and it took her utmost to keep her fingers to herself. To not touch Louis in any way whatsoever as she had accidentally done in the kitchen earlier. Because, Allah forgive her, the feeling that had spread throughout her body then had been utterly inappropriate. And here it was again, rippling through her veins even though they had not touched.

'These are heavenly,' he said.

'Yes.'

He chuckled when he reached for the plate and found there was one left. 'It's yours.'

'I ate more than my constitution can handle. Please, it's yours.'

He pursed his lips in refusal. Mervat had to blink twice, remind herself she shouldn't be staring at them.

Allah, but he was handsome.

The *shaykhs* at the mosque might further remind her as they did the faithful to glorify the Creator by saying *Subhan al-Khaliq* when faced with such perfection.

'We should begin,' she managed.

Louis stood to collect his notebook and pencil; he'd left them near his shoes when he'd entered the house. He pushed aside the plate with the lone guava when he returned and was closer when he sat down again, his muscular thigh nearly grazing hers. Mervat drew on all the fortitude she possessed to focus on their task.

'I would have been ten or eleven when Anne sent word she had family visiting from Turkey and I was to come home. By home, I do not mean here. In the first few years of my life, we lived at the old palace, the one before Sesostris, with my paternal grandparents and their heirs.'

'The current khedive and his family too?'

'Yes. Hussam and his siblings were like my own, but Baba had bought this land a few years into my parents' marriage, when it became clear that my grandfather meant to appoint an heir and he did not want to be considered. My mother refused to stay away from court and he and I moved here—visits between them were scant and by the time my aunt came, it would have been clear to those at court that my parents were, if not divorced officially, then certainly separated.'

'It must have been difficult for you.' There was kindness in his voice that she couldn't dwell on, lest…it stirred those forbidden emotions of hers further.

'Baba braided my hair the day we went to see my aunt. He dressed nicely too. Hussam's father was the khedive by that time, and he greeted us at the gate, suspiciously at first, but my father was as he was earlier with you. His own internal gate, closed to any he isn't sure of. I remember this because when Anne kissed Baba's cheek in greeting…'

Mervat told herself she shouldn't cry, but she recalled her mother's effect on her father. How he would have loved for his wife to understand him better, but she did not.

'When Anne kissed him, he was touched. Pleased. And Anne, she continued the charade. She pretended to be a caring mother, acting like we were always together. The three of us, a happy family. Even then I knew it was only a show for her sister. But my aunt didn't care. Aunt Feride was grouchy, a frowning woman who barely paid my father or me any heed.'

'Why was she upset?'

'I only recall my mother crying at the end of our visit because my aunt had said that none of us could ever return to Turkey.'

Mervat had forgotten that and wondered if it was why Anne wouldn't listen to her suggestions for them to visit her homeland. She tapped the chest. 'Anyway, my aunt had brought this. Anne shouted at Baba to throw it out, by then dropping the pretence of us being a close family. But my father collected it, kept it all these years. It means it is not garbage.'

Louis said, 'Let us see what is in here, shall we?'

When she nodded, he lifted the lid to reveal paintings. Small canvases, neatly and tightly arranged, each with the same black frames.

And as they started pulling them out, a pattern emerged.

The paintings were dark, all demonstrating an obsession with death.

Mervat had always thought there were multiple sides and histories to artifacts. After all, did she not occupy herself with the investigative aspect of tracing their genealogies? But there was no other way to judge this body of work.

This wasn't a collection inspired by a beautiful garden. Unless there were bodies buried under it. This was a collection inspired by a cemetery, by a mind that yearned for a place there. Done by a talented artist, no doubt, but one who was likely disturbed.

In one painting, dead babies dropped from a cloudy sky.

In another, a crocodile hung from a noose.

A few paintings were of skulls: a singular one with a cobra emerging from the eye socket, another was of a litter of them forgotten in a field of listless weeds.

Mervat had the strongest urge to cry, as if the desperation in the paintings or the unbearable sadness of the artist had reached into her soul so that she could feel something of what it had taken to produce the works.

Louis put a hand on her knee, his touch was hesitant, so light she mightn't have believed it was there if she wasn't looking down at it. 'We can stop.'

'They would not make for a happy wall in a museum, would they?' Mervat blinked, straining for a lighter mood

He tried to help her along. 'Oh, I don't know. A museum can be a place where any number of emotions are experienced.'

Mervat didn't know how to respond to that without pulling herself entirely away from the task. 'Is there indication of the painter's name or the dates when they were done?'

They examined a few closely, separating them from their frames, but found nothing.

'Your mother would know more,' Louis stated the obvious, but he might as well have declared that their investigation of the Cleopatra Cerulean had, unironically, died.

'She would not tell me anything even if she did.'

The tears Mervat had been holding back slipped at last. She pressed her eyes with the back of her hand, angry at herself. Angry at Anne. 'You will think me weak. That I should demand she answer—or we'd have wasted the day otherwise.'

She got on her knees to collect the paintings back inside the chest, but she was frustrated and they weren't fitting properly. When Louis covered her hand with his own, her emotions churned and shifted into something…else.

'You have a unique relationship with your mother and I will not presume to tell you how it should be conducted. But you're wrong to say I think you are weak, Mervat. Nor would I ever count a day spent in your company as wasted.' When she looked up at him, Louis smiled kindly. 'We will think on it some more and an idea will come tomorrow. I promise.'

She watched him as he took over, arranging the paintings as they had been. And though she ought to look away from the scenes, one caught her attention. And then another.

Mervat took them from Louis, her vision clearing. The first was of a tomb, covered in sheets, the figures of dervishes bowing before it. The second was a river bank. The Nile? A cloaked woman sat there. Not a woman, no. Her legs weren't legs, they were fins. And next to her was a jewel. A blue one.

Excitedly, she showed Louis. Pointed to the spot in the grass. 'Is that…?'

He squinted. 'The Cleopatra Cerulean gem? It might be. But there is no crown? You think the woman is Cleopatra?'

'She is not a human woman.'

He spotted the fins. 'A mermaid?'

'El-Naddaha. She's a legend in villages near the Nile. Mothers warn their sons to be careful when playing by the river, lest they disturb the spirit jinn who dwells there. El-Naddaha is said to lure men to their deaths with her siren song. And that tomb in the other painting reminds me of a landmark in Tanta. It is a place where a thirteenth century mystic named Sayid el-Badawy was buried. Some hold it be a holy site.'

'Tanta? As in Amu Taha from Tanta's home city?'

Mervat broke into a grin, but before she could answer in the affirmative, Mishmish meowed and sauntered around them. They were pushed closer together, her head, practically on Louis's chest, his hands holding her shoulders as the cat passed.

She looked up at Louis and despite the dimming light, could see how he stared at her lips. 'Maybe we can talk to Amu Taha next in our pursuit of the mystery around the Cleopatra Cerulean?'

'We can,' he agreed. He met her gaze and what she saw in his eyes was a slow, gentle examination of her own. As she searched his face, he searched hers.

'Don't be sad, Mervat,' he whispered. 'Nothing should upset you. No one.'

The corners of his mouth turned and then, ever so gently, he lifted his hand so that it hovered near her face. He stroked the line of her jaw with the back of his thumb. And when he made to take it away, she clasped his wrist. Keeping his thumb on her face. Mervat leaned into it, turning her neck until the tip of his thumb was nipped between her lips.

The sound he made, the desperate groan of it, gave her a taste of her own strength. Louis might think she could not stand up to her mother, but here she was making him weak.

She quite liked the feeling, forbidden as it was.

She inched her face closer to his. He twisted his neck until the tip of his perfect nose grazed hers.

'Mervat.' Her name was a shuddering breath. 'We mustn't.'

'Kiss me,' she urged, possessed by a vixen's spirit. Maybe el-Naddaha's or a culmination of the novels and love poetry she'd read and dreamt of exploring in the dark recesses of her mind. A yearning she buried, like dark paintings in a chest.

Mervat focused on knowledge through words and text, but at that moment she wasn't thinking. She only wanted to *experience*. Hadn't Louis once said that was what he valued most?

Yet, he protested. 'It's inappropriate. You are a princess. Your reputation. My goal. My sanity.' The excuses came like rain after a hot day, the kind to lap up. She rubbed the line of his jaw as he had hers with the back of her thumb. His stubble pricked enticingly, seemed to scratch the very pit of her stomach.

Mervat cupped his chin almost roughly. 'What does your sanity require, Viscount?'

'For you not to tease me.' His eyes were lowered, his voice as if trapped in a deep crater.

'I told you want I wanted. Clearly and without teasing. Kiss me.'

He held her back ever so slightly. 'You will regret it, Mervat. It has been a long day. The paintings took an emotional toll.'

He cupped her face in both his hands and now that it was getting dark she could barely see him. Maybe Louis was right. Baba was in the next room. If he were to wake, find them in this position, she wouldn't know how to explain it. And what would happen if his kiss only led to more? What *haram* would she fall into?

She'd read about what a woman would feel like in the arms of a competent lover, heard whispers in the harem about the chore of one-sided lovemaking or the pleasures to be had when a man was adept at knowing a woman's desires and when she, in turn, desired him. And when the hands that cupped her face slid to her shoulders and then past the very thin material of her kaftan, she believed Louis would indeed be a competent lover. And every nerve in Mervat's body throbbed with the awareness of how much she desired him.

But he was right. She could not demand he kiss her.

Chapter Eleven

Louis

It was the last thing he wanted, but Louis let her pull back from him.

What he wanted was to kiss her. Press his lips to hers, nibble and prod. Sample and gorge. But would it be enough to satisfy him? He dropped his hands from her waist, brought his knees close to his chest. Even as he imagined pushing her back, laying her flat, sliding that loose kaftan of hers up and away or ripping through it so he could touch her bare flesh. Or maybe turning her on her back, tugging her hair from its binding to lose himself in her long, luscious curls. Press his body over hers and kiss the back of her neck, under her earlobe, until she asked him again for that kiss. Begged him for it.

'I apologise,' she said.

It was getting dark and people did things in the dark that they might regret in the light. His grandfather had told him that.

'Live a life with no regrets, yes, my boy, but that is not carte blanche *to act with abandon. Remember that it is what happens in the light of day that matters most, that lasts.'*

Louis would hate it if she regretted any action when it came to him.

But it took all his might not to lean forward and kiss her anyway. He inhaled deeply, exhaled a steadying breath.

She rose to light the lamps. Outside, the *athan* was sounding from a faraway mosque. And her father's snoring had ceased.

He watched her smooth out her dress, adjust the binding around her hair. Without looking at him, she said, 'Wait here until I go and pray *maghrib*? Just in my room, it shouldn't take long.'

'Certainly.'

Indeed, she was barely gone for a few minutes before returning and he hadn't had a chance to think what he would say when she took the seat next to him. 'I hope you aren't upset with me, Mervat. I would be remiss if I did or said anything to risk your good opinion of me.'

It sounded too stiff, even to his own ears.

'Only I think of how Hussam is with Nadine, how if she asked him to kiss her, he wouldn't have come up with excuses why it is wrong. She is prettier than me, more desirable, I know, but I thought an Englishmen would have even less cause to come up with reasons why he should not kiss me.'

Louis didn't know if he should be insulted or aghast. 'Firstly, you are a beautiful woman, prettier than any I have seen. Secondly, being an Englishman does not mean I am not also a gentleman.'

'To my understanding, charming, handsome Englishmen would likely have been with any number of women. What is one kiss amidst years of them?' Whether Mervat initially spoke out of hurt, Louis could not tell, but when she added, 'I only wished to experience what I had read in books,' it was his own hurt that marked his next words.

'You were using me?'

'In the kitchen earlier, I thought we had…that you *wanted*… the same. That we might try.' Mervat stumbled on her words.

Louis knew he should let it go, yet he could not.

He leapt up, paced in the small space, feeling much too tall for the lower ceiling.

She had wounded his pride. He believed Mervat's tenderness towards him was indicative of a growing admiration, a desire to learn who he was as much as he wished to know her better, as well. Were the moments they'd shared throughout the day not real?

He asked, 'You're saying you wished to kiss me as some sort of experiment?'

Before she could answer, he continued, 'I am not Hussam, with a convoluted love plan. I am not a Casanova or a gigolo. I am not a cad. I wish to respect you only because—'

'Only because I am like your friend's sister,' she cried, finishing his sentence with her own thought. 'And though you might need an arranged marriage for Allenborough, the truth is that you also want a proper English woman to be your wife.'

If he was confused about what she meant by that, the sadness he perceived in her face and tone, was enough to have Louis covering the distance between them in a single stride and taking each of her hands in his. 'I was going to say, only because you are the tenderest person I have ever known and you deserve to be treated honourably.'

He would have said more but the door slammed.

At its threshold, a woman from the harem, marked by the way she was dressed, lifted her face veil.

'Anne!' Mervat's face flushed crimson as she pulled her hands from his and moved towards her mother.

They had been found alone and in a compromising position. Exactly what Louis had feared for her.

He could not understand any of her mother's tirade in Turkish, but he knew it was heated.

When Gulnur Hanem saw the chest, she was further disturbed. Her yelling became louder and more furious, prompting Louis to stand between her and Mervat.

The woman stared at him, snarling as if he were but an inconvenience.

It was Mervat's father who came between them and was finally able to quell her.

'Gulnur,' Abbas pleaded. *'Min fadlik.' Please.*

She calmed as he closed the chest and pushed it out of her sight. When her mother sat down and buried her head in her hands, he turned to Mervat.

She was crying, but they were silent tears she worked quickly to wipe any trace of.

'What can I do?' he wondered, helplessly.

Before she could answer, her mother hissed, *'Zuk!'*

Louis didn't know what it meant but assumed it was some sort of Turkish sentiment wanting him to shut his mouth while she went on talking. It was Abbas who translated for him.

'Gulnur says you will bring shame on our daughter.'

'Kindly let her know it simply is not true. I have the utmost respect for the princess. The prince is my dearest friend and even he knows my intentions. We are working together on a project. That is all.' Louis wasn't sure why it felt wrong to reference Hussam, perhaps it was because Gulnur Hanem thought he would be marrying her daughter. He had done it only to remove the pressure from Mervat.

But if the look Mervat gave him then was any indication, he'd said something wrong.

For his part, Abbas translated nothing. Mervat's father stepped away from all of them, withdrawing. *'Fin howa* Mishmish?' he mumbled in Arabic as he spun, looking for the cat.

Gulnur threw up her hands and pointed to Abbas's back.

Again, Louis did not comprehend her speech but it was clearly a rebuke of her estranged husband.

Mervat moved to her father, rubbed his arm kindly. They exchanged whispered words and when he nodded, her wide, tear-filled eyes turned to Louis. It was all he could do not to whisk her away right then and there. Her unhappiness broke his heart.

She explained her mother thought it best if he went to the palace first. 'Anne wants Baba to take you from the back road, rent a *hantoor* at the end of the street so that the palace carriage and driver she came here with will not know we spent the day together. That he would not spread gossip.'

'What about you? Will you be returning to the palace?' He didn't want this to be the last he'd see her, but Louis was damned if he didn't also know that this was Mervat's home. That she was most herself and happy away from court.

'Anne says I must.'

Louis sighed with relief. 'When will you return? I do not want to leave whilst both of you are upset.'

She mustered a small smile. 'All will be well. As you said, tomorrow we will continue on our quest.'

Mervat's sad wave was Louis's parting image. He and her father scurried like thieves in the night to the back of the house, narrowly managing to avoid the royal carriage and driver who waited beyond his garden. Abbas shook his hand kindly enough after commissioning a new driver to deliver him to the palace.

The trip passed in a blur and Louis was grateful to see Hussam waiting for him near the gates of Sesostris. He'd had a table set up near the steps with a sheesha contraption and two chairs.

In the top bowl, the coals burned ash and orange, the water

in the decorative lower bowl bubbled without a care in the world. Hussam held the hose out. 'You look like you need it.'

Louis collapsed in the chair and threw his head back, utterly spent. He hated the way he'd had to leave Mervat alone with her mother. Hated that they'd been arguing beforehand. But how could he explain that to Hussam? He barely understood it himself.

Instead he took his friend's offering, inhaling deep and long.

'No drags,' Hussam advised. 'Remember how I taught you? That time we snuck out to London's East End?'

He remembered. Louis blew out the honey tobacco smoke from his nostrils. It really was a relaxing endeavour.

When he finally returned the hose, Hussam asked, 'Gulnur Hanem gave you a hard time?'

'You know what happened?'

Hussam nodded. 'I'm sorry. She caught me and Nadine on our way back, dragged her back to the harem by her ears. She blamed her for leaving Mervat, shaming her for not knowing the simple rule that someone entrusted with a princess should remain with her at all times outside of the palace. Said she'd have Nadine sent back to her father in shame if she said anything to anyone about her faux pas. She was vicious with her and when I protested, Gulnur Hanem further scolded me. She urged I take better care of the woman who will be my wife.'

Louis bristled at that last part. 'How does this affect the plan?'

He sighed. 'Nadine and I *were* seen in the city and the carriage drivers would gossip, but I didn't expect Gulnur Hanem's strong reaction this soon. She will be more vigilant now, but not yet bring my father into it.' He turned to Louis. 'How did you and Mervat get on?'

For a second, Louis thought he was asking about the near kiss between them, wondered what excuse he would offer. He and Hussam were close and could talk about anything, but he was pretty sure the prince would not like Louis to regard his cousin with any real sentiment beyond friendship or what his plan entailed.

'You mean with the crown jewel mystery?' Louis asked. 'Actually, there is a servant in the palace from Tanta who we intend to interview next.' Louis didn't want to expose what Mervat had shared with him about her aunt's visit from Turkey or the paintings they'd rifled through. It wasn't his story to tell, but he mentioned to Hussam that the princess and he had reason to believe the city was significant and might hold further clues.

'Do you know the servant's name?'

'Taha.'

Hussam rattled off his features. 'Elderly, very dark brown skin, thinning white hair. Clean shaven. His livery fits awkwardly.'

'Sounds about right.'

'Brilliant work, mate.'

'Glad you think so.' Louis wondered how long he might push their sitting there whilst watching for Mervat? He needed to make sure she was all right before retiring for the evening.

'What do you think of not only interviewing Taha, but having him also chaperone us to the site of your enquiry?' Hussam said. 'We four will visit Tanta in a party large enough to escape any protest Gulnur Hanem may muster.'

Chapter Twelve

Mervat

She laid her forehead on the door after Baba and Louis had gone, unable to muster the physical strength to do anything else. Mervat was embarrassed, hurt. Frustrated that Anne should interrupt her and Louis —when they were arguing, after they had been about to…what? Surely, she should be grateful for that. She'd been lost in her emotions, wanted him to kiss her desperately. But if he had, who was to say it would have stopped with the one? And what would she have done then? On the other hand, Louis might have only been acting kindly, making it seem like he was being honourable for her sake, maybe he didn't want to kiss her at all. Whichever it was, she felt as mortified with her behaviour as she was shocked by it.

Mervat detested the dishonesty at Sesostris—the disrespect, the drinking, the decadence—because she was a Muslim woman, and she believed those things were fundamentally wrong. She'd not been raised with the experience of what love or marriage was like when two people truly wanted to be with each other, but she had a sense of what they *should* entail. She knew that lovemaking in its physically intimate sense was supposed to be between two people who were committed to one another. Two people with similar values and traditions, who wanted to love each other in all ways and on an equal footing. Outwardly and inwardly.

It was why she'd refused the prospect of marrying Hussam in the first place. And why, secretly, she had found his relationship with Nadine problematic. Not that she could judge them after what had almost happened with Louis. In fact, now she could better empathise with their plight. If her cousin wanted to marry Nadine and make their love a *halal* arrangement, then she should be especially glad for her part in his plan to help him do so.

'You could have been ruined. You should thank me—the things I do to save your honour.' Anne found Mervat's *milaya* and veil, tossed them her way. 'Put them back on.'

As she did so, she mustered her defiance. 'Hussam would rather marry Nadine.'

Anne refuted, 'He needs a princess as a wife and that girl is ill-bred. If Hussam wants to have other women later, you can let him as his mother does his father. But if you are smart, he will not want to. After what I've seen, how you can look at a man and how he can respond to you in turn, I'm confident in your abilities. You only need to redirect your adoration.'

What did Anne mean by that? What had she seen in Louis's look?

She wanted to ask her mother the questions, confide in her the worry that she would never be as desirable as Nadine.

Louis would have never been able to resist a kiss request from her.

'I cannot marry Hussam,' she managed.

'Because of the Englishman?'

Mervat lifted her chin. 'Even before the viscount arrived, I said I would not marry Hussam. In Paris, when you first informed me, I said the same.'

Her mother didn't know she'd met Louis by then, but it didn't matter. Mervat was certain she would have refused, regardless.

Anne stepped towards her. She took both of Mervat's hands and her tone softened. 'I didn't have guidance at your age and married your father, choosing the wrong heir. I thought a soft man who did not look at other women was better, not realising that Abbas didn't look at *anyone*, including me. Just as he had no desire for power, no manhood for it, my bed was often empty. You know why I stayed at court, Mervat?'

'Because the khedive wanted it?'

'He might have wanted it to prevent your father from having any sons, yes, but for my part, I knew that getting pregnant with you was a miracle since my bed was mostly empty even in those first days.'

Mervat saw in her mother's eyes the understanding. She knew her daughter was physically attracted to Louis. That she desired his touch. The feel of his lips on hers. She couldn't admit it aloud.

'Then why did you stay, Anne? Why not come home? Baba loves you. He would have worked to become the man you needed if only you'd made the effort to know him better. Taken the time. Shown him the patience he shows to his garden.'

'Perhaps,' she admitted. Anne took a deep breath. 'My childhood in Turkey was...difficult. The harem here offered privilege and prestige. Protection. Things I had lacked and feared to lose. Even now, I still do. But in those early days, I had a mission. A purpose that kept me away from you and Abbas. I was working to build the khedive's trust, making him see that a marriage between our children would assure his legacy.'

Anne let go of her hands to cup Mervat's cheek. It was the

most loving she'd ever been with her and yet Mervat could not help but be suspicious. Her mother was guilting her into accepting the marriage with Hussam.

She resisted and her eyes pounced on the abandoned chest where her father had hidden it. Her mother had seen it. Did not comment. She knew what was in there. The disturbing paintings of a mad woman. A woman Anne must have known.

Louis thought they should talk to her, but Mervat had not wanted to risk her mother's ire, or refusal. But now, if she was talking of the past… 'I remember your sister visiting the old palace when I was a girl. She brought that chest of paintings and said we could never go back to Turkey. Why, Anne?'

'Zuk! Bas,' her mother dismissed.

'Why have we have never been to your home country, never met your family?' Mervat insisted. She hated to see the paintings again, but she strode towards the chest with purpose. Drawing one out, she brandished it and asked, 'Who did this?'

When she had no answer, she repeated the question with the next painting and then the one after it. On the fourth, she wondered. 'Perhaps I should ask the khedive if he knows?'

'He knows nothing,' Anne snapped. She closed her eyes, and when she opened them again, she chuckled.

It was a change that had Mervat asking with trepidation, 'Did you paint these?'

Anne finally shook her head, spent. 'Not me.'

'Then who?'

Mervat could be patient. Listen when she had to, instead of talking. And this was one of those moments. She led her mother to the dining table, made her sit down and took the chair opposite. The one Louis had sat in. She wished he was still here, taking notes in his journal. And maybe too, Mervat wanted him to be witness to her strength in demanding answers from her mother. Would he be proud of her?

'My grandmother painted them. Her name was Omnia. She was Egyptian, a beautiful girl my Turkish grandfather found on one of his visits to the delta where he owned farming lands. He caught her bathing in the Nile, a girl in the wrong place at the wrong time. Or, others would say, part of a plan to be naked at the exact moment he was passing.'

'Women's stories are often twisted by those with their own motivations.' Mervat knew it was true from the genealogy projects she'd followed and said so in the hopes her mother would continue.

'Maybe the story came from the fourth wife my grandfather had to divorce in order to make room for Omnia.' Anne scoffed but it was a sad sound. 'Omnia was a girl, but old enough to be in love with a village boy and poor enough that her father would sell her to the richest offer.'

Mervat could barely believe Anne was sharing this with her. She listened with bated breath, hoping for more, and then was rewarded.

Her mother continued, 'When I was a girl, they'd send me to give my grandmother food. She liked me for some reason— they said it was because I looked most like her. She'd yell at everyone else, throw the food in their faces. But with me, she'd sit down. Eat. Bid me call her Omnia. In her mind, I was a childhood friend. She told me about the boy she loved. How they planned to run off with the jewel he'd been given by the Nile Djinn. He'd sell it and they'd be rich. But the *djinn* tricked him. Omnia said that el-Naddaha took the form of a crocodile, gobbled her lover.'

'Even as a girl, I recognised the delusion she'd created in her mind. I figured it was her father who killed the boy and threw him in the Nile, rather than risk his daughter's virtue or the wealth and honour that was coming to him by virtue of her marriage to my grandfather.'

In that last bit was a warning for Mervat, one she didn't care to dwell on then. 'It was in the painting *El-Naddaha*. The jewel was next to her. The Cleopatra Cerulean?'

Anne shrugged. 'I think it belonged to her. A gift from her lover, but my grandfather didn't know where she'd gotten it from, only that she loved it. She had these fits when he took her to Turkey and he tried to please her, getting a jeweller to set it into the crown they thought belonged to Cleopatra. He had purchased the crown as a wedding gift for her. Her *shabka*.'

That was it? The mystery was solved? Mervat fought a wave of disappointment. What would she work on with Louis now?

Her father wedged himself through the door, joining them.

'It is done, Gulnur,' Baba told Anne. 'The palace driver didn't see me either way.'

'And the Englishman?'

'On his way to the palace. I found my favourite driver, a discreet man who does not insist on talking.'

Anne stood, patted Baba's cheek as a mother might a child to show her approval. Mervat hated the way her father savoured it, the littlest affection from his wife. She didn't get the chance to see it often now and she wasn't even sure that it had ever bothered her, until today.

It occurred to Mervat that the day they'd visited her aunt was the first time she'd witnessed it.

Had Mervat somehow copied her father's patterns with her mother? Louis paid her a bit of attention, looked at her with longing in the kitchen or said something kind beforehand and so Mervat desperately wanted more? Yes, she'd asked for the kiss and only his gentlemanliness had prevented it. But if he'd given it and then prompted her for more than just the kiss, she might have been swept up in his affection and obliged.

It was a scary thought. Mervat *had* to be stronger willed. Louis was going to return to England, marry an English bride, raise his future heirs. He would leave her and she needed to be better considered with her own chastity.

Baba said, 'You are free to go now.'

'Anne was telling me about her grandmother, we cannot until she is done.'

Her mother's brow furrowed. 'There's nothing more to tell.'

'What happened to your family that made you unable to return to Turkey?' Mervat gestured to the chest. 'What do those paintings have to do with it?'

'You should not have kept them,' Anne told Baba. 'They are worthless and you may toss them now.'

Mervat pleaded, 'They are not worthless. They tell a story of Egypt and Turkey, their relations and peoples. Even if they were not always happy, our histories make us who we are today. Who we can be tomorrow. Please keep them safe, Baba, as you have these past years.'

'So long as you come back with me now.' Anne answered for him, pulling down Mervat's veil and then her own. 'Bring a lamp, Abbas. Guide us to the palace carriage and then return to your solitude.'

Baba's energy for guests must have been spent because he dragged his feet to do as she asked, barely looking at Mervat as their carriage set off.

They rode most of the way in silence, but when they were near Sesostris, Mervat dared once again to ask the question that remained foremost in her mind. 'Why can't you go back to Turkey?'

Mervat thought it unlikely she'd get an answer, but her

mother spoke, her body swaying back and forth with the carriage's movement like a leaf being battered in a brash breeze.

'In Turkey, it was said Omnia was a witch who'd brought a curse upon my grandfather, his entire family. He'd been a rich nobleman, acclaimed throughout the country, highly respected in the Ottoman court. After he married Omnia, disaster after disaster beset him, until our name was one associated with poverty and bad luck. My grandmother had one daughter, my *anne*, who begged for scraps at court. Did things a woman shouldn't be asked to do. My engagement to your father was a boon, we thought the sultan favoured us once again, but he was merely gambling at our expense. If somehow Abbas became khedive, our family would owe him. If not, then any resurgence of my grandfather's wealth upon the death of my grandmother and the curse that came with her could be seized by him for monies lost on the arrangement he'd brokered.'

'Your grandmother was still alive when you married Baba?'

'I told you she was a child. She'd given birth to my mother at fifteen. When Feride, your aunt, came to visit me it was only to announce that despite Omnia's death, our curse had not lifted. We were still poor in Istanbul and I had embarrassed them by marrying a man who had chosen to live in a slum instead of a palace. She'd come to tell me I had failed them all.'

Mervat felt a pang of sadness for her mother, the secrets she'd borne over the years. 'Thank you for telling me, Anne.'

'It is best you know now, so to do what I could not. *You* will marry a future khedive.'

Chapter Thirteen

Louis

Louis had taken many a train ride in his lifetime and while Cairo's central railway station could not compare to the marvel of engineering that was London's St. Pancras, here they were afforded luxury treatment that was unlike any other. A carpet was put out for their small party—the four of them involved in Hussam's plan, along with Amu Taha in full livery, Faisal, the English-speaking servant, and one of Hussam's aunts who got wind that they were travelling to Tanta and who wished to visit a renowned dentist there, one she swore was the only man of medicine who knew how to handle her delicate teeth.

'Meaning she has very few left,' Hussam joked.

'Is she the one who calls you "hussy",' Louis asked, 'because I definitely want to hear her say it.'

The hearty laughter that that drew from his friend had everyone looking their way. Including Mervat. His eyes were immediately drawn to hers, which were wide and stark, the only part of her face visible because of her harem veil. Was it going to be awkward between them given their almost kiss? For her part, he wasn't sure, but for his, there was a crucial moment in that instant when their eyes met, the steamy smoke chugging from the train around them. As if they were the only two on the platform. Before he could think better of it, of who might be watching, he had tilted his head, arched his brow, and given Mervat a slight nod of acknowledgement which, he was happy to witness, she returned.

They'd not had a chance to talk since her mother had walked in on them. It had been two whole days and Louis found that more than anything else, he quite missed their conversations.

Which was probably a very foolish sentiment because once the Cleopatra Cerulean mystery was solved and her engagement to his friend officially off the agenda, they would have no reason to spend time together. And because Louis needed to focus on securing his career in order to help his family back home, it really was foolish to hang *any* sentiment on missing conversations with a princess who could not be his anyway.

Hussam clamped his shoulder good-naturedly. 'She is indeed the said aunt, but I have warned her to be on her most official behaviour. She acts as chaperone to the two young ladies joining us today. It is the only way my father relented and allowed this outing, for though he was amiable, Gulnur Hanem fussed to no end when she got wind of it.'

'It was smart of you to get your father on board beforehand.'

'He's excited about you reporting on the railway lines. Insists that we not spend much time in Tanta before we arrive in Alexandria—where we will, thankfully, be chaperone-free.' Hussam leaned in, lowered his voice. 'Nobody knows we will let Taha spend the day with his family in Tanta or that I may have fudged my aunt's appointment time so she will require more time at her dentist or that the four of us will picnic on the shores of the Mediterranean. Starved by that time as we are.'

'You really have a cad's mind for strategy,' Louis remarked.

'Write a good piece to secure my father's gratitude and it will be your mind and pen we shall have to thank for mine and Mervat's freedom.'

Despite the reservations he'd had with Hussam's plan, Louis couldn't deny he was having a good time. Even if being in Mervat's company was at once baffling and wondrous, troubling and exciting, articles that required traipsing across Egypt under the most luxurious of conditions were damn good fun.

A fact underscored as they boarded the train.

Besides the main locomotive, there were three cars in this special run between Cairo and Alexandria with a stopover in Tanta which had been reserved for the prince's party. The one for the servants was akin to a slightly glorified boxcar, and the caboose car would be used by Louis, equipped with a writing desk. The main car, reserved for members of the royal court was seventy feet long with plush leather lounge seating for ten, mahogany wood detailing on the walls and roof, a thick Persian carpet, any number of amusements to pass the time and even a built-in lavatory.

All of this was stressed to Louis by one of the conductors. The man who spoke impeccable English himself had been assigned to apprise him of the railway line's history. As he continued his lesson, the whistle blasted, but Louis was conscious of the fact that Mervat wasn't aboard.

He turned to see her scrambling towards a quartet of beggars; he hadn't seen them, but that corner of the station was hidden, easy to overlook. Not for Mervat, apparently. The mother and her two daughters were dressed in rags. A baby wrapped in a filthy blanket lay before them—one so still, Louis wondered if it might even be dead. He held his breath, hoping that Mervat wouldn't get a shock, but as she crouched the baby squirmed. She even put a finger to the baby's cheek and he sensed she was smiling beneath her veil.

Hussam's aunt gestured for Nadine to get Mervat and as she ambled to pull her away, the beggar mother rose, as well, squeezing the princess's hands in a grateful gesture. Louis couldn't hear what they were saying and even though he'd been watching and not seen Mervat give the woman anything, she must have.

'Alas, such large buildings cannot completely be rid of vagrants,' the English-speaking conductor said. 'I hear London's stations are beset with them, as well.'

Louis turned to him after making sure that Mervat was on board safely. She had talked of the discrepancies between what was contained within the walls of Sesostris and what was beyond it, but watching her acting, her kind loveliness, moved something in him too. It made him ashamed that he had not noticed the woman and her daughters or that he ignored the dismissal of them as mere vagrants.

He sighed before returning to his task of diligently taking notes. The conductor talked about how the tracks they were on were the first railway line in the whole of the Ottoman Empire, Africa and the entirety of the Middle East. He mentioned how the short-lived French occupation at the turn of the century initially wanted to expend monies only on the canal, but the foresight of the khedives of decades past envisioned connecting the whole of the country through train travel.

'You should not write of the unfortunate accident in the late eighteen-sixties of the drowning of the prince who fell from the car float as the route crossed the Nile. The khedive would not like that. Rather, you might focus on the marvellous suspension bridge built after it,' the conductor stressed.

Louis smiled complacently. It would not be gracious to say anything bad regarding his host, but he disliked the implication. He hadn't had cause to dwell on it too much before taking on his column, but Louis believed in the freedom of the press.

People should be able to write what they liked, in as honest a way as possible and without fear of ruffling feathers.

It made him proud to think Mervat would approve of the thought. Before he could repeat a politer version of it to the conductor, she appeared. Louis had noticed that Hussam's aunt had removed her veil as soon as she'd stepped on the train, but he'd been immediately pulled to this car before he could see whether Mervat followed suit.

She had, in fact, done so. And he was, once again taken aback by her beauty. God, but he really had to stop being so surprised by it. Indeed, it took Louis a full minute of staring at her in the connecting doorway of the car to come to his senses.

Her hair was still mostly covered with a silky scarf, the ends of which were tossed over her shoulders. She wore a dark green skirt with a delicately embroidered blouse cinched at the waist with a ribboned belt he'd have enjoyed tugging loose. He shook his head, steeled his nerves. This was the sort of *noticing* of details that would spark more tension between them.

'I have enough for now, sir.' He thanked the conductor and walked him to where Mervat had moved to let the man pass between the cars.

'Princess,' he greeted her, 'what can I do for you?'

Before she could answer, the train lurched and Mervat with it. Louis's left arm came around her waist as his right rose to grip the frame of the door. His face was inches above hers as she looked up to him and he instinctively inched closer. Her eyes darkened; her body tensed in his embrace. He knew because his reacted in much the same way.

They were out of earshot, but Louis didn't know if anyone could see them from the main car at that angle. Nor did he want to pull away to check.

She gently fingered a vein in his forearm before stepping back from his grip, forcing him to drop the arm he had around her waist. 'I wanted to speak with you. Hussam's aunt was sleeping, but I fear the train jolt will have woken her.'

Louis kept his other arm draped over the doorway, too taken by the flush in Mervat's cheeks as she looked up to him to let her escape too quickly. Despite his better instincts, he asked anyway, 'Perhaps you would like to come inside?'

'And were she to wake?'

'Now who is finding excuses?' He was talking about their near kiss, but would she recall it? He held his breath, both in anticipation of her answer and to temper an instinct to kiss her regardless of her asking.

'That evening at my father's…'

'Mm-hmm,' he urged, keeping his gaze locked on hers. This really wasn't a position for serious conversation, but he needed to know if she'd thought of that missed chance as much as he had. Louis's pulse quickened when she paused to lick her lips.

He should offer her water. Train rides were dehydrating. He was thirsty himself.

'I spoke to my mother after you left,' she began.

She hadn't been thinking about their near kiss.

'Anne told me everything she knew about the painter, about the crown. The mystery around the Cleopatra Cerulean is quite solved. This trip is unnecessary.'

'Oh.' Louis fought a wave of disappointment. Their project was done? How would they spend time together after today? He knew he should ask what she'd learned; instead he wondered, 'Why did you join us then?'

Mervat searched his face. 'You are angry.'

Maybe he was a tad miffed. 'Only because you have not sought me out before now. It's been two days since that evening. Days I have spent in the study at Sesostris. Quite accessible.'

She dipped beneath his still-lifted arm and walked towards the end of the car. Clutching the railing to watch the passing scenery, she said, 'It is sensitive family history. My mother's. I was trying to work out how you might write the article but still keep it private.'

'I can be sensitive. Delicate,' he said, then clarified, 'In my writing, I mean. Will you trust me, Mervat?'

She sat in the seat the conductor had vacated while he sat in the one opposite. As the story tumbled from her lovely lips, he did his best not to stare at them, instead occupying himself with taking his notes.

In the end, it was the plight of her great-grandmother, forced to marry a man she did not love which was the angle that called to Louis most. Hussam had said his pen could be central to winning their freedom. He hadn't been sure how, but now an idea was forming. One, for the piece on the mystery of the Cleopatra Cerulean, but also a greater look at how women like the princess he was staring at now were talented, strong.

How they should be allowed to make their own decisions, marry whom they loved. Or never marry at all if it suited them. And it wouldn't be just a call for women of Egypt. Heaven knows, women of noble birth in England were as much, if not more, constrained.

'Huh,' he mused as he flipped to a new page.

'What is it?' Mervat had come around the desk to stand over him. It was his turn to look up at her.

'It occurred to me that I used to heartily believe in arranged marriages. Allenborough could have and still can derive great benefit from a well-appointed one. Both my father and grandfather married for love, and I have always been—*am* still—determined to do the opposite because of the estate's need. I have never allowed myself to think about the consequences of doing otherwise. Yet, your great-grandmother, what happened to her after she lost her devoted Egyptian boy makes me wonder about the consequences of *not* marrying the person you love.'

Mervat teased, 'That is what you derive from the account? Not the magical *djinn* lady? Not the family curse?'

He chuckled. 'And what of the connection to Tanta? Is this trip utterly futile?'

'Actually, I talked to Amu Taha about the location in the painting yesterday. He can tell you more and we will see it in the flesh, but the short version is that it is indeed the tomb of Sayid el-Badawy. It is close to where my great-grandmother lived as a girl and my best guess is she prayed to the Sufi saint to somehow counter what she considered el-Naddaha's interference. I believe the gem itself was a gift from the boy she loved. He might have found it near the Nile, not knowing how precious it was. It could have come from some mine at the river mouth or had been buried in the flow from the time of the ancients. Because my great-grandmother's Egyptian boy died and remains unnamed, there is no way to ascertain for certain.'

'Are you sure he is dead and unnamed?' Louis asked.

'He must be.'

Louis would not push. It must have been hard to talk to her mother. He knew she'd not wanted to. Gulnur Hanem was not the easiest of mothers. He was happy to hear that Mervat had learnt the story from her, hoped she was proud of herself.

He made a final note in his journal. 'Then her Turkish husband whilst he was still rich, had it placed as an addition to the Cleopatra crown he'd purchased from the same find as the Elgin Marbles?'

'He fashioned it as a symbol of the Turkish-Egyptian bond. He'd been a collector before things went awry for him. The crown was hidden away until my great-grandmother gave it to Anne, knowing she, a Turkish bride, was to marry my father, an Egyptian.'

'Thank you. I will honour the story, write a piece that respects the family's history.' He reached for Mervat's hand, held it in both of his. He meant the gesture to be a reassuring, quick thing, but it was hard to let go. 'You can approve it before I submit.'

She answered the question he had asked earlier, 'I trust you, Louis.'

Chapter Fourteen

Mervat

They barely spent an hour in Tanta. Only long enough for a quick visit to the mosque and burial site of el-Badawy, the Syrian-born mystic who had settled and died in the city in 1276 and to accept the *halawet el-moulid* sweets brought on board the train by Amu Taha who was glad to be let off to spend the day with his family.

She could not speak too much to Louis at the site since she knew very little about Sufi traditions or why there was quite a crowd circling around the encased tomb in one corner of the very exquisitely rendered *masjid* named after him. Nor could they find anyone who spoke enough English to help in that regard. She might have asked someone in Arabic, but did not want him to wait while she translated. And Mervat did not wish to intrude upon anyone's rituals.

'I promise to research it more before your article,' she apologised. Hussam had told them they could not spend long touring it since the rest of their journey was time constricted.

Louis had been examining the high ceilings, his neck awkwardly angled to take in the geometric patterns painted in squares akin to a giant chessboard. No, not really a chessboard, for the artist had not confined the blocks to two colours, but a mosaic of them—and seemingly without any rhyme, yet somehow they all still matched as if part of one grand design. *Subhan Allah*, she thought.

When Louis looked back down at her, his smile was an earnest one. 'I am glad if it means we are not done yet. Our project is not done yet, I mean.'

Mervat had dreaded telling him what she'd learned about the Cleopatra Cerulean because it meant they would no longer have something they could work on together. Was it possible that Louis too was not eager to stop spending time with her?

'It will be an easy task, even the harem library will have it.'

'Then we should consider engaging a different, more complicated project.'

As they walked back to the waiting train, she noticed how especially handsome he was today. It was muggier in Tanta and there was a sheen to his brow, the waves in his hair damp. He'd grown it out, perhaps not yet found a barber he liked near Sesostris. His golden locks nearly reached the shoulders of his brown chemise and Mervat would have liked to show him how deftly she could tie it back for him. As it was, he kept raking through it, whipping his head or blowing it out of his eyes.

When they mounted the car and the train set off to Alexandria with just the four of them in the car now, Hussam and Nadine chatted intimately in one corner, completely oblivious to her and Louis at the other.

She untied the ribbon on Amu Taha's *halawet el-moulid* package and pushed it towards Louis. He picked a finger-length sesame candy cylinder from the assortment which included discs dotted with dried peas and squares of crimson Turkish delight with pistachios. The perfume of caramelised sugar and blossom water filled the air between them, cooling now the train was moving and the soft breeze from the Nile was blowing through their open window.

Louis's face registered surprise when he bit into it, the crunch causing it to splinter into shards he had to brush off his chest.

Mervat laughed and then felt bad lest he think she was making fun of him. So, she picked the same candy for herself. 'This one needs to be moistened first.' She demonstrated how, putting it between her lips, sticking her tongue out a bit to lick it.

She watched him watching her as she did. His gaze never left her mouth; his Adam's apple bulged in his throat. It was a long minute before she understood that the action wasn't just about the candy.

Louis finally shifted his eyes upwards to meet hers. 'Mervat.' Her name was a low, frustrated growl. 'Please stop.'

Which, of course, only made her want to continue.

Mervat twirled the cylinder in her mouth, knew her lips were plumping with the sheen of it until she finally pulled it out to show him the sharper tip. 'Now, when you bite into it, it will not make a mess.'

He had no response, only gave her a wry grin before finally pulling his gaze away. 'Hussam,' he shouted, 'the princess has confections she'd like to share with you both.'

'Then why does she not bring them over?' Hussam boomed.

Louis smirked, nodded his head in her cousin's direction.

'You're trying to get rid of me.'

'Never that.' He pushed his head into the cushioned seat back, 'It's simply that I need a minute to gather myself because a man can find himself in danger around you.'

He said it in a way that made her want to keep doing whatever he considered dangerous, but she got up and crossed the car to Hussam and Nadine, wondering if Louis was watching her, but he'd moved to the window, his back to them.

'*Ya salam,*' Nadine said, biting into a Turkish delight.

'Don't eat too much,' Hussam insisted. 'In Alexandria, we *have* to eat fresh fish and I have a picnic planned.'

Mervat wondered if they'd be back home before nightfall, and he admitted it'd be late because they had to pick up his aunt. 'You're not afraid your father will be angry?'

Nadine answered before Hussam. 'I am afraid my time at court will end soon.'

Mervat guessed Anne would have something to do with that. 'Maybe we are provoking them too much, Hussam.'

'Is that not the point, cousin? Modernity might be uncomfortable, but it is what my father wanted for Egypt. This locomotive is proof of it—the ground we are covering that would have taken days, if not weeks, otherwise.'

'Well, just remember that there aren't many days left before he announces our wedding. He needs to know we are not getting married before then.' Because Allah knew that Anne was not about to believe it unless the khedive did.

'There is time, I'm sure. But if this is to be one of our last outings, then we should have fun. And since I will be making the most of it with Nadine, I will be too busy to host Louis. Will you be attentive to our guest, cousin?'

Because they were speaking in Arabic and in low tones, Louis didn't hear it, but Mervat couldn't help but wonder why the request was so innocently rendered on the part of her cousin. If Louis had feelings for her, surely he would confide them to Hussam, his close friend? Maybe she was reading more into what was between them then was there. But just now when Louis had sent her away, she had thought it meant that he was attracted to her. Wanted her. Perhaps, it could have been any other woman.

'Your cousin does not need to be reminded. Her talent is her graciousness,' Nadine reprimanded Hussam.

'Maybe that's why my father wants her for me and not you,' Hussam teased Nadine and then added, 'Look at you, chastising me and you're not even my wife!'

'Yet,' Nadine added, wagging a playful finger. 'Are we not practicing for the day when I am?'

Their easy banter pricked Mervat, and she stepped back, leaving them to it. She wasn't jealous of them, only of the ease with which they spent their time together, knowing that they loved each other and wanted to be together. Could be together if this plan worked.

But between her and Louis? It was fraught—at least from her point of view. Perhaps, he was only biding his time in her company. Making the best of it because Hussam had asked him to as he'd just asked her. Even if this plan worked for him and Nadine, she wasn't the bride Louis needed or wanted. Not for his future. Not for Allenborough.

Before she could resume her seat, the conductor entered with an announcement. 'We'll be at the Sidi Gaber Station in Alexandria shortly.'

She moved to where Louis stood watching the passing buildings.

'That's the Mediterranean?' he noted about the hint of blue in the distance.

'Alexandria is a coastal city where, no matter where you are in it, the sea is always close.'

Mervat had been here a couple of times with Baba, always in early September when the crowds had lessened and usually near the western harbour where her father had spent his own childhood summering in the Ras el-Tin Palace.

She thought that was where they were going, but Hussam asked the conductor to tell the train operator that they wanted to get off earlier. 'We will be checking on plans for a new khedival palace in the Montazah, but I am cognizant of the time and think we do not have much to spend in Alexandria were we dropped off all the way into Raml Station.'

After checking with the train operator, the conductor returned to say that he knew where it was and would save time via a yet incomplete track near the Montazah.

It sounded dangerous, but, as it turned out, they were fortunate that the track they disembarked upon had not yet been open to the public, so it was easier to go into Alexandria without the summer crowds noticing them as a party that included the prince of Egypt. The conductor flagged a carriage and ordered it to come as close to the track as possible, but the four of them had to walk a bed of rocks to meet it. Nadine clung to Hussam whilst Mervat thought it best to rush ahead and not have to take Louis's arm. She nearly tripped for her efforts but was the first to board without anyone's aid.

The carriage horse trotted alongside the corniche, a bricked pathway that overlooked the sea and ran nearly the length of the city. The salty breeze whipped the scarf she wore, reminding her of the last time she'd been to Alexandria.

She and Baba had eaten freshly grilled corn and roasted watermelon seeds. They drank *erk-soos* juice from peddlers who carried tankards of it strapped to their bodies. They were innovative contraptions with a place for cups and a water hose to cleanse them between customers. Mervat disliked its licorice taste but had been entertained by the songs the peddlers sang and the costumes they wore to stand out amongst the multitude of vendors along the corniche.

Mervat would insist that she and Baba come again this September. The wedding season would be over, but she'd be back home, Anne likely upset with her. And Louis…though he might still be in Egypt with his new post, he'd only be biding his time till he could go back home and find a wife to benefit his estate.

The thought caused her chest to tighten and Mervat dragged her gaze from the blue sea to the blue of Louis's eyes. He'd been watching her.

'They call Alexandria the "Bride of the Mediterranean",' she said.

'I can see why.'

The smile he gifted her felt too intimate. Mervat glanced at Hussam and Nadine but they were oblivious, too besotted with each other to notice her and Louis.

The carriage passed a fence that was still being constructed with red bricks and white cement. The servant from Sesostris who'd come with them and was sitting next to the driver had to talk to the soldier stationed at a gate to let them pass. When they came to a stop at the end of a long newly bricked road, the area was completely empty.

This time, Mervat could not be the first to descend the carriage and Louis leapt off to offer her his hand. It would be rude to refuse it and although she braced herself against the rush of emotions at his touch, he steadied them by holding on even after her feet were solidly on the ground.

He said, 'I sailed this very sea from France to Egypt, but this view is without equal.'

'Wait till you see what's ahead,' Hussam said, jostling between them so that Louis was forced to release Mervat's hand. He glanced at her when he did and she was almost certain that it was with regret.

The Montaza gardens were immaculate. Unlike Sesostris with its manicured lawns, the palm trees here and the wildflower bushes were less planned out, more untamed with the sea breeze thrashing them about. The line between green land and white sandy beach blurred. The sound of the waves crashing forward then scrambling back grew louder the closer they got. The four of them practically ran towards it, unable to resist the water's invitation.

Hussam had ordered a large umbrella to be set up and a moderately lavish buffet.

The best part was that they were entirely alone. If there were servants about, they must be very discreet, because before them was a private beach all to themselves.

Nadine squealed with delight, giving Hussam a proper hug and he lifted her off the ground, twirling her until she was dizzy.

'She's telling my cousin he is very romantic,' Mervat said but Louis didn't seem to want a translation. He was already removing his shoes and rolling up his trousers. He unbuttoned his shirt as she continued, 'Hussam says that he will build a grand summer palace here and she will be mistress of it. Nadine is further saying that she will never love a man like she loves him.'

She finally stopped talking, too occupied with her examination of his bare chest. It was perfect. Not so pale, tanned. Arms perfectly muscular, the broadness of his shoulders perfect too. His stomach flat, taut, perfectly defined. It was hairless mostly, save for a perfect line of light brown threading below his navel to... Mervat swallowed. She needed to stop using the word *perfect* to describe him and *really* needed to stop staring.

'Do you swim, Princess?' he asked, drawing her gaze upward, his tone telling her he knew well and was quite pleased with the effect his half-naked body was having on her. 'Only, you look flushed, like you could use a cool-down.'

He might be teasing her or daring her, but whatever it was, she rose to the occasion. Mervat slipped off her own shoes and stockings, took great pleasure in unfastening her belt and removing her skirt and blouse, knowing that the kaftan she'd worn beneath was decent enough she wouldn't be naked, but he didn't know that and she revelled in how his face flushed a little too. 'Perhaps I will. Take a swim.'

Then she raced Louis to the water. When they neared the edge, he gestured to let her go first as if it were a doorway to enter, but when she jumped in and screamed at the cold, he dived quickly after her with an apology. 'I should have tested the temperature first.'

She laughed in response and sprayed him with water. 'That would have been the gentlemanly thing to do, Viscount Wesley.'

He dunked her then, catching her waist so she didn't go too far under, and lifting her before she'd been under enough. She laughed and dunked herself while he swam around her.

The salt water burned, but it was gloriously cleansing.

Rejuvenating.

Louis stood before her, stopping to slick his hair back, dark with the wetness.

She did the same. But her hair was more abundant, longer and curlier and...she'd lost the binding. She fished after it, nearly catching it before a large wave took it further away. By the time she grasped it, they'd gone far enough that the sea water was at her chest and when a wave knocked into her, she lost her footing. Louis grasped her waist, bringing her towards him. Their bodies clung to each other. He pushed the hair off her face, held it back for her as she readjusted her hair binding.

'Mervat.' Her name on Louis's tongue was a whisper amidst the mewing of seagulls overhead and the swirling water around them. 'Ask me to kiss you again.'

She wanted to.

She didn't want to fret over whether his feelings for her

were more than a physical attraction. She didn't want to fret over a future they could not have.

She wanted Louis to kiss her. Now.

She raked her hands through his hair, clasped them at the back of his neck. Felt his body harden against hers. He lifted her by the waist so that their faces were nearly touching, so close, Mervat perceived the droplets caught between his eyelashes, smelt the sesame candy on his breath. Fingered the tiny mole on his left cheek she'd not noticed before.

'Ask me,' he repeated, roughly, 'to kiss you again.'

She could have him here, open her legs in the water, let the blood his body might bring after penetrating hers be washed away in the sea. A wedding night between them that could never otherwise be, here in the city that was the Bride of the Mediterranean.

The last time they'd been in this position, Louis had not kissed her because he'd known where it might lead. And now, here, Mervat knew it could easily lead to the same. No Baba in the next room. No chance of Anne barging in. Even Hussam and Nadine were nowhere to be found. It would be just her and Louis.

She wanted his kiss. But what if she wanted more?

What if they couldn't stop? What if they fell into *haram*, that which was forbidden? They weren't married. They never could be. And yet...

'Before I ask,' she said, 'you must promise that it will only be one kiss.'

'One kiss and then we are done?' he asked.

Mervat couldn't decipher the expression in his face. Was it hurt? Frustration for having to wait so long for a single kiss? 'Yes.'

Louis closed his eyes for a long beat and when he opened

them and met her gaze, searching, there was only determination, clear as day. 'You have my promise.'

'Kiss me.' Did she whisper or yell it? Was it a plea or a demand? Mervat didn't know because the question came from something deep in her soul. A compromise with the wanton spirit who lay dormant there, waiting for the kind of unbridled love that would sweep her off her feet. Have her soaring in water.

Keeping one hand on her waist, Louis cupped the other around her neck, then he slowly lowered his lips to hers not taking his eyes off her until the end, when he turned them to where they would land. It was wet at first, lush and soft. A nibble that demanded she suck. She wrapped her arms around his shoulder so that he wouldn't end it yet. Louis's lips hardened around hers, prodding, licking, feeding. And hers responded in kind.

It was glorious. A sensation that stretched to her toes and had her believing the whole sea was alive with it.

Neither took a breath, prolonging the single kiss until they had to gasp for air. It was over.

Louis kept her hand in his but pulled away, putting distance between them as he dragged her past the water and its white spitting foam.

He wants more and is frustrated with his promise, Mervat thought, because that was what she was experiencing.

If Louis was frustrated then, he calmed and was amiable soon after, commenting on how well the grilled sea bass tasted or wondering how the freshly squeezed mango juice remained cold. He chatted with Hussam almost as if nothing had happened between them. *Almost.* He held her glance when their fingers brushed reaching for a *balady* bread half and he gave up the one he'd taken to her before taking another for himself. Or the jealous smile as she tried to gather

her hair and needed to ask for Nadine's help. As if he would have volunteered instead.

'You will suffer for it tomorrow,' Nadine said. Mervat looked at her, wondered if the girl had seen her and Louis's kiss, but she only pointed to her head. 'My sister has the same type of curls. Egyptian hair needs fresh water after the drying saltwater. The knots will be impossible to untangle.'

Tomorrow too she might regret what had happened between her and Louis. But right then, nothing could dampen the joy of their kiss and by the end of the day, Mervat decided it had been the best one of her entire life.

Chapter Fifteen

Louis

Louis had taken to strolling in the Sesostris gardens or standing by the foyer, anywhere women of the harem passed in order to catch a glimpse of Mervat, but since their return from Alexandria two days ago, it seemed that they'd closed her off. Having submitted a piece on rail travel in Egypt—working in the study in hopes that she would appear—he was already finishing up the one on the Cleopatra Cerulean and was quite pleased with it. He would have liked to share it with Mervat, thank her for the research on the Sufi saint of Tanta, but the fact she'd sent it to him via Amu Taha in written form rather than spoken to him directly about it, indicated that either her mother was likely upset with their trip or that Mervat herself was avoiding him.

He had felt unmoored since their kiss. Although, at her request, it was only supposed to happen once, he couldn't stop thinking about it. Mervat had smartly known that there should not—could not—be more between them. To attempt it was to court disaster in a court built on traditions, no matter how much the khedive spoke of modernisation.

'My father,' Hussam said, as the two of them sipped lime cordials on the palace verandas, 'has been strangely silent.'

It was a hot day and unlike in Alexandria, there was no sea breeze coming in to cool them. Louis might have splashed in the fountain pool were it not so picturesque with its Andalusian tiled design. Instead, he watched a pair of larks sipping from its tiered basin and listened as they chirped happily thereafter.

'Perhaps that is a good thing? An indication your plan is working.'

Hussam scraped at his beard. 'I fear not. What if he has guessed at it and is deciding what to do about Nadine? If he sends her away before...'

Louis frowned. Hussam should be concerned with the impact on Mervat, as well. 'The princess hasn't been seen. Have you checked on her?'

'I assume my cousin is in her room, working on one of her projects.' Hussam swirled the drink in his hand and went back to fretting. 'Remember Montague at Eton? His father had holdings in the West Indies where the lime cordial was discovered. And when I brought it to mine, I had two weeks of praise. The khedive rewards behaviour he likes vocally, withholds it when he's displeased.'

'You're telling me you're worried that a plan of your devising *is* working? Do you not realise the lives at stake here?'

Hussam finally noticed Louis's frustration. 'I'm sorry, my friend. I hoped my father would be easier to read, but whatever his mood, I won't let it affect you. You'll have your post, your articles. His being upset with me will not hurt you. I'll make sure of that.'

Louis appreciated the sentiment, but he wanted the same for Mervat and was about to say as much when they were interrupted by one of the servants.

He spoke in Arabic and Louis understood that Hussam had been summoned to the khedive.

'Speak of the devil and he shall appear,' Hussam whispered to Louis in English as he stood to leave. 'Excuse me.'

But the servant said something more and Hussam frowned. 'My father is asking for you too.'

As they followed the servant to the khedive, it was reminiscent of them being called to the headmaster's office at Eton. When Hussam winked nervously, Louis knew he'd had the same thought. They moved through a long corridor and then up a set of wooden stairs to a meeting area that might as well have been a separate castle in itself. With only two small windows, the sheesha smell, a molasses-drenched smoke, nested heavily in the air. The room was fairly plain in comparison with the rest of Sesostris, its walls papered in pallid yellow stripes, the odd paintings that hung on them were of past khedives, of which there were not many.

The current khedive paced at his desk, a glossy monstrosity that absolutely could have also belonged to the Eton headmaster.

'Hussam. Viscount Wesley. Please come in.'

Hussam took his seat while Louis bowed, unclear of Egyptian traditions, but feeling that his purpose here, like it had been when they were students, was to save Hussam from himself. This time, he was aware it might also involve saving Mervat.

'Your Highness,' he greeted, his voice dripping with charm, before assuming the seat next to Hussam.

The khedive tilted his neck rather than nod and Louis realised this was not Eton and the man before him was not the kindly, if frustrated, headmaster there. Egypt's ruler, up close, looked like a lion one did not want to rile.

Even as the khedive thanked him for the pleasant articles he was writing about his country, Louis fathomed the apprehension rolling off Hussam, the tension around them.

'Egypt has been a pleasure to write about. I have fallen in love with your country, sir.'

'Have you also fallen in love with a member of my harem?' the khedive asked.

Next to him, Hussam sputtered but his father was already turning to him, 'Or was that you?'

'Baba,' Hussam started.

'I am your khedive,' his father reprimanded, sharply.

'Khedewy.' Hussam adjusted the title, shifted in his seat. 'No doubt, there has been gossip but I assure you, it is nothing for you to concern yourself with.'

Louis would have added something to defend himself, but he didn't know what. He could hardly disclose his feelings about Mervat—he was barely sure of them himself. She was a princess of Egypt. He was but a guest here, depending on his friend's father's favour to obtain a diplomatic post in order to support his family and title back in England

'You would not know if the viscount had his sights set on your bride, Hussam. You are often obtuse.'

Hussam looked back at Louis and he couldn't tell if he was surprised by the claim—hadn't that been his plan after all?—or trying to think of a retort.

The khedive continued, 'Or perhaps your ogling of Nadine has blinded you.'

Hussam sputtered again. 'With all respect, Khedewy, you have it wrong.'

'The little tricks you have been playing, I know them. Mervat's project, the visit to the Azhar, to Tanta that turned out to be Alexandria. I know.'

Louis protested, 'We *were* researching a project. The Cleopatra Cerulean piece will be—'

Hussam held up a hand and tilted his face so that his father could not see when he mouthed the words to Louis: *Follow my lead.* 'The piece will be phenomenal. But you are right, Khedewy. Louis does love someone in the harem. We tried to be discreet about it, but he was afraid you would not approve, what with us being his hosts here. But her sweetness, her beauty, made it hard for him to look away.'

Had Hussam seen Louis kissing Mervat? Did he think he was in love with her? What the hell was his friend talking about?

Hussam continued, 'And with Nadine not being a permanent member of the harem, I suggested the outings. If my old friend could make her fall in love with him too, no harm in getting a leg up if he gathers the courage to propose.'

'Nadine?' Louis couldn't stop the name from escaping his mouth, an expression of his complete shock.

Hussam grinned. 'You see how he is? Every time he is in her presence he is thus flustered.'

The khedive finally sat down in the chair behind his desk. Though he did not smile, he looked more at ease; his expression of malice dwindled. 'Nadine's father is a wealthy man but seeks power through his daughter, knowing she is a beauty. Although you are a viscount in England rather than an Arab noble, he *might* be persuaded. You will have to convert to Islam, of course, were you to marry her.'

'Louis knows that,' Hussam answered on his behalf while he himself was sure his mouth was agape. He could not trust himself to speak even if he understood what had just happened. 'And with the position Louis will have in the embassy, they could travel between Cairo and London easily.'

'Which reminds me that I have been meaning to talk to Sir Stuart,' the khedive said.

'We can hardly fault you for delaying it, the man is an insufferable bore.' Hussam did not miss a beat—as if he hadn't just transferred his own love for Nadine onto Louis.

'I will assure Gulnur Hanem then that there is nothing to fear. Hussam?'

'You may, Khedewy. I am your most humble son and servant.'

His father waved to the door, dismissing them.

Louis and Hussam were almost out when the khedive added, 'Cairo's first opera house is opening in two days' time, Viscount. Consider this a formal invitation since there are precious few of them.'

'Thank you, Your Highness, I am honoured by it.' Louis didn't know how he managed to sound coherent.

'And Hussam,' the khedive added, 'the French ambassador's wife, Madame Lamoureux, is in the ballroom, teaching women of the harem dances for the Midsummer Festival. She requested male accompaniment earlier, but we thought it inappropriate. Take the Viscount there now—I will send a messenger saying I have changed my mind and that he may be of use to her.'

'Certainly.'

Hussam shut the door but only showed his agony when they were a good distance away.

An agony matched by Louis's anger. 'What was that?'

'I panicked. You saw how he was. You don't know that look, forcing me to call him "Khedewy", like I was taking him for a fool. He was about to banish you and Nadine from the palace! I had to lie.'

'And how long is that lie supposed to go on? Till I marry Nadine and you and Mervat are the happily married couple visiting us in Allenborough where you can have at my wife?'

Hussam arched his brow at him in a way that made it seem like he was considering.

'I was being sarcastic.'

Hussam folded his hands on top of his. 'I know. It was

wrong of me. But why are you upset? Even if you were to marry Nadine, her father's wealth would shore up your estate. Wouldn't it be the sort of arranged marriage you've talked of for as long as I've known you?'

'I won't marry Nadine, Hussam!' If Louis admitted that he didn't love her, his friend would remind him that he never used to care about that sort of thing anyway. But it was what he wanted to say because he realised that knowing Mervat *was* changing him.

'You're right. If you did, I would kill you.' Hussam faced him, patted his chest kindly with the palms of both his hands. 'I will fix this.'

Except Hussam always used to say the same thing when they were called to the headmaster's office after one of his terrible ideas. And it would still always be Louis who did the fixing. But he had no idea how he would do it now. Yes, Allenborough was his priority and he still wanted the diplomat's position. But Louis also needed to live with himself and if he had to give up the latter for the former, he would. An arranged marriage to a wealthy bride back home might be the only thing to quell the hollow feeling in his stomach now. The one that would not let up until he could ensure both the freedom and happiness of Hussam and Mervat.

Hussam was not permitted to stay in the ballroom, but Madame Lamoureux was overjoyed with Louis's arrival. She had been informed of it, clearly, for she handpicked Nadine from the younger ladies present, proving the swiftness of the khedive's influence.

Before he began, his gaze instinctively found Mervat's. She smiled openly enough, but her mother was near her, frowning.

Louis forced his eyes away.

Mervat had never looked so much like the young lady he'd first met at the Louvre. The one he'd sketched and thought about for months until he'd come to Egypt. The same young lady who had repeatedly shown him her kindness since. The one whose lips tasted like the sweetest fruit on the brightest day in the most heavenly of earthly places.

But her mother knew Louis cared for Mervat enough to voice her worries to the khedive.

A man who had his own son trembling, telling a lie to save them all. Maybe Louis needed to do the same.

He should think of Mervat and not be so presumptive. He'd been the one to encourage her to stand up to her mother. Chided her because he did not wish her to be trapped in a marriage she did not want.

But what if he'd been hurting Mervat in the process? She might have done fine by herself, refusing the marriage to Hussam in her own gentle way. And when his friend first thought of this plan, Hussam had taken his advice on what defiant love looked like from an English perspective. Was it Louis's presence then that had encouraged Hussam's folly? Or would the two of them have found a way to love each other? Because the Hussam Louis had seen with the khedive would absolutely marry Mervat if his father demanded it, excuses be damned.

Louis had never believed he had any real chance to be with the princess. It was why he had doggedly focused on the Cleopatra Cerulean, his writing and the hope for a diplomatic post in order to help his estate. But what if he had hurt Mervat in the process? Or if she began to care for him more than he realised? He'd not anticipated that when he'd first agreed to Hussam's plan.

And that was on Louis.

So he squared his shoulders and danced with Nadine and tried to pretend that his heart was in it, when, in truth, it was somewhere else entirely.

Chapter Sixteen

Mervat

'To think it is only you chosen to attend the opera tonight, from the entire harem!' Anne grinned at Mervat as she adjusted the pearl pin in her daughter's swept-up hair. 'Along with the khedive's wife, of course.'

Mervat and her mother were getting on better now, but because she was sure it would not last when Anne finally realised there was no hope of her marriage to Hussam, she wished to please her mother in other ways. An exclusive invitation to the opening production of the Royal Opera House and a chance to wear one of the dresses they'd brought from Paris? That was one such way.

'Do you not think this gown will cause a scandal, Anne?' she wondered.

The dress was nearly bare-shouldered and her mother had to add all the pearls in her possession so that Mervat's cleavage would not spill from it. While the white gloves she wore were long, the capped sleeves meant the top of her arms would be exposed, as well. But perhaps it was the colour and fit that was most shocking. Scarlet-red, cinched tight at the waist and pleated at the back, the material that flowed in the front outlined the length of her legs without hiding the breadth of her hips.

And though she'd had no word that Louis would be coming, the thought of him seeing her in it excited Mervat in ways it should not.

She'd been jealous after his dance with Nadine the other day. Nadine and Hussam were in love, Mervat knew she had nothing to fear in that regard, but Nadine had the sort of beauty which could captivate anybody. Maybe Louis, disappointed in his kiss with Mervat, had been taken by her.

'This is a gown to make any man think you are the most stunning woman he's ever seen.' Anne seemed to read her thoughts, but then she bobbed wickedly. 'Hussam will not be able to resist you.'

'But what of a scandal with the harem?'

'Everyone knows the khedive is making changes—your fashionable outing will prove it. My sources tell me it is to impress the English investors. He has called it a celebration for the Suez Canal completion. I would have advised him that it is foolish to favour the English at a French-Italian opera, but then he chose only my daughter to attend so I cannot complain.'

Anne further warned, 'I do not know if this viscount of yours will be there, but do not fawn over him, if yes. Do you understand?' Mervat feared her mother might see proof of their kiss in her flushing cheeks, but Anne continued, 'My sources tell me the viscount remains in Egypt in order to secure a diplomatic post with the ambassador's office. He writes of my crown because of it.'

'I have told you this, Anne. Another source was not necessary.'

'What happens if he does not get this post, hmm? What if the time spent with you is part of his plan? He could blackmail Hussam by saying you love him?'

Mervat nearly laughed with the irony in that one considering that her cousin was the master planner. 'He and Hussam are friends. I promise you that is not the viscount's intention.'

Again, her mother acted as if she heard nothing, 'I have seen the viscount at the British consul's ear often and have lived long enough at court to know that Sir Stuart is a weasel. Not as smart or handsome as his French counterpart, but he knows that what he lacks in charm the young Louis more than makes up for. He would use him even if the viscount does not intend to be used.'

'Mr Wesley is, as you say, a viscount with his own land and title in England which he is sure to return to.' Mervat felt the need to defend him even though from what he had told her, Allenborough *was* in dire need of monies and a suitable English bride. She knew he wanted a post. Needed it to accomplish his goals for Allenborough. But she could not abide her mother's accusations.

'You are innocent, naive,' Anne patronised. 'You must be warned.'

Mervat's patience thinned. 'Warned of what?'

'Were you to fall in love with him, act outside of our traditions—' her mother leaned forward to whisper the next bit even though they were quite alone '—and let us not forget that evening in your father's house, the looks between you two. Louis could very well bribe me. Hussam. The khedive, perhaps. He could threaten to write about the half-Turkish princess he had a love affair with in the Egyptian court. Think of the scandal it would cause, the political ramifications, Egypt's standing in the history of the Ottoman Empire.'

Anne must be exaggerating, but before Mervat could tell her so, the door rapped and her mother rushed to open it.

'Gulnur Hanem, *marhaba*. The carriage to the opera is ready for my cousin.'

Hussam. Picking her up from here? A room inside the harem?

Her mother lifted a vindicated brow when she turned and gestured for her to come forth. When she did and Hussam saw her, he whistled in appreciation.

His gaze ran the length of Mervat before turning to her mother to dole out the compliment. 'Your daughter looks beautiful, *mashallah.*'

'And you are handsome too, my son.' Anne cupped Hussam's bearded chin in a motherly gesture that irked Mervat to witness. But she was right. In his black tailcoat and starched trousers, he struck an imposing figure.

Her mother retrieved a handkerchief from her kaftan pocket to fold into the one at Hussam's chest. It had been cut from the same material as Mervat's gown. 'A perfect couple.'

Mervat grimaced as she took the arm Hussam offered her, and they made their way to the winding staircase. The servants had all come out in their finest livery for the occasion, members of the harem too. And there were quite a number of press people there. Egyptian and foreign reporters; a photographer had set up a camera in the centre.

'All this, for us?' she whispered to Hussam.

He grinned. 'I am surprised by it too. Perhaps we are merely the preshow and my parents to follow, the main. But I have seen them, and we are definitely dressed better. The French designer of your dress is sure to be inundated with new orders.'

'You're teasing me!'

'Not at all,' he insisted and then as if to prove him right, one of the cameramen asked them to pose for a picture. As soon as their photo was taken, Mervat subtly scanned those gathered below for *him.* And though her gaze easily found

Nadine who looked very comely dressed despite not having an invitation, Louis was much harder to spot.

Until she did, leaning on the grand pendulum clock.

It was evening and all the lamps were lit in the palace foyer, so that if he were trying to hide, the lights shining around his golden handsomeness would make it impossible. Mervat could not stare with everyone watching her and Hussam, but her glance was long enough to catch Louis's dapper dinner jacket, the cravat around his neck.

And the frown on his face.

The royal box was lined from top to bottom in velvet, its seats a smaller theatre within themselves.

Mervat assumed that she and Hussam were supposed to sit there with the khedive and his wife but was grateful when they were asked to move to the central rows below. The khedive had not said anything to her on the carriage ride over— or ever in her life that she could remember. She wasn't sure if that was because of who her father was or simply his personality in private, but his silent air of disdain made her uncomfortable. And while Hussam's mother was certainly more familiar to Mervat, it was odd being in her presence without her own mother.

The usher apologised profusely to the khedive's guards. 'The conductor is a fickle sort, an Italian, and the director expected more of a public presence.'

Hearing it, his father said, 'Hussam, take your cousin and sit below.'

'As you wish, Khedewy.' Not Baba. Hussam's foul mood was apparent as soon as they left the royal box. 'I hate it when he orders me around like I am only his subject.'

'You are upset.' Mervat suspected it was because Nadine wasn't invited but wondered if there might be more.

'An opera is the longest, most boring invention of Western civilisation. I was hoping to snooze in the back of the box where none could see, now I have to sit and pretend to enjoy where everyone can,' he grumbled, barely lowering his voice before the usher who clearly understood the Arabic. Mervat gave the man an apologetic smile as he led them to their seats. It was quite dark and from her vantage, the row had no vacancies, but when he held up his lamp the light showed them the two empty spots near the end of it.

'Itfadily.' Hussam gestured for her to go first, and it might have been a difficult thing to navigate the guests in any other dress, but Mervat was grateful that the fit made it so there was nothing to gather as she moved between tight spaces.

She might have been bashful to be seated in the front row in such a dress, but it was reassuring to see that the women she passed—mostly French ones—were similarly fashioned.

A few *'excusé moi'*s later, Mervat fell into the empty seat, spent with the effort.

'Princess Mervat.'

Louis.

Her heart leapt at the sound of his voice, thumped with the awareness he would be her seating companion.

'Finally, a friendly face,' Hussam answered, leaning over her from his own seat. 'Did you sneak any spirits in a flask like a good lad?'

'Afraid not.' Louis spoke discreetly, his voice hushed. 'Maybe loosen your tie and try to enjoy it. One can always be pleasantly surprised.'

If those last words were for her, Mervat dared not acknowledge it. His proximity brought with it both a draught to her skin and a heat beneath it.

'Always the voice of reason,' Hussam said. He fell back

into his seat as the remaining usher lamps were extinguished and the focus turned to the spotlights on stage.

When the curtain rose, Mervat craned her neck to observe Louis's profile. The hand on his knee, his arms politely tucked in so she would be comfortable. The outline of his straight nose, his strong jaw, the way his hair curled at the nape of his cravat.

The whites of his teeth appeared as he smiled. Louis sensed her watchful gaze.

'You will enjoy it,' he whispered.

'I know nothing of the story. The language.'

'An opera is to be *experienced*. Besides, I am here for you, Mervat. Ask me…ask me for anything you need.'

It had been days since their kiss, the thing she had asked of him.

But this time we are not alone in the sea. It is a theatre full of people.

Why then did it feel like they were?

Instinctively, Mervat pressed towards him. Since returning from Alexandria, she'd avoided Louis. It was due to a combination of guilt on her part but also the fear that he had not been as moved by their kiss as she had.

He'd danced only with Nadine during the harem lesson and then there was the frown earlier at the palace. Louis had been avoiding her too. Why?

The director's voice boomed from the stage. He welcomed the audience in French and Italian to their opening night, then he switched to English 'for the critics amongst us.'

He was glad, he said, to have an all-Italian cast of actors and sopranos and thanked Egypt for the generous hospitality they'd been met with. Here, the lights shone in the direction of the royal balcony where the khedive waved.

The director further claimed that the sets and costumes had been shipped from France.

'As has my gown.' Mervat thought she'd mumbled it to herself, but Louis had heard.

'I wished to compliment you in it,' he answered. 'You are exquisite. Ethereal and devastating at once.'

'Yet you were frowning when you saw me in it at Sesostris.'

Even to Mervat, it sounded like an accusation, one that necessitated a defence. And his came quickly, a begrudging hiss. 'Because it was not I whose arm you held, Princess.'

How did his icy blue eyes manage to pierce the dark and how was it that when Louis looked at her, she felt like he could see her utterly naked?

It is a theatre full of people, she reminded herself.

Mervat clutched the pearls her mother had wrapped around her neck but feared they would burst so she let go and then didn't know what to do with her hands.

She peeled off one glove, then slipped it on again.

For his part, Louis seemed to be taking deep breaths, as well. The hands so casually palming his knees were fisted tightly there now.

It was a blessing when *Aida* began. Its music churned the air around them, demanding Mervat's attention.

In the first act, they were introduced to Radamès, an Egyptian warrior called to serve an old kingdom pharaoh as the threat of a conflict with Ethiopia loomed large. Radamès was torn between serving his king and his love for an Ethiopian slave girl they had previously captured. Aida had also fallen in love with Radamès, but she could not reveal her true identity as the princess of Ethiopia nor could she let on that her father waged war on Egypt only to save her. And then there was Amneris, the daughter of the Egyptian king, who was also in love with Radamès but knew her love was unrequited.

In act one, Mervat was most effected by Amneris's song. That she should be a princess who any man would want to marry but was denied the one man she wanted above all others touched Mervat. But this sentiment would not last long.

In the second act, Amneris turned cruel. Guessing that Radamès and Aida were in love, she told the prisoner that he had fallen in battle in order to see if it would garner a reaction. Meanwhile, he returned alive and victorious, crossed into Egypt with a host of Ethiopian prisoners, one of whom was the king, Aida's father, also in disguise. When the Egyptian king declared Radamès would be his son as a reward and then asked him what he wished for as a prize, Radamès said he wanted the prisoners released. Once his Aida was free, he committed to marrying Amneris, the Egyptian king's daughter.

Mervat cried when Aida and her father found each other in the parade meant to mock them. Before she could ask Hussam for the silk kerchief her mother had tucked into his pocket, Louis offered his own. She inhaled *him* as she dabbed at her eyes, but that brought even more tears. Ones of longing. Melancholy. Allah had destined their meeting at the Louvre all those months ago. And here they were, sitting next to each other in a dark theatre in Cairo. Yet, when she thought of his future in England, she knew there was no place for her there.

In the third act, Amneris and others of the Egyptian king's army followed Radamès to a secret rendezvous with Aida on the banks of the Nile. They wanted to run away, be together.

Mervat marvelled at how one moment in time could determine a lifetime. How a couple's hopes and dreams were entwined with infinite possibilities *before* a decisive moment from which they could not return. What if they'd not hesitated? Run right away, rather than plot their escape? Maybe then Radamès would not have been captured and he and Aida would have had their happily-ever-after.

In the fourth act, Amneris desired to save her love and urged him towards a strategy that would squash the accusations against him as a traitor for conspiring to have the Ethiopian princess set free. But Radamès refused to speak a lie and deny his love for Aida. As he faced his judgement of death, his only assurance was that Aida had run and made it back safely to Ethiopia. Unbeknownst to him, Aida had already sealed herself in the dark vault of the temple he too was to be sealed in until his death.

'"The fatal stone now closes over me", Radamès sings,' Louis translated for her. '"To die, so pure and lovely."'

Louis's hand found her gloved one in the dark. Without removing it from under his, Mervat slipped the glove off to feel his skin in contact with hers.

She wished Louis could be hers as Radamès was Aida's.

And, as morbid as it might be, Mervat had the overwhelming sense that she wanted to take her last breath in Louis's arms. She weaved her fingers between his, letting the sensation overtake her, anchor her. And he held on for as long as he could before the lights came on and the audience rose for a standing ovation.

'Heartbreakingly beautiful,' were the words she managed to muster as she rose to join them.

Louis beamed next to her. 'Utterly,' he agreed.

Except, as he was looking at her when he said it, Mervat had the feeling he might not have been referring to *Aida*.

Chapter Seventeen

Louis

Hussam put the finishing knot on Louis's *keffiyeh*, a white cotton headscarf wrapped in an Egyptian traditional styled turban to cover his blond hair. 'It's good a thing I caught you before you shaved, the stubble will make you stand out less.'

'I will stand out, nonetheless.'

The *galabaya* he'd been prompted to wear was comfortable, but fairly billowy with wide sleeves that made Louis feel out of sorts. The leather sliders on his feet in lieu of shoes were no more than slippers. Were they meant to go wading in the sea, it might be appropriate attire, but Hussam had planned an excursion to the marketplace.

'We are hiding in plain sight as it were, and you are to play husband to my cousin. With her darker hair and customary kaftan, no one will doubt you two are a couple.'

Which was the only reason really that he'd agreed to this dangerous outing. Louis had already decided that he would back off—Hussam's desperate move claiming he was in love with Nadine was proof of the danger they were courting with the khedive—but the pull Mervat had on him was impossible to resist. The night of the opera was proof of it.

'Are you sure she's all right with it?'

Hussam led him down to the gardens. They slipped past the doors when the servants there moved inside. He hadn't answered Louis's question around this latest covert outing of his.

'I should think you wouldn't complain about getting out after being confined to a penguin suit for hours seated in the stuffiest of chairs, ears assaulted every time we tried to get some shut-eye, with voices that could shatter glass!' Hussam broke a branch as he brushed past it.

'I quite enjoyed it,' Louis argued. 'I daresay your cousin did, as well.'

He'd thought little of the opera outside of the woman sitting next to him, had only wanted to experience it through Mervat. When the evening started, he'd been unnaturally jealous at the sight of her on Hussam's arm. He knew they did not want to marry, but at the top of the stairs they looked as though they belonged together. And despite Louis knowing he could not be in Mervat's life in that way, he hated thinking of her holding on to any other man.

It was a petty notion and he should be above it.

Then, by the end of the evening, how incredible it had been to have Mervat by his side. The opera was an emotional experience, no doubt, but Louis's desperate desire to never be without her on his arm was maddening to say the least.

'Still, I cannot believe you would risk your father's ire *again*. Do you not recall the lie you had to tell about me being in love with Nadine?' Louis had a sudden, scary thought. 'You haven't told Mer… the *ladies* about that have you?'

Hussam chuckled. 'And risk Nadine falling in love with your good looks and charm? No, mate, I would not want to give her any ideas. She will be mine, one day, no matter what.'

Louis cared for Mervat's good opinion of him so he was glad for that, but Hussam's declaration piqued his ire. 'You take too many risks with all of our lives.'

Hussam searched beyond the trees for a minute before speaking. 'The truth is that I risk this outing because I'm scared to lose Nadine. She is upset to not have been invited to the opera. Her father has written, says he expects the khedive to ask for her hand on my behalf and in preparation for that he is calling her home. She told him she will return home with him after the midsummer festivity which he will be attending.'

'As Mervat's timeline approaches she will want you to make your lack of engagement officially known to your father.'

Hussam groaned with misery. 'Which is why we need this outing.'

'By pretending to be someone else besides a prince, you hope to gather the strength to tell your father the truth?'

'I don't know.'

Louis wished he could help his friend, had tried to think of a fix. A sacrifice he might make. But no matter how much he thought about it, the best thing that Hussam could do for himself and for Mervat was to corroborate what she'd been trying to impress upon her mother. 'You have to tell the khedive that you will not marry your cousin. That you want to be with Nadine. It is the only way I see out of this.'

Hussam said, 'I know you are right but…'

Nadine appeared then, alone. Louis tensed because as much as he reprimanded Hussam, he himself was eager to spend time with Mervat. He couldn't tell his friend, but the limited time they had left as a group might be just as much as a knell for him as it was for Hussam. Once the khedive knew that his son and Mervat would not marry, she'd have to leave here. And Louis may not get his position. How would he check on her welfare once he was back in England, looking for a new opportunity to seize? He was afraid that an arranged marriage would not make him as happy as he once believed.

'*Ruhti feen?*' Mervat ducked from under a tree and looked surprised to see the group of them. She did a double take when she spotted Louis, took in his attire. He couldn't tell if she liked what she saw or not.

Her eyes widened at Nadine who was smugly leaning on Hussam. 'Why did you lead me here?'

She had spoken in Arabic, but Louis understood. 'You said the princess was aware,' he accused Hussam.

Hussam held up his hands. 'It is a surprise. Arranged by Nadine and me.'

'Arranged *for* you and Nadine,' Louis mumbled. He turned to Mervat. 'We do not have to join them.'

'I am sorry. I was afraid neither of you would come,' Hussam answered them both. 'My plan has failed. You tried to warn me from the start. And I have been a coward. Let us have one last outing, the four of us. A bit of fun, us pretending to be other than who we are before we are forced to be who we are.'

Louis stiffened. Part of his jealousy at seeing Mervat on Hussam's arm the night of the opera was because he *could* picture them being together. Theirs would be an arranged marriage that should be right by all accounts. They were a prince and princess who were supposed to be together.

Louis could not figure out why Hussam's tone, his words, had been irking him, but now he was starting to. What if his friend had no plans to talk to his father at all? What if when Nadine left, Hussam would do as the khedive asked and marry Mervat?

He stared at his friend when he asked, 'Have your parents set a wedding date?'

'No. Because there will not be one,' Mervat's answer came so suddenly that Louis was reassured, but Hussam joked.

'Have you ever met a woman who disliked the idea of marrying a man more? Do I smell bad, cousin?'

Which was not the response of a man who was about to tell his father the truth.

Louis had ignored his history with Hussam, how he'd always been the best at coming up with ideas for adventure, pulling him and their friends at Eton along for his ill-conceived ploys.

But then, when things got too tough, Hussam would back out. Leave it to Louis to clean up the mess he'd started.

Even now, there was a plea in Hussam's expression. 'I have commissioned a *hantoor* to take us to the Khan el-Khalili bazaar. We shop like locals, drink a spot of tea, return before anyone notices we are missing.'

Hussam shook Louis's shoulder happily. He asked Mervat, 'Does he not make a handsome fake husband for you?'

Fake. Louis twisted free of Hussam's grip and threw him a reproving glance.

'Would you like to?' Mervat asked Louis.

The way she looked at him so intently caused him to ask, 'Be your husband?'

'I mean, would you like to *go*,' she clarified, 'to the bazaar?'

Because Louis had been confused with the question she was really asking, he answered in the affirmative with a bit too much enthusiasm and despite him actually thinking it wasn't a good idea, 'Yes, most ardently.'

Hussam clapped, but it was the smoothing of Mervat's furrowed brow that made Louis happy with the acceptance.

'Very well then,' she said, 'let us go.'

The four of them walked through the garden rows. Between the tomato bushes, it was narrower. While Hussam and Nadine were practically one body, hugging each other as they moved, Louis and Mervat walked cautiously, their pace slower. Was she thinking as he was how dangerous it would be were their bodies to touch so freely?

'Is it strange, dressed in clothing that feels foreign to you?' she asked.

'It is comfortable, cool in this heat. I can see why Egyptian men like it.' It wasn't a direct answer, but Louis wondered, 'You prefer me in my plain English garments?'

'Never plain,' she said with a small smile. 'Only I know what it is to wear frocks one is not accustomed to.'

She might have been talking about the night of the opera, but Louis could not mention it now. To do so would be a great peril for then he might divulge how he'd wanted to slip her garments off her—if only they *were* free to touch. He'd have begun with the gloves, finger by finger. He'd have untied the sash at her waist, spinning her around to find any bits that needed undoing at the back. Pressing her into his body as he did so. He imagined how the red silk would pool at her feet and he'd gallantly offer a hand for her to step out of it. Then, he'd turn his attention to the undergarments she had on beneath. A corset or stockings. Both. There would be nothing left when he was done. Except perhaps the pearls. He'd leave those. And he'd have said to Mervat, 'I dare you not to rip them off as I seduce you.'

Louis had written the script for it in his imagination, played it out in the nights since the opera again and again. He cleared his throat now and hoped she would think any red in his face was related to the hotness of the day.

'Hurry up, cousin,' Mervat called back in reprimand.

Somehow, they'd overtaken Hussam and Nadine and were walking along a wider pebbled road towards the commissioned *hantoor* with a colourful canvas umbrella. It was gaudily bedecked, but what it contained in loud decoration was contrasted with the quietest of drivers.

Hussam and Nadine took the more shaded back seat, while Louis and Mervat sat facing them. And though their snuggling was uncomfortable to have to witness, the more they got into the city, the more there was to distract them from it.

Mervat described the things they were seeing. He'd taken the same route with Hussam before, but seeing Cairo through her commentary was something else entirely.

'Salahuddin Citadel.' She pointed up to the high hills over the core of the city. 'It formally ceased to be the seat of the government this year, but it's been on the decline as such for years. It is where my parents used to live before…before Baba and I left.'

He thought of Mervat, what a sweet little girl she would have been eagerly going to visit her mother and aunt there. How sad her disappointment would have been.

'I recall,' he said quietly.

She nodded quickly before continuing. 'My father talks of the days when he would climb to watch his grandfather work. He hated it, said there was nothing green at the top, too much brick. I believe the architecture is the most "functional medieval" you can experience in Egypt. The aqueduct system is phenomenal. During the time of sieges, it wouldn't be useful, but it climbs up hexagonal towers that pull water from the Nile. Watching it rise from Joseph's Well is incredible. It was named by the commander Salahuddin after one of his eunuchs who had the smart idea to dig it and did the very dangerous excavation that the work entailed.'

'It sounds amazing.'

'Also inside the complex is what is called the Alabaster Mosque designed by a Turkish architect. Anne talks of how she only liked to pray inside it.' She nudged Hussam's foot with her own. 'I think the complex would make a great museum. You should tell your father so that all of Egypt might benefit from it.'

'Perhaps we should tour it,' Louis added.

Hussam shook his head. 'Too many of my father's men still patrol it. And we've already been to the old things, they're too religious for me.'

'The Azhar, cousin?' Mervat reprimanded, with a wave to Nadine, 'Watch out, your *illit adab* is on display too much today.'

His lack of manners.

Hussam laughed, 'There is an infidel in me who wants to let loose, Mervat! I want *shaa'bi* things to do, for my English friend too.'

'Shaa'bi?' Nadine recognised the one word in Arabic from her paramour's mouth and he tapped her hand placatingly before adding more, *'Raqs balady, Khan el-Khalili,* sheesha and *chai*. The poor man's authentic Egyptian experience.'

Mervat turned to Arabic for Nadine's benefit but made it easy enough that Louis could follow. 'Then you didn't need us women. We have no interest in smoking sheesha or watching *raqs balady*, which, for the viscount's benefit, means belly dancing.'

Hussam pointed to a band of drummers they were passing. It was a street corner and, seemingly an impromptu demonstration. People gathered to watch, a few hung from their balconies as the beat began. A woman moved to the centre, lifting her arms and shaking her hips to the music. People clapped, encouraging her and some started singing at the top of their voices until it was so loud it seemed the whole street had joined in.

The refrain, Louis understood: *Il yawm il hilw da*. What a good day this is!

'You see,' Hussam said, waving to the crowd as if he knew them, 'even the locals are welcoming us.'

Mervat chuckled as he and Nadine swayed to the beat.

Louis tried to relax and forget what was at stake, but he had a hard time of it. He knew that unless a miracle happened, the four of them would never be like this again. It was more likely to only ever be Hussam and Mervat travelling together. Officially. Like they had the night of the opera.

Married, no matter if she refused it or not.

And that bothered the hell out of Louis.

A herd of sheep gathered at the market gates. Horned and with darker coats, they butted heads over the scant fodder in the containers set out for them. These weren't the same docile lambs grazing on the grassy hills of the English countryside—these were city sheep with attitudes to match. And, as they descended from the carriage, one came right up to Mervat and baaed so loudly that Hussam jumped. Louis offered Mervat his arm, but she joked, 'Maybe my cousin needs the protection.'

'Some of us didn't grow up on farms,' Hussam teased back. He tucked Nadine's arm in his and urged Louis to do the same with Mervat. 'You have to pretend she's your wife, my friend. None of that British decorum nonsense. Egyptian men are not afraid to touch their women.'

Hussam was irking him to no end today, but his desire to hold Mervat close *did* press upon Louis. He angled his arm towards her, 'May I? If you would care to...'

She hesitated only briefly before folding her arm into his. Louis was awed by how the whole of his body felt at ease. On fire, yes, but at ease too.

Many were linked in pairs—mothers and daughters, brothers and sisters, friends too, he guessed. It was necessary in order to navigate the tight corners, and the mass of people. Better too if one wanted to not lose who they were with or protect them if threatened in any way.

'The Alfishawy café will be our final stop, meet us there in an hour,' Hussam yelled in Arabic right before he and Nadine drifted away. Louis had no idea where they went, but it was a relief to be alone with Mervat. Well, alone, amidst hundreds of people.

'Speak to me in Arabic,' he said, in the little he'd learned. 'I would like to practice.'

She smiled. 'You already sound impressive, even without formal lessons.'

'My grandfather encouraged a love of languages, knew a little of Dari and Pashto from his time in Afghanistan. He used to say the more people we can communicate with, the better the world would be.'

'He was a wealth of wisdoms. *Allah yerhamoo.*' When Mervat prayed for mercy on his grandfather's soul, warmth spread through his own. It was growing increasingly difficult to not think of her with all manners of affection.

They moved as one body, in step, fitting too well. Mervat happily showed him everything. She pointed to the rainbow melody of colourfully painted *fanoos* lamps and talked of how children use them in Ramadan to collect money gifts or candies. She rubbed the material of cotton shirts between two fingers, demonstrating how the fabric milled at private farms in the Nile Delta were superior.

'Malden Trading Company brings them to England,' Mervat mentioned. 'Probably more expensive, but undergarments made with this cotton would last a lifetime.'

Louis did not allow his mind to wander on the subject of undergarments.

But soon enough, Mervat had wandered from him. She'd

followed the sound of a crying child to find a boy. She crouched to talk to him and found out he'd lost his mother. Louis lifted him to his shoulders and the boy squealed, nearly forgetting his predicament. 'Tell him to look for her now,' Louis instructed Mervat. And soon enough, from that height, he'd pointed the woman out.

She wasn't very far at all, and her son couldn't have been lost to for long because his mother looked surprised to see he'd been crying. But when he lowered him from his shoulders and Mervat looked at him approvingly, Louis felt the hero. He could get used to doing good deeds, even such small ones, if that look of hers was his reward.

At the date seller's stand, Mervat sampled a few, taking bites and then giving him the rest or holding out the first bite for him and then taking for herself what he left behind. It was a very intimate thing, him putting his lips on something that had been in her mouth or vice versa, but Mervat didn't seem to notice that intimacy. It was natural. She whispered to Louis in English while explaining their geographical origins. Unripe red dates were from the Red Sea, plump golden ones from palms on their western borders, small dried ones from villages near Luxor.

From her facial expression, Louis knew which ones she liked best, and he pulled out some money from the large pockets of his *galabaya*, which she took in order to haggle on his behalf. The seller, smelling that Louis wasn't Egyptian—'For they can absolutely smell it,' Mervat explained— sought to charge him a higher fee.

When she gave the seller the amount she thought fair, the young man winked at Mervat forwardly, flirtatiously. *'Ashanik, ya helwa.'*

Louis deciphered the comment, 'For you, because you are beautiful.'

Mervat must have realised his ire because when the seller turned to package the dates, she reassured him, 'They're like that with everyone. It's how they sell their wares.'

He was sure it wasn't everyone, she *was* a beautiful woman. When the man handed her the dates, it was Louis who took them.

Mervat was on his arm. Not the date seller's and not Hussam's.

It would not last longer than an hour, but right now, Mervat was *his* beautiful woman.

Chapter Eighteen

Mervat

The viscount was jealous of the attention other men were paying her!

No one had ever been jealous over Mervat in that protective way men sometimes might have. Jealousy was not in her own *baba's* nature, but her mother talked of hers and how, before he died, he was extremely vigilant over ensuring his wife and daughters were treated with the utmost respect. Anne said he once yelled at a boy who'd whistled in her presence and challenged a man to a swordfight who'd 'bumped' into his wife in an empty street.

Mervat wondered if it was only because Louis had donned traditional clothing that he acted more like an Egyptian husband might. Her mother's warning that he might use her and bribe them to get the post he wanted jumped into her mind then. It conflicted with her own attraction to Louis and what she knew of the gallant gentleman he was, but it was hard for Mervat to believe he could have deep feelings for her. That he could truly love her as a husband might his wife.

The night of *Aida* had been an experience that would always be engraved in her heart. At the same time, what if she couldn't trust the hope it engendered in her because of the emotions that the music had stirred? The fact of the matter was that whatever had happened between her and Louis over the summer—including one very passionate kiss—had been exactly that: between them. He hadn't told Hussam, his supposed good friend, of his feelings.

And though she had not explicitly done so either, both Anne and Baba could guess that she cared about Louis in a deep way. Maybe even loved him. It was why her father welcomed Louis into their home and why her mother was afraid he would risk her plans for Mervat.

They rounded a corner to run into a trio of Europeans perusing a newspaper stand with dailies from around the world in any number of languages. None spoke English or French that Mervat could understand but as they left, two words jumped out at her: *Cleopatra Cerulean.*

Louis had heard it, as well, 'That sounded like Portuguese. How would they know it?'

Behind the stand, a thin boy chugged from a clay olla that looked double his weight.

Mervat spoke to him in Arabic, 'Are there English newspapers left?'

'None. Big news today.' He wiped the dribble of water from the side of his mouth, then let his sarcasm drip. 'An Englishman found a crown in the khedive's palace. An artifact lying around. Are the servants there so stupid they steal the cheap silver instead of the real treasures?'

She turned to Louis. 'Could it be your essay on my mother's crown?'

'That would have been quick.' Louis twisted his head to where the trio of men had been. 'If they read it in Portuguese, that means the *Telegraph* sent it to affiliates across the Continent.'

She was proud of him, immensely so. 'How exciting!'

'"Exciting" would be my sentiment too.' Louis's tone was measured. He looked younger than his years, sad even. She had an impulsive urge to hug him close, reassure him like the lost boy they'd met earlier.

'What's wrong?'

His eyes searched hers. 'Though I have often tried to seize opportunities per my grandfather's encouragement, they have not always borne fruit.'

'Not always?' Mervat teased.

He opened his mouth to say something, then thought better of it. To distract him from whatever he was fretting over, she pointed to the bag of dates. 'Were you going to offer me one of those?'

He opened the bag and held one out, waiting for her to take it.

Mervat bent her neck to pluck it between her teeth. Slowly, she looked up at him in that position and saw he did not look...displeased, though taken aback at her flirting.

'You are sure you're not the Naddaha, a siren bewitching me? And in public no less!'

She let go of the date and rose. 'Look around, no one pays us any attention. Cairo is not the harem at Sesostris!'

He did look around, then took her hand to lead her to a gap behind a nearby stall. 'I am starting to see that, but we British, we aren't so cavalier about displays of public affection.'

Was he trying to say that he felt affection for her or wondering if she felt it for him? They stared at each other for a long moment that stretched. Finally, she took the date still in his hand. She ate the whole thing while he watched—and despite the hunger she perceived in his gaze.

'The man who sold these,' Louis said, his voice strained. 'Did you find him...handsome?'

'I did not notice him.'

'Because he is only a date seller?'

'Because he is not you.' Her honesty surprised even herself. She wanted to read his reaction, but he looked down, stared at her hands. Then, he took them in both, the bag of dates acting like some strange curtain. Not heavy enough that it blocked the sparks being ignited in her stomach because of his touch.

'You know why I have done what I have done since coming to Egypt,' he started. 'The plan of Hussam's, the articles, researching the crown, it has been to make something of myself for my family, my siblings. Allenborough.'

'I know.'

His lips hovered over her forehead, his breath so hot there, she wasn't sure if he pressed them to her skin, but the sensation was nearly the same. 'But somewhere in it all,' he continued, 'my priorities have been obscured. You have proven quite the distraction.'

Mervat was unsure of what he was saying. Doubts creeped into her mind, the insecurities she had and the warnings her mother had placed there rearing like wet worms on dry soil. 'Oh?'

'Yes, *oh*.'

'You like me.'

'Very much.'

'You haven't told Hussam, though. Why?'

'Have you told Nadine how you feel about me?'

The image of him dancing with her came to her mind and she fought a wave of jealousy.

'We do not have a history like you and my cousin. We barely talked until the day of your luncheon.'

He dropped her hands to cup her cheek with one of his own. 'Hussam is a close friend, but in this I fear he will disappoint me. God, Mervat, you have to know how much I care for you, worry for you. The khedive, your mother. If you are hurt in any way because of my feelings for you, it would destroy me. You have been nothing but gracious in ensuring I will not suffer due to his plan.'

She mostly only heard one part of his speech. 'Your feelings for me?'

He repeated, affirming, 'My feelings for you.'

'Which are?' She stepped closer until her waist was pressed into his. His arm came around it and he dropped the bag of dates. His breath was still hot at her brow and she wanted to lift her face up to him, but he was kissing her there and she didn't want to risk it ending so she pressed her palms on his chest, instead, felt the pace of his heart quicken beneath them.

He started, 'Which are—'

But he didn't finish. They were interrupted by the sudden appearance of Hussam.

'What's going on here?' he demanded, distancing himself from Nadine to insert himself between Louis and Mervat.

She stepped back. 'Hussam, this is none of your concern.'

But he didn't seem to hear her, his ire directed at Louis. 'I trust you with my cousin and you drag her to a dark corner to do what, exactly?'

A line appeared in Louis's brow. 'Am I merely a "fake" chum, pretending to be in love with whomever and whenever *you* need me to?'

'I did not imagine you'd take advantage of Mervat who is supposed to be *my* fiancée,' Hussam said with a huff.

'Louis did not take advantage of me,' Mervat insisted.

Hussam turned on her, his face a jumble of accusation and disappointment. 'You have no excuse for this! Are you that lonely as to not know pretence from reality?'

She understood why Hussam was upset, but she was hurt

by his words. And then Louis was pulling him back. 'Hussam,' he warned. 'You go too far.'

Not understanding the English, and perhaps fearing for her lover, Nadine yelled and drew a crowd. She'd exposed them all but at least it had the effect of calming Hussam.

He smiled pliantly at those gathered and reassured them in Arabic, *'Monaqsha beeny wa ben sahbee. Kulu tamam.'*

It is only a disagreement between me and my friend. All is well.

Mervat was relieved Hussam hadn't forgotten that he and Louis were friends. She saw Louis's shoulders ease as well. She would hate it if they their bond was broken because of her.

When it was only them again, Hussam was chastised. 'I am sorry.'

Louis crossed his arms. 'You disrespected your cousin.'

Hussam swallowed and faced her. 'Forgive me, Mervat. For what happened now and this whole fiasco of a plan. I should have respected your position, known better than to draw you into a plan to irk your mother, my father. Never thinking about how you would be affected. Louis is a handsome, charming man, it would be natural if you...but I know he is honourable and would never intentionally hurt anyone. I blame myself.'

Her cousin's apology was sincere, but it did not acknowledge the reality of what was.

And what was, was that Louis had feelings for her. And she for him.

Yet, when she met Louis's gaze, she knew he was not going to correct Hussam. Knew that he was not going to name those feelings.

She would be lying if she said it did not trouble her. If Mervat was going to stand up to her mother and the khedive and fight for them, shouldn't Louis be willing to tell Hussam the truth?

With the tip of her shoe, Mervat herded the bag of dates that had been stomped upon to the wall's edge. *Maybe a needy creature would find them.*

She lifted her chin. 'We should get back to Sesostris.'

Chapter Nineteen

⸙

Louis

Their return to the palace was swift, as if they were racing to outrun a dark rain cloud. None of them spoke the whole way, Hussam took it upon himself to sit beside Louis in the carriage and to walk with him through the gardens. He had suddenly become a proper chaperone and though Louis would have been peeved, he could also see that Hussam was regretful.

And that, Louis could begrudgingly admit, Hussam was right to be protective of Mervat.

When they reached the point in the gardens where the ladies would take a different path from theirs, they stopped to say their goodbyes. Hussam barely nodded at Nadine but caught Mervat's hand and squeezed it.

'*Samihini bint ami.*' Forgive me, daughter of my uncle.

'*Misamih.*' You are forgiven.

Of course, Mervat was not one to hold a grudge, but he almost wished she would. She acknowledged Louis with a modest incline of the head as she passed. 'Viscount.'

'Princess.'

And that was it.

He'd have said more or asked to speak with her later. But Louis knew he had to sort things out with Hussam first.

'I want to show you something.' Hussam sounded unchar-acteristically thoughtful. Louis nodded, agreeing to follow.

They went to the back of the palace, round the area that passed the kitchens. The sound of the staff shouting com-mands in Arabic and Turkish mingled with the pungency of smoking meat and garlic. The two of them dodged a few servants angling pails of water from a well, then slipped into the palace via a nearly hidden door.

As soon as they entered, the sounds of women came to them. Dangerously close.

'We're in the harem,' Hussam whispered.

'Do you want to get us flogged?' Louis amended, 'Well me. You're a prince who will probably face no reprimand.'

'Always, you are safe with me, my friend.'

There was sincerity in the words that prompted Louis's guilt. He could have told Hussam from the start about him and Mervat, but he hadn't. And today, the prince had had a shock seeing them together. Were their roles reversed, Louis would have felt the same.

They moved towards an inner balcony that looked over a small quiet area. It was empty, except for Mervat. She was praying.

'She'll see us,' Louis said. It didn't feel right watching her, intruding on a private moment between her and God, but he felt a pang of tenderness. Knew she was sobbing in her pros-tration. 'We need to go.'

'You care for her,' Hussam said when they were outside the palace again. 'I missed the signs but only because I wasn't looking, caught up in this plan of mine. Before you arrived, I was content to marry Mervat. Do you know why?'

Louis gritted his teeth. 'No.'

'Because that mosque is meant to be used by everyone in the palace. We are technically in the harem on the upper level, the lower one is an in-between space. Nadine told me to meet her there, that no one ever uses it, and she had a way to sneak in. When Mervat entered, we hid up to the place we were just in so as not to get caught. Nadine and I had been fooling around in the mosque and my cousin is the only person in this whole palace of nobles who believes that houses of Allah should be used for praying. Imagine that?' He scoffed. 'I felt guilty. Had to hide it from Nadine, of course, but I realised then that Mervat was the kind of good woman who would make me a better man.'

Louis's jealousy pricked because he felt the same about her. She made him question so many of the assumptions he'd long held—why wouldn't she have had a similar effect on Hussam? 'When I first arrived, I got the impression you wanted to marry her only because she would be gullible enough to let you have affairs.'

'Mervat is not gullible, but that is how men talk is it not?'

'They should talk fondly of women they love, wives they will spend their lives with.'

'You yourself used to talk of arranged marriages being superior to love matches,' Hussam accused.

Louis countered, 'Mervat has changed my opinion.'

Hussam nodded, but he noticed how he'd grimaced when Louis had called his cousin by her name in an intimate manner. Without her title. 'I should have seen how she is with you. Happy, confident. Willing to share her knowledge without fear of being reprimanded for talking too much. Yet, I fear for her once you are gone. And you must, one day, be gone, my friend.'

Now it was Louis's turn to grimace with what he knew in the bottom of his heart to be true. Still, he resisted, 'What do you fear for her when I am gone?'

Hussam sighed. 'Mervat hates the court, only stays because she wants to please her mother, would do anything for that connection because she has missed it all her life. She will not go against Gulnur Hanem, it would break her heart to. I knew it from the moment I saw her praying there. And why I wanted you to know that the main reason why I did this plan was to help her, a last-chance attempt for my cousin's happiness because she is a good woman and deserves the best.'

'You sound like you would have her marry you and talk her into believing it would be for her own good!' Louis knew he should be calmer, but frustration was getting the better of him.

Watching Mervat, her sadness, her loneliness in the mosque had hurt *his* heart and he suspected that was precisely Hussam's intention in taking him there.

Hussam took a deep breath, released it slowly. 'What I am saying is that I will do whatever she wants in order to make her happy. But what if Mervat decides she wants you? The two of you defy my father and her mother. She could be stripped of her status and be no credit to you, to your estate. If both of you could get past that and get married for love, you'd have to take her to Allenborough. To live with your family, a penniless burden. When you become the earl and she your wife, she will live with you and do her duty and would not mind the lack of monies, no doubt, but I promise you that the girl praying down there, that girl crying because she has such a sensitive, spiritual soul? *She* would not be content with defying her mother for long. Mervat might travel to Europe, longs to see Turkey, but in the end, she is her father's daughter. The earth beneath her speaks Arabic. Did you know she hopes to fund a museum? That she put in a commission with my father as soon as she came to court for one? Her comment earlier today about the old palace? It tells me she has not given up on it and I dare say it would be her life's work.

Make no mistake, my friend—Mervat Abbas is not only a royal, but as Egyptian and as Muslim as they come.'

The truth of it all was too much for Louis. 'And I am none of those things.'

Hussam agreed, 'You are not.'

Hussam watched as Louis paced for a few moments and then asked, 'What do you want to do? Tell me and I will support it. Support you.'

Before he could respond, they were intruded upon by Faisal.

'Prince Hussam,' the servant said with a huff, slightly out of breath. 'The khedive and the British consul have had us looking everywhere for the viscount. His presence is urgently requested.'

Louis was not eager for such a meeting.

'Permit us a change of wardrobe,' Hussam said, speaking up.

'And a quick bath?' Louis added.

'My prince, with respect, it is not you requested, only the viscount. And I fear if there is further delay, a man or two might lose their positions.'

Louis sighed. 'Very well.'

'Good luck,' Hussam said, trying to sound reassuring.

Faisal practically dragged Louis through the palace and mumbled that the khedive hated having to spend any extra time with the British consul. He pushed the office door open and with a soldier-style salute, he announced, 'Lord Wesley, Viscount of Allenborough.'

'Your Highness.' Louis bowed with trepidation. He could not read the look on the khedive's face and while the British consul seemed pleased, that was suspect since Louis assumed that the man did not like him at all. 'Sir Stuart. A pleasure it is to see you both.'

The khedive took in his *galabaya*, the scuffed slippers. 'My son bamboozled you into another one of his adventures?'

'I shall not trouble you with the details.'

The khedive wrinkled his nose. 'I should hope you would know better by now.'

Sir Stuart chirped, 'You can trust an Englishman to know better, sir.' As he strode closer, he waved a copy of the *Telegraph*.

His article about the Cleopatra Cerulean! Louis had forgotten all about it given what had transpired in the bazaar with Hussam and Mervat.

'If there was any doubt, look at how this has taken the world by storm, reviving Egyptomania in a way unseen in decades. Not just in Europe, either. I am told that print runs are expanding the world over—China, India, the Americas. Our office just fielded an enquiry from the *New York Times*! We could not have predicted the response towards an ancient crown.' Sir Stuart patted Louis's back. 'Certainly, we owe it to this young man's way with words. I'm proud to say I noticed his talents that very first day at the luncheon.'

Louis nearly choked at the man's hypocrisy, but he couldn't help but wish his grandfather were alive. He would have been elated.

The khedive countered, 'Yet it was my son who told me to put him in contact with an editor at the *Telegraph*.'

Louis graciously said, 'I am most grateful to you and Prince Hussam. As I told you the last time we spoke, Your Highness, the opportunity to write on Egypt's marvels, the railway, the opera, this very palace, has been my honour. But I am glad that the Cleopatra Cerulean exploration was the article to make its mark since Princess Mervat helped with the research.'

'I had forgotten Mervat's part in it,' the khedive said, his shrewd gaze examining Louis closely. 'You kept her name out of it.'

Louis had not meant to draw the khedive's attention to her. Only to give her the credit. 'At her request, Your Highness. She is a humble young lady.'

He rummaged his brain for a change of subject, turning to Sir Stuart in hopes of inspiration, but the khedive would not let it go, 'Did Mervat have something to say about the "marriage" angle?'

'Pardon me, Your... Highness?'

The khedive rounded his desk, waved one of the *Telegraph* copies. 'It seems to me that the purpose of this essay is different than the others published.'

'Oh?'

'In those you were only "reporting", in this you are making a central argument. Perhaps that is why it is garnering traction, people's attentions. This piece has meaning attached to it.'

Louis tried to contain his trepidation. He did not want to do or say anything to get Mervat in trouble with the khedive, but he felt caged under the man's scrutiny. When Louis looked at Sir Stuart for help, he found the consul lingering in the shadows, waiting for this—whatever 'this' was—to resolve itself before he would say anything further.

Louis asked, 'And what meaning or argument do you suppose that is, sir?'

The khedive looked peeved to have to answer but said, 'That women should be allowed to marry whom they wish. That people should not be forced into marriages based on station or arrangements.'

If words coupled with stares were daggers, Louis had no doubt he would be dead then. What did the khedive hope to ascertain with this assessment? And how might it harm Mervat?

It was that fear for her that had him grasping for anything at all that would shift the khedive's attention. *Nadine.*

'Perhaps I did have marriage in mind, as you well know, Your Highness. For it was you yourself who recently and very generously afforded me the opportunity to woo a certain young lady in the ballroom?'

The khedive's smirk was a relief. 'Ah, yes, your dance partner. Madame Lamoureux mentioned you were most accommodating, but the ladies require more practice. Alas, there is not much time left before the Midsummer Festival.'

'Then I will have to sort matters on that occassion.'

'And the father of the lady in question has accepted our invitation. I may help your suit with him to secure a beautiful and rich wife.' The khedive turned to the consul. 'Do you not agree, Sir Stuart? We must stress to the young viscount here that modern love marriages needn't dismiss duty or financial arrangements that would be of benefit too.'

Feeling himself safe again, Sir Stuart stepped forward. 'I agree wholeheartedly. And speaking of duty, the by-line will do his family proud, as well. Further to this goal, I am come to formally offer Viscount Louis Wesley of Allenborough a diplomatic position in the British Embassy.'

Louis experienced a rush of emotions and had to sit down. This was the opportunity he'd wanted most when he'd arrived! Matters had changed with Mervat's presence in his life and his coming to care for her so desperately. But she was still a princess, part of the family of a very menacing khedive. The only way Louis had been able to defy him just then was to use Nadine like a bone tossed to a predator in order to divert their sniffling elsewhere.

The popularity of Louis's article, an appointment in the embassy, would not change anything for Mervat. And even if she was able to free herself amicably from the khedive and her mother, that would not change things between their stations. They were too different and he would eventually have to return home to claim his title, a world that would not make her happy. Would it not torture him to carry out his appointment knowing all that? To be in the same city as Mervat, having the realisation that she was near yet could never be his?

When Louis did not make any answer, Sir Stuart spoke. 'It will be most lucrative. A post in service of Her Majesty, Queen Victoria, is the largest boon, no doubt, and although it might be crass of me to say but even the most endowed of titles would not sneeze at the salary that comes with it. Allenborough would benefit enough to, dare I counter the khedive, *not* need a rich wife.'

The British consul wanted him to agree, but Louis himself felt conflicted. This was what he'd wanted since his arrival in Egypt, but now he wasn't so sure.

'No one counters me,' the khedive warned with a menacing smirk. 'But I will allow you to claim him *if* he still writes his dispatches.'

They continued discussing him as if Louis had left the room.

'He could demand more money of those now too. Embassy lawyers would be happy to negotiate on his behalf.'

The khedive added, 'A tour of the Suez Canal is in order, perhaps.'

'Certainly,' Sir Stuart agreed, 'especially since British investors will now understand that Egypt's centrality necessitates a robust streamlined, global network.'

The khedive nodded, 'I will think on how to incorporate the Cerulean Crown discovery at the Midsummer Festival, but since it is a wholly English occasion, perhaps the viscount has some ideas for the festivities.'

Sir Stuart said, 'It is quite the jolly time throughout our

countryside! Allenborough likely has its own traditions Louis would be keen to share.'

He'd not got a word in edgewise, nor agreed to the post and the fortune and honours that came with it, but Louis had never been so wholly rewarded in his life. Work that he had done had led to this moment. Coming to Egypt, his ambition to ask the consul for the job at first, participating in Hussam's ill plan but continuing to publish his articles, despite it going off the rails. Louis's persistence in writing about the crown in a way that did not expose Mervat's private family history had resulted in a piece with a universal sentiment.

Louis had seized an opportunity that had, at last, come to a realised fruition.

So why was he hesitating?

Here, in Egypt, was a chance to make things right for his family and be near to the woman he cared for. Not care for. Loved.

He loved Mervat.

He would have told her as much if Hussam hadn't interrupted them at the bazaar. He had planned to say she was a distraction he'd not anticipated because he hated that he wanted to prove himself worthy of her love. Her respect. Her hand.

That he would do anything to make her his, but that he feared he would never succeed. He had seized an opportunity to speak to her at the Louvre, he had fallen in love with her. He dared to believe that she too held similar sentiments for him. But nevertheless, theirs was a love that could not result in a marriage.

Yet…what if she were willing to consider a life with him? Maybe he could speak to her about England? Ask if she could see herself coming home with him, eventually? Becoming his viscountess? Maybe this was his chance to be accomplished enough so that it wouldn't be just *talk* of love. That a life with Mervat could be his reality. That he would earn enough, *be* enough to make her his.

The consul thrust his hand forward, forcing him to attention.

'It is not the palace, but the furnished lodgings included with this position come with the most modern of amenities *and* a magnificent view of the pyramids. You'll have embassy transport so you may come to Sesostris anytime you wish. Your family can visit too.'

Louis missed his siblings, he imagined taking them to the bazaar and buying each one those colourful *fanoos* lamps. He had been ready to head back to England, return to Allenborough and aspire to a well-appointed arranged marriage. If he worked in Egypt for a few years, he'd earn enough to help his father and the estate, afford his brothers' education and dowries for his sisters.

He did not have a choice, really. Louis had a duty to them and Mervat would want him to fulfil it.

'I am most honoured to accept the position, Sir Stuart. And I look forward to working with His Highness, the khedive, to strengthen the bonds between our two nations.'

When he shook their hands in turn, Louis could've sworn he heard his grandfather's joyous laugh from the heavens.

Chapter Twenty

Mervat

Since she'd come to court, Mervat could not remember her mother in a better mood. Anne had invited her to join the hammam for the first time, paraded her around the pool like a prized trophy. Embracing her, kissing her cheeks. Even asking her to talk and telling people to listen carefully when she did because there was much knowledge to be gained from her speeches.

If she had not been so out of sorts because of Louis's absence, Mervat would have enjoyed the connection she had been craving with her mother for so long, but it had been a full week since the incident at Khan el-Khalili and though there had been much talk around the Cleopatra Cerulean, there was not a word about the man who'd written the story.

Mervat had finally sent a note to her cousin, enquiring, when Nadine proved no help. Nadine herself was put out because Hussam had not contacted her either.

Hussam's response to Mervat had been brief and somewhat cryptic.

The viscount is well. He ponders returning to England but has, for the time being, taken a post at the British Embassy.

She was happy to hear about his post, and hoped it was the one he sought, but could she be sure it was? And what did 'the time being' mean? Was he supposed to be return to England? Surely, Louis would have come to bid her farewell or sent a note at least? Maybe he was upset or embarrassed not to have told Hussam about his feelings for her. In fact, she realised, they had been interrupted at the bazaar before he shared them with her, as well.

Tonight was the Midsummer Ball and the invited guests numbered in the hundreds. If Louis didn't come then Mervat might have to assume he was no longer in the country.

The palace was a beehive of activity for the largest party Sesostris had ever witnessed. It was the first public occasion for its ballroom, an exquisite space with a glass-windowed wall that overlooked the palace gardens. For the evening, it had been decorated to look like the gardens had spilled into it. Greenery and twigs decorated the tables and chairs that had been made to look like tree stumps and arranged like a hedged fence for the dancing and merriment to be contained within. Tables were being piled with all manner of fruits and dainty delicacies. Hundreds of lanterns had been hung from the ceiling and a makeshift stage had been set up as an extension outside. Mervat had heard a production of William Shakespeare's *A Midsummer Night's Dream* was going to be performed by a troupe of young Egyptian actors.

'You would think they are building pyramids for the occasion,' Anne announced to the women of the harem. 'It will be an evening to remember for ever!'

The Turkish hammam, a nod to the ways of the past, was clearly her mother's domain. While some soaked in the perfumed bath, others took their turns getting ready, having their hair combed in braids or ironed straight, their eyes kohled and their cheeks rouged. When Anne and Mervat's turn came to get out of the water, they sat together at the beautifying station, her mother never letting go of her hand the whole while they were being primped.

'I insisted that the khedive send an invitation to Abbas,' Anne said. 'But even if he decides not to come, we will see your father soon. Tell him what it was like this night.'

'*Tamam*, Anne.' Mervat's chest expanded with joy. 'I would love that.'

Her mother demanded from the girl who attended them, 'Make my daughter glisten. She is *the* fairy princess tonight.'

The women of the harem were not given a gown requirement, but all were provided garlands to wear in their hair, fresh flower tiaras, like every other woman guest would be given upon palace entry. The men guests would be offered corsages for their suit lapels.

Anne chose matching fuchsia rose ones for them, and though they were nice, it was the gown she'd asked her to wear that took Mervat's breath away.

They stood far from the others, behind a dressing screen when her mother slipped it over her head.

'Saved for you all these years,' she said. 'My father had it embroidered by a woman famous for her *zardozi* work for Indian royals. I wore it on my *kina geseci* but was afraid it would get henna on it.'

It was a simple cut, almost kaftan-like, but that was where the plainness of the gown ended. Its rich ivory silk was as smooth as butter on Mervat's skin, the sleeves were a shimmering chiffon, nearly opaque. The same material acted as an overlay for the dress's body and held its gorgeous paisley-designed embroidery, threaded with turquoise beads and studded with cyan sequins. At the waist were bejewelled blocks of gold, neither gaudy nor subtle, but right enough to seem like a belt on its own even though it too was part of the exquisite design.

And although the gown looked like it would be heavy, it was nearly weightless. With minimal undergarments—there was no space for them, the fit was snug—it rested like air on Mervat's frame. Because it had long sleeves and a collar that rose to her neck, it did not require either pearls or gloves like the Parisian gown she'd worn the night of the opera.

As much as this gown was beautiful, it was modest, as well. Mervat stood taller in it because she felt comfortable. And because it had been her mother's, it had a history. It was truly perfect for her.

'Amar,' Anne exclaimed. It was the Arabic word for *moon* and Egyptians liked to use it as a compliment, a symbol of beauty.

She kissed her mother's cheek before adjusting the garland in her own hair, 'I am only afraid this one does not match.'

'You may not be wearing it for long.'

Before Mervat could ask what she meant by that, the women were called to greet the palace guests.

The festivities had begun.

Mervat lost Anne in the crowd gathering in the foyer to enter the ballroom, but she was glad for it when she spotted Louis.

What a handsome vision he was himself! In his silver suit, lighter than the droll outfits of most of the other men in attendance, Louis stood apart—like summer in the candlelight; he had come with an understanding of the party's theme.

Mervat knew she had missed him, but actually seeing him underscored how desperately. She had to stop herself from running to him and knocking down any in her path.

The viscount had entered with the British consul and his wife. And because most of the other foreigners had also come with women on their arms, she feared Louis might have brought someone, as well. But when he stopped at the table of corsages and allowed a servant to fasten his chosen one, she breathed a sigh of relief. And the closer she got, the more she realised that it was the perfect shade of fuchsia.

'We couldn't have matched better if we tried,' she whispered when she'd got close enough that only he could hear her.

Louis's face broke into the warmest grin when he turned to face her and she could have kissed him right there, in front of everyone. 'Princess Mervat.'

'Viscount Wesley,' she curtsied dramatically. Her stomach throbbed. She wanted to tell Louis so much—about how she and her mother were in a good place and how his article was to thank for that. She wanted to tell him that she had fretted over the incident with Hussam. She wanted to tell him that she worried she'd never see him again and what a miserable life she feared she'd have without him in it.

Instead, she pointed to his chest, the flower there. Then turned her finger on her own crown. 'I mean, the colour matches.'

His eyes followed her finger and then locked on her. 'It does.'

When someone accidently nudged them on his way to the table, Louis gestured that she should join him behind the grand pendulum clock where it was somewhat quieter. 'Every time I see you, I think, "She cannot be more beautiful", and each subsequent time, I am made the fool. You are stunning, my lady.'

She closed her eyes, inhaled *him* for a quick beat and then wanted to scream because she knew they were not alone. 'You have taken up a post in the embassy?'

His brow furrowed a tad. 'Is that what Hussam told you?'

She nodded. 'He also mentioned you were thinking of heading back to England?'

'Did he? He and I haven't had a chance to talk, since...'
Louis took a weary look around before focusing on her again.
'I was sent to the Suez Canal, focusing on a piece for it.'

'Oh? Why not return to the palace then?'

'The embassy post comes with a residence. A lovely flat
with a view of the pyramids.'

Her heart leapt with the confirmation. So Louis would be
in Egypt, permanently then? 'Congratulations and bravo! It
is all you wanted.'

'It *was* all I wanted.'

Servants were ushering guests into the ballroom and
though she would have liked to take Louis's arm, walk together as they had in the bazaar, he did not exactly offer.

He must be aware, as she was, that this was a much larger
group than any before gathered at Sesostris and anyone could
be watching. Including her mother.

As soon as they passed the threshold of the ballroom, Hussam found them. He was with a stout fellow with pale skin
who looked like he could be Nadine's father.

Indeed, Nadine was close behind, in a dark dress that
seemed too dull for the occasion.

Mervat hadn't seen her in the hammam earlier and she
gave her a small hug in greeting now but Nadine barely responded to it, remaining limp in her embrace.

Hussam introduced Mervat and Louis to the man, who did
indeed turn out to be Nadine's father. He shook hands heartily with Louis and tried to use him to practice his not-so-
skilled English. She would have tried to help Louis's struggle
to decipher it, but Hussam turned to her.

'Mervat, you look lovely,' he spoke in Turkish which she
thought was rude both because of Nadine's presence and because it seemed like there still was tension between him and
Louis. Before she could reprimand him, he pulled her away

and apart from the others in their group. 'Might I speak with you? A quieter place for a few minutes?'

She didn't like the fretting in Hussam's face. 'What is it?'

'*Wa'Allahi.* I have tried multiple times to talk to my father about our dilemma, after what happened in the bazaar and since Louis has been gone. I know I have done wrong by both of you and I was ashamed, trying to make it right…but my father is not listening. Even now I tried to get a moment with him, but he only bid me introduce his friends to mine.'

Mervat knew what it was like to talk to a parent who refused to listen. Perhaps if she and Hussam faced their parents together, they could make their position clear.

'Is that why Nadine is upset too?' she asked.

'We broke it off this morning when she demanded I speak to her father, ask for her hand. My father would have never agreed to it and it was unfair of me to keep making her empty promises.'

He looked miserable for it, and Mervat put a comforting hand on his shoulder which he covered with his own. 'I am sorry to hear it, Hussam, I know you loved her.'

'Ladies and gentlemen, honoured guests, welcome to Sesostris for our first Midsummer Festival!' An announcement was made and everyone's focus was called to the front of the ballroom where the khedive had appeared.

But Hussam's father wasn't there with his wife.

He was with her mother.

Chapter Twenty-One

Louis

He finally felt like he might be triumphant. Louis Wesley, a viscount by birth circumstance but nearly a pauper by that same circumstance. He'd been forced to make his way through good society on a menial allowance from a home desperately in need of funds; every opportunity he'd tried to seize a failed one. Until now. Until Mervat. Until Hussam.

Maybe that was why it pained him to see them together.

Hussam had thrust Nadine and her father on him and pulled Mervat away. Then Louis had watched them in an intimate moment, and he felt wretched.

And now, as they took their seats, next to one another, he feared he was too late. That somehow, they'd found one another and agreed to the marriage their parents wanted for them.

His dear friend who, despite his faults, Louis loved.

And the girl he'd met at the Louvre who, because of her virtues, Louis loved.

His time away from the palace hadn't diminished that at all. If anything, Louis wanted more, hoped for more. Was willing to act on more. He had come here tonight hoping to have a heart-to-heart conversation with her about the future. Come to some sort of understanding. He had planned to ask her if she would be willing to one day settle with him at Allenborough. Be his viscountess?

Mervat had not yet said her heart belonged to him—at least, not in so many words. Yet she had sought him out as soon as he'd entered the room, the joy in her glorious face there for all to behold.

But as he watched her now, it seemed like she'd never been farther from him. To add insult to injury, while she and Hussam were sitting next to each other, Louis found his seat was between Nadine and her father.

Nadine's father was ostentatiously wealthy and he did not try to hide it behind any semblance of modesty. Everywhere he could put gold he did: his cufflinks, pocket watch, ring, buckles of shoes; there was even a gold chain around his neck competing with his silk cravat.

Perhaps it was Mervat's influence on Louis, but now he lived in the heart of Cairo and had seen for himself those who suffered from poverty in Egypt, it was difficult to reconcile the extravagances at court. Or with men like Nadine's father. Not that England did not have her share of poor people, but because he had been removed at Allenborough which wasn't rich either, he'd never experienced such disparity. He might not have even known to look for it were it not for Mervat's sensitivity, her impassioned speeches.

'Some believe that Midsummer Day—' the khedive began his speech in English, but wove in Arabic and Louis found he was better at not needing translations '—goes back to England and has its roots in pagan traditions in a time when men roamed the earth living at the mercy of the land. For them, this festival was about asking the skies and the land to be good to their crops.

'What many do not know is that it is also an ancient Egyptian tradition. When the summer solstice aligned with the rise of the River Nile, Ra, deity of the sun and purveyor of life, was honoured through the people's worship. And so this party is an honouring of our two traditions. England and Egypt. Tonight we celebrate the bond between our two countries forged in the Suez Canal investments and pray for our collective prosperity and more projects to come.'

There was a round of applause.

'It will be a night of merriment, feasting and dancing. There will also be fireworks and bonfires in the garden where the world's largest Victoria sponge cake awaits to be sliced. Additionally, we have an Egyptian troupe that will entertain you with scenes from Shakespeare's play, lest you find there is not enough to do!'

Another round of applause and cheering.

The khedive had become a master of ceremonies, but it was not a role he was familiar with for as he moved to resume his seat, someone whispered in his ear and he rose again.

'I am told we must begin with the dance known as the "quadrille." I ask those familiar with it to form lines in the centre for the traditional dance.'

It looked a mess Madame Lamoureux was trying desperately to arrange. Louis might have sat it out if Nadine's father hadn't pushed the two of them to join and if he hadn't caught the way Hussam had grabbed Mervat's hand and swept her off to the front of the line of women to stand opposite for the line of men.

Mervat was laughing when Louis dropped off Nadine and she smiled at him as he moved back to stand by Hussam.

'I want to hear all about your first week in your new post.' Hussam smiled. 'And there are other matters to talk of. Perhaps we can find a quiet moment later?'

Louis nodded, unable to get the picture of Mervat's hand on

Hussam's chest out of his mind. Louis could not help feeling angry despite the innocently affable look on his friend's face.

There were seven women in the line opposite and the men's side was short by one until Madame Lamoureux dragged her husband, the French ambassador, to it. He made a joke that she should know better than to call on him because if anyone knew of his two left feet, it was her.

When the fellow turned to the khedive to say, 'What we do for our women, *n'est-ce-pas*?' Louis noticed that it wasn't Hussam's mother at his side, but Gulnur Hanem.

What did that mean?

People were still laughing as the band struck up the music and the dance began, but the ambassador's comment proved to foreshadow chaos. No one seemed to be doing the quadrille correctly and those gathered were either being too silly or too serious. Madame Lamoureux faulted her husband and pushed him away as he laughed in response.

She ordered the band to stop the music, then rushed to the podium to say something to the khedive while the lines of dancers were once again unmatched and waiting for direction.

When the khedive rose, he was forgiving. 'I am told anything can happen on midsummer night so I would ask all the men to resume their seats save for the esteemed friend of ours, the essayist who now enjoys a new post in the British Embassy, Viscount Louis Wesley!'

Hussam gave him a shake of the shoulder before abandoning him as Louis bowed to the podium. The khedive addressed Louis, saying, 'Madame Lamoureux suggests you show everyone how it is done as you were such a help to her before.'

'The waltz,' the woman added, speaking to the band.

Louis could hardly refuse, but when he looked at the

line of ladies still standing there, still not dismissed, he responded, 'The waltz is with a single partner.'

With a knowing look and gesture towards Nadine, the khedive responded, 'You have my permission, Viscount, to choose the partner you wish from the line of young ladies.'

Louis did not meet Mervat's gaze. He struggled internally but how could he ever choose anyone except her? He knew he would be defying the khedive, and upsetting Hussam if he chose anyone besides Nadine as his father clearly wished him to.

But Mervat was right there. With her heart-shaped face reflecting the goodly beauty of her entire soul. And it was her soul that called to him.

How could he not want her to be his partner in all things?

He stepped forward, shifting until he stood before her. He bowed low, 'I choose the princess Mervat.'

He saw nothing after that, didn't care that they were being watched. Or who he'd infuriated.

'Do you know the dance?' he whispered.

She bowed before him, her face flushed. Whether it was because of everyone's attention or the anticipation of being in his arms, he wasn't sure but her smile said she wanted to dance with him.

'I watched you in Madame Lamoureux's session.'

Which meant that she knew exactly what she was doing because she was brilliant and the quickest of studies.

When the music began, so too did the magic. It was not like it had been in the sea that day he'd kissed Mervat for he did not forget they were not alone, but their dance was in tune, each step precisely done.

When he held her in his arms, she leaned into his embrace, their bodies fitting together as if they were made for each other. She surrendered her body to him, let him sweep her closer or pull her back, twist her arms between his or spinning her in the air. She danced without any reservations. Trusting him.

Mervat was a bird flitting amidst the clouds. A fairy-tale princess.

His.

But too soon the music ended and the dance was over.

They separated reluctantly and when the applause started, it surprised them both. He bowed graciously before her and Mervat tilted her head in the most becoming of nods.

He waited, savouring the moment, hoping for more. But the music had gone silent. Louis dared to look at the khedive but he could not tell if he were upset with him for not choosing Nadine as his partner.

The khedive only waved them back to their seats.

Mervat went to hers, to Hussam. And Louis went to his, next to a now-sulking father and a frowning Nadine. Surely she was not upset at him too? She could barely follow the basic steps during Madame Lamoureux's lesson and until recently, she had been in love with Hussam. What had changed?

The khedive called Mervat to join him on stage along with Gulnur Hanem.

Mervat threw Louis an apprehensive look before rising and taking her mother's hand as she rose up to the podium.

'Some of you would have read the recent publication on the Cleopatra Cerulean Crown by Lord Wesley. What you may not know is that the crown has been in Princess Mervat's family—from her mother's Turkish side—for decades and it was her motivation to learn more about it that was a major factor in his quest.'

While the khedive translated in Turkish, presumably for Gulnur Hanem's benefit, Louis watched Mervat who watched the procession coming in from behind her. A man carried a large canvas and another behind him carried a tray—both were covered with white sheets. The first man looked familiar and even before he'd uncovered the canvas, Louis remembered him.

He was the artist Louis had seen on his first night in Cairo. The one who Hussam had commissioned to paint Mervat's portrait.

As he uncovered it now, the lights shining on its mastery, on *her* extremely princess-like magnificence, Mervat gasped. Then, she clapped her hands over her mouth. This was obviously the first time she had seen it and her reaction was so endearing and genuine, the room burst into further applause.

'As you can all see, Princess Mervat is wearing the crown, a crown that Gulnur Hanem has graciously allowed us to display.' As he spoke, Mervat's mother pulled the tiara from her daughter's head and replaced it with the Cleopatra Cerulean Crown.

'Beautiful,' the khedive remarked when the task was completed. 'She wears it tonight on loan from her mother, but the crown will come to Princess Mervat one day,' The khedive went on but then paused to call up Hussam. As his son came to the stage, he took his hand and Gulnur Hanem gave him Mervat's.

The khedive announced, 'It will be hers on the day she marries my son, Prince Hussam. Please join me in congratulating these two on their engagement.'

The tiled marble at Louis's feet seemed to quake. No one was looking at him, but everybody in that room seemed to be laughing at him. His utter foolishness and hope.

He fingered the fuchsia rose at his lapel, chosen from the table, not because it complemented the ones in Mervat's hair, but because he thought it was from the bush outside of the palace study. The one that had reminded him of a wall of defence. It offered no protection of his heart now.

And even though Louis could probably think of a saying or two of his grandfather's to help him remain strong, he didn't want to.

He wanted to storm that stage and declare his love for Mervat in front of all.

Were you not all witness to our dance? She is my partner! She chooses me!

Instead, he stalked away.

Louis did not hear what Mervat had to say because he was afraid that in the end, she would not choose him at all.

Chapter Twenty-Two

Mervat

Mervat blanched, stupidly, not processing what had happened. How had she gone from the whirlwind of being in Louis's arms to being tossed down a dark hole and buried in flowers, dying, cloying with their overpowering smells.

She caught Hussam's eye behind his father's back, but there was only shame there. He had tried to warn her that he had not been able to get through to his father, but even he didn't know the announcement was coming today. Her mother did, though. That's why she'd been nice in the hammam. Given her this dress. What a betrayal it was! Had their closeness been only a lie? Was Anne only proud of Mervat because she thought she got what she wanted?

She clamped down the pain of it, a pain she would save for later when she was alone. But right now it hardened into questions: Had any mother in history ever used her daughter as Mervat had been used? Did Anne care nothing at all for her happiness?

And Louis? What would he think? She had to find him, tell him the khedive was wrong. She wasn't going to marry Hussam.

She searched for Louis in the mass coming to congratulate her, but he was nowhere to be found. Not even with the British consul and his wife.

And while her beaming mother fielded well wishes from Turkish nobles, Mervat panicked. What if she'd have to do it right then and there? Marry Hussam before she had a chance to walk away? Before she'd got off that stage. She would be her cousin's wife and Louis would be out of her life.

She was physically weak with dread. When she stepped back, none noticed, but Amu Taha found her. From his tray, he gave her a bowl of *umm ali*, sweetened with nuts, coconut and cinnamon.

'Thank you, Amu,' she said, taking a bite and then another until the dish was finished. He took it from her and gave her a glass of water to wash it down.

'One of the other servants said ladies become dehydrated from the hammam. And you looked especially ill. You aren't accustomed to such attention.' But Mervat knew it wasn't the only thing making her feel unwell.

'Begging your forgiveness,' Amu Taha said, his words little more than a whisper, 'but there is an… Englishman in the gardens, looking somewhat miserable himself.'

She nodded, unable to say anything else. How could she go to Louis? Tell him it was all a lie, that she wouldn't marry her cousin. She'd been saying it all along and yet…she was closer to a wedding date with Hussam then she'd ever been.

She handed Amu Taha the empty glass and watched as he went back to work. His presence had reminded her how much she disliked court life. And now she'd have to add the hammam to her list.

Yes, Mervat felt things for Louis, but even if he remained only a memory from a Paris museum, she needed to free herself from her predicament now. She would not marry if she was not in love with Hussam, she would not marry to please her mother. She would not marry in deference to a khedive content to use her as a tool to secure his line. A man who, if he did not care for the wishes of his son to marry the woman he loved, would never treat her and her wishes with respect.

There was only one thing left for her to do.

Anne would be upset, but as much as it pained Mervat, she knew that there was no way to move forward without crossing her mother now. If there was, she would have taken it.

She marched to the khedive, sitting back in his throne chair, listening intently to a pair of diplomats. Before she got there, Hussam caught her arm, dragged her to a corner of the stage.

'What are you doing?'

'What I should have done weeks ago.'

'You're upset about Louis and I agree with you and I know he cares for you. I see it now. Saw it earlier. Everyone saw it when the two of you were dancing. My father must have too.'

'Your father planned this, regardless.'

Hussam took a deep breath. 'But you will make it worse if this is the stance you take now.'

'You're missing Nadine. You loved her and should have fought for her. You want me and Louis to be as miserable as you.'

'No, *w'Allahi*. I want you to be happy and him too. And I don't even know how or if it is possible, but I promise to help both of you. Only, Mervat if you do what you're thinking of doing now, defying my father in such a public way, it will be a disaster.'

Hussam was adamant. He knew what she was thinking and wasn't about to let her do it. But she wasn't about to let him convince her into following another of his doomed plans either.

'I'll find Louis now,' he said, 'tell him that the three of us will speak to the khedive tomorrow in his office, alone. We will say that while we respect him, none of us can see this marriage through. I will put myself at my father's mercy, say he can marry me to whoever he wants *if* he leaves you and Louis alone to love or marry as you wish.'

If there was any logic in Hussam's words, she did not hear it. 'What makes you think Louis would agree to this?'

Hussam lifted a brow. 'As I said, *everyone* saw how he looked at you. Did *you* not?'

'Very well, find Louis. Tell him of your rational plan,' she said but she wouldn't let him sway her.

Something in her voice must have put Hussam on alert because he asked, 'Will you come with me? I dare say you can convince Louis better.'

Mervat had convinced Louis once before to be a party to a plan of Hussam's. She would not do it again. With a weary glance at her mother, she found an excuse, 'I will find you both shortly, I need to speak to Anne first.'

When she was sure Hussam was gone, she brushed past her mother, past those still in line to offer congratulations to the khedive. When she stood before him, his look of scorn suggested that he knew exactly what she was going to say.

It was a look that had been buried in her mind. He'd given her father the same one when he'd brought Mervat to visit her aunt from Turkey. It was a look that said, *You don't belong here.*

He had not been wrong then and he was not wrong now.

'Thank you kindly, Khedewy.' She lifted her voice and chose to speak in English because it had become the most common language used in Egyptian politics. Her declaration had to be official for all who were standing around him. 'It has been a pleasure discovering more about the Cleopatra Cerulean.' She gestured to the painting, 'And that portrait is a beautiful gift, but I cannot accept it. Hussam and I, while good friends and cousins, have no intention of marrying. I am but a simple girl caught up in the grandeur of court life while visiting her mother but is most eager to return home to my father. I am Abbas's daughter in all manners. As this day marks midsummer, my *baba* will need my help with his garden harvest, and I thought this lovely evening with the traditions you spoke of earlier would be a fitting occasion to mark my final evening at court. That was to be *my* announcement were I not surprised by yours.'

Anne was by her side, shushing her, addressing her loudly in Turkish so that the khedive would hear, '*Zuk, kiz!* Your future father-in-law is not yet accustomed to your ramblings.'

Mervat felt a pang of regret, felt sorry to do this to her mother. Anne hadn't understood what she'd said but would have sensed the gist of it.

If only she'd listened to her before now!

The khedive sneered then spoke in English, as she had, to those gathered, 'This modern era, they cannot fathom arranged marriages. Girls have minds of their own. Even those who would be given crowns.' He stood and glanced at Mervat's head. He hissed, in Turkish, 'Best to take it back, Gulnur Hanem, for your daughter refuses my son.'

The khedive was done with them. He turned back to his guests as if she and Anne weren't standing there. 'Midsummer night is mixed all up, like the first dance, the Shakespeare play follows a few confused couples. Shall we proceed to watch it?'

The khedive would not wish to turn her refusal of Hussam into a comedic stage, for indeed a crowd had gathered to see the fuss. Mervat dared a quick look around, hoping Louis had found his way back, that he had witnessed this break, her strength in defying the khedive, yes, but also in prioritising herself rather than hoping her mother would know how desperately she had wanted them to be mother and daughter. Because, in truth, the hardest part of that moment was knowing what Mervat said would be seen as a betrayal of Anne.

And when everyone had gone to watch the play, her mother turned on her.

'You did that because of the Englishman? Because you think he loves you?' She scoffed. 'Foolish girl. Now you will be no one and he will not want you outside of this palace, outside of your princess status. In fact, I predict that Louis will ask Nadine's father for her hand this very night. The man is wealthy and looks to fund an estate in England. With her blond hair and pretty eyes, she would fit right in, do you not think? Unlike you who only belong in a hovel with your father.'

It was a cruel thing to say but Anne was hurt and she would forgive her in hopes that she too would one day forgive Mervat.

Anne snatched the crown from her head and left her there, bereft.

Mervat yearning for Louis's steadying presence, went to search for it. She would ask if his grandfather had had advice on dealing with an opportunity seized when the result of it was losing a mother's love.

Chapter Twenty-Three

Louis

Louis paced near where the troupe of young Egyptian actors were setting up for their play. He did not feel like celebrating anything, could not even think straight with all his frustrations—ones that were enlarged when Hussam found him.

Made worse still when his friend looked at him with pity.

'You are upset and so am I, but we will talk. Me, you, Mervat. Decide on a course.'

Louis shouted, 'It should have been done with. Your plan, the outings. Everything we risked. *Done.* Instead, an engagement is announced. Forgive me if I no longer trust your plans.'

Hussam gestured to the people around them, those listening and watching. 'I do not want to fight with you, and we cannot talk here.'

'By all means consider this an invitation to my new home. Join me for a spot of tea. Bring your betrothed, since you are now officially engaged, it will not be inappropriate.' Louis hated the bitterness in his tone and thought of his grandfather's adage. *Perhaps when one has known the sweetest of the sweet, after an all-consuming hunger for the salty, what is left but the bitter?*

Hussam exhaled sharply. 'Out of us all, only you got what you wanted. A post. Acclaim.'

'It means nothing without *her*, do you not see?'

Hussam held up his hands in surrender. 'I need to check on Mer—'

'By all means.' Louis waved him away with an embellished flourish.

'Find a quieter spot. Have a drink, my friend. I will find you later, when you have calmed down. We will make this right. I promise.' Hussam rubbed the top of his head vigorously before sighing and walking away.

Louis knew it was good advice, knew his friend was trying to be a good one. But Hussam hadn't succeeded in calming his frustrations. Louis should have gone home but had come in the embassy carriage and was supposed to wait for Sir Stuart and his family. The consul was expected to cut the cake later on in the evening and would not be leaving before then.

He'd also told him in the carriage ride over that he trusted that Louis would use his 'considerable charms' to further enhance relations between England and Egypt which were in a good place at the moment but 'one never knows the fickleness of future politics.'

It was about as ambiguous as much of his post had been thus far. But Louis couldn't dwell on that now. People started taking their seats for the play and he didn't want to be the main act.

He stalked towards a pair of large trees. He'd not seen them before and wondered how they'd been planted in the Sesostris gardens in the short time he'd been gone.

It was not long before Amu Taha found him pacing there.

'Eat,' the older man encouraged, handing him a bowl from his tray and doling out a sympathetic smile.

Louis made a show of loading the dainty spoon with a

hearty bite and though it tasted fine, much like a baked bread pudding, he only swallowed to appease Amu Taha. The servant liked Louis because of Mervat and likely had only singled him out with the dessert because of her. It meant that Amu Taha thought that she cared for Louis and it warmed his heart that someone besides him believed it.

He thanked him and watched as Amu Taha left.

Mervat had never told him she loved him. Although he had tried to do what was honourable and right by her all along, how would his behaviour have changed if she had?

Louis groaned, throwing back his head against the spindly branches and then losing the dessert spoon he still held. It was dark between the trees, only the moonlight pecking between the droopy leaf branches high overhead. When he crouched to find it, it glinted in the dirt.

While he pondered whether he should pick it up and ruin the dessert by trying to eat with it or if he should simply abandon the dish next to the spoon, he heard a rustling. He held out both dish and spoon, ready to give them back to Amu Taha but it wasn't the servant.

It was Mervat.

She held a lantern to his face, and though it was dim, the candle in it small, Louis felt too exposed. As if she could see his helplessness, read the hurt in his face like words on a page.

'Are you not going to finish the *umm ali*?'

She neared, pointed to the dessert dish he still held in hand like a fool.

'The spoon fell and I...'

Mervat dipped two fingers inside and scooped them up into her mouth in a move that muddied his insides.

This really is not fair of her, was all he could think as he tried desperately to curb his desire for her and to focus on what she was saying and why he should not be listening to her say it.

'The dessert was the winning prize in a competition between Egyptian bakers for a celebration of the death of Shajar al-Durr, a woman who married two kings. The first of her husbands was named As-Salih Ayyub. When he died, it marked the end of the Ayyubid era in our country. In 1250, Shajar al-Durr, whose official name was Asmat al-Din Umm Khalil, became sultana with the aid of the Mamluks. Eighty days into her rule, she abdicated by marrying her first husband's commander and his food taster, Izz al-Din Aybak in a rushed ceremony, and making him the first Mamluk king of Egypt. But his rule too would not last long. And soon after she was killed, as well. The Mamluks only wanted a grip on power and they used her to get it.'

'Umm Khalil?' Louis wondered. 'I thought the dessert was named *umm ali*.'

Mervat grinned. 'You have little patience.'

'When you speak, I am lulled with all the patience in the world.' Louis knew the aching truth of it. 'But I am a man who needs clarity when confused.' He was talking about their relationship too.

Mervat reached up and hung the lamp between the ginger root–like spindly tree branches, freeing her hands and illuminating the space between them. The moonlight hit the embroidery in her gown, one that was beautiful enough for a wedding ceremony.

Not to him, he knew, and yet Louis yearned to clasp her waist by its cinched design. To bring her close to him, let her feel his physical need if his words would not suffice. Instead, Louis thrust the dessert between them, another line of defence where none had sufficed.

Mervat's eyes trailed downwards, then back up at him.

'Shajar al-Durr was a controversial woman. She was first purchased as a child slave, then became a concubine to the sultan even before he took the throne. When she had his child, he married her and when he died, she was part of the Mamluks' plans to conceal his death from the people because the seventh European crusade was nigh, literally en route to Cairo. Her ambition to rule made her quick marriage to the second husband necessary. But that food taster and commander? He had to forsake his first wife to marry Shajar al-Durr. His first wife, the forsaken one, was called Umm Ali.'

'Hmm, I see.'

'It was a terrible mess with numerous sides, lies, variations of the truth. Umm Ali claimed that Shajar al-Durr ended up killing their shared husband because she wanted power returned to her— —a crime for which she ended up paying with her own horrible murder.'

Mervat shrugged, then smiled. 'But we Egyptians, we like our desserts.'

He had nothing to say to that. Her smile bewitched Louis and then she was taking the two fingers that had been in her mouth and scooping up a bite for him from the *umm ali*. She brought it to his lips and he was sure he'd die of frustration. He tossed the spoon and grabbed her wrist before taking it. The tips of her fingers in his mouth had all the nerves in his body ricocheting against each other.

He took the bite, slowly, licking her fingers as he did. In truth, he tasted nothing of the *umm ali*, only heard her groan and saw her eyes flicker closed and it was satisfaction enough for him.

'You surprise me, the different sides of you.' Louis was confused and hurt by her too. 'At once innocent, gentle. Now, the vixen. Teasing.'

'I told you from the first time we met that I like to explore the different sides of things, delve deep. If clay, a statue has much story infused in it, cannot a person too? Cannot I, Viscount?'

'Certainly, Princess but I did not think cruelty would be one of your sides.'

She stepped back. 'How am I cruel?'

He set the dessert dish near her *fanoos*, letting down his guard. 'You come here to me, knowing I lo…*care* for you. But tempting me with all that I cannot have. Knowing you are engaged to Hussam.'

'How do you care for me? That day in Khan el-Khalili, you were about to tell me.'

Did he dare now?

He pointed to the palace somewhere in the distance, and declared, 'I love you Mervat. Since the day I arrived in Cairo and first saw that portrait the khedive just casually showed everyone, because it was meant for Hussam, I have loved you desperately. The next day, when actually faced with the mysterious Louvre lady that had haunted me since our encounter in the flesh, I have loved you selfishly, because I knew you were meant for Hussam. Every day since he first conceived of his stupid plan for defiance, I have loved you foolishly because I knew no good could come of it!'

He said with a huff, 'Hell, even before Hussam was in the picture, I have loved you. The only innocent moment, the pure moment of that love in this entire debacle was when I saw you standing near *Psyche Revived by Cupid's Kiss*, and I didn't know you were a princess engaged to my oldest, dearest friend. Mervat Abbas, I have loved you since the moment you opened your mouth to explain what a genealogy of artifacts entailed.'

It was an impassioned speech that drew too much from Louis. He closed his eyes, embarrassed, afraid that he had made a fool of himself by it. He waited for Mervat to speak, dreaded what she might say. He wouldn't ask her if she accepted his love. If she returned it.

When he opened his eyes, he could see she had shed a few tears.

'You asked for my feelings and there they are. Honest as can be, though I hate to be the cause of your grief.'

When she finally spoke, Mervat's tone was assured. 'You say I am cruel for tempting you because I am engaged. You are wrong, Louis. I am not engaged to Hussam.'

'As you have been saying.' Louis pointed beyond their enclave as a burst of applause came from the direction of the play. 'The khedive, he whose rule is supreme in this country, says otherwise.'

Mervat shook her head. 'His announcement was unfortunate, but I am glad my uncle made it. It forced my hand. When you left, I told him he was wrong. I did it officially. With witnesses present, embarrassed him even, so there could be no mistake and no coming back from it. I told him that I will not marry Hussam. It's over between us, once and for all.'

He gaped, disbelieving, his heart thumping with hope. 'Truly?'

Chapter Twenty-Four

Mervat

'Truly.'

Mervat would have said that she loved him, but he cupped her face in his palms and kissed her forehead before she could. The kiss was chaste but intense too. She wrapped her arms around his neck and melted into the slow sweetness of it. She couldn't say how long it lasted but she was shivering when he finally pulled away. The night cold was settling in.

She didn't want to let go of him and as he clutched her waist and seemed to not want to either, Louis had to wiggle free to shake off his jacket. When he finally managed to put it around her shoulders, he said, 'We should go inside.'

'I won't be welcome there now,' she answered.

'Your mother? Did she hear what you said to the khedive?'

'Yes.' Mervat thought about the cruel things Anne had said and implied. About how Louis needed Nadine's wealth. About how he would not want Mervat if she were away from court.

Hadn't Louis just declared his love for her? Hadn't Mervat's soul wept for his words?

He searched her eyes with an intentness that further tore at her heart. 'Are you all right with her?'

'No. But I do not know what more I could have done to make it right.'

Above them, the sky was lit with the boom of colourful fireworks.

They watched it for a moment, but they kept looking at each other and grinning sheepishly. Maybe he wanted to hear Mervat say she loved him too.

She wanted to say it. She did. But was suddenly afraid to; afraid of the future. What could theirs be if they had different aims in life? Maybe there had been too many revelations tonight and she was too spent to think on the ramifications of any more.

So instead, Mervat said, 'I am sorry our project is done.'

Louis fingered where the Cleopatra Cerulean Crown had sat then bent to kiss her forehead. His lips stayed there like feathers drifting in the air, and *not* where Mervat wished them to be.

He said softly, 'We can find more things to research, although now that I am living away from the palace it will be harder to plan the time.'

She hesitated. 'I won't be here either. It is best if I return to my father's home either tonight or early tomorrow.'

He gently cupped her chin, lifted it to meet his gaze. 'You are a princess with the right to be here for as long as you want.'

'You have inspired me, Louis. Your honesty, your commitment to your family. Even as you are far from them, every opportunity you have seized has been for them.'

His brow furrowed. 'Why does that sound like a goodbye?'

'I do not mean it to.'

Talking about his family was dangerous territory. Mervat couldn't ask Louis for any promises, wasn't sure she could make any herself. Not now, not before she had worked out her feelings over losing her mother's love. Not when she wasn't sure that she could ever belong with his family either.

And what if Louis knew it too? He'd said he'd loved her, yes, but everything she knew of what he wanted for his future suggested that there was no place for Mervat in it.

He smiled. 'Perhaps I was only motivated by pride, by how I want society to see my family, to see me. You said that to me once.'

'Does not pride come from knowing oneself and being content with who you are, even if society perceives it differently? Is that not a kind of honesty too? You are a viscount, even without the typical trappings and outside of your country whilst I have only ever been called "princess" within this court. Tomorrow, I will be gone from it.' She laughed at herself. 'I don't know if any of that made sense.'

'How about we simplify things and make the most of this evening then? I will only be but a viscount for the Egyptian princess. Does that make any more sense?'

She shrugged, happy that the mood had been lightened. 'What would you like to do?'

He took a deep breath, then gave her one of his charming smiles. '*A Midsummer Night's Dream* is my favourite play. I was Oberon as a boy—a school production but easily the most important player.' He cocked a playful brow at her headshaking. 'And what is your objection to that, Princess?'

'Only that I did not see how adorable you must have looked in your costume!'

Louis winced. 'Green silk hose and a doublet, wings that kept falling off—it was quite ridiculous. You most definitely would not have liked to see it.' He touched the tip of her nose in mock reprimand. 'Would you like to watch how Egyptians do the bard?'

She pursed her lips. 'I don't want to be in anyone else's company right now.'

He sighed, deep and heavy. The finger he had touched to her nose, slipped, tracing her cheeks, his eyes piercing hers the whole while, but when his finger touched her lips, his gaze was pulled towards them. Mervat very much liked to watch Louis watching her.

She rose on her toes instinctively, cupped his cheeks, her hands so cold that his own moved instinctively from her face to cover them, warm them.

'You have to ask me,' Louis said.

'Every time?'

'There has only been once before.'

It was true, but it felt like a lie. Even though she'd not dared to believe they could be together, Mervat had made love to Louis in her waking dreams, so much so that it wasn't hard to imagine there'd been more than just the one kiss they'd shared.

'A body grows weary of words,' she said with a huff.

He'd lowered his mouth to hers, his breath hot. 'Ask,' he demanded, his voice rough.

But she really was tired of talking. She inched forward and kissed him. So sudden it surprised him, at first. She didn't care. Mervat quite enjoyed taking the initiative. And he let her for a bit.

The meshing of their lips thereafter was like a meeting of entities with minds of their own. Gentle in turns, testing the waters. And then hungrier, as if hers hadn't eaten and were sampling everything he had had that evening. The hibiscus punch. The caramelised *umm ali*. And then it was the taste of him. *Louis*.

He resumed talking.

'You are a summer day that starts temperate, mild.' He dotted her cheeks with kisses. 'Then sweeps you away with its beauty, surprises you with its perfection.' He nibbled behind her left ear. His tongue tracing her neck stopped at the collar of her dress. 'Joy upon joy in each of its moments.' His lips moved to her right ear and she thought then that her knees would surely buckle with the heft of sentiment in her body.

'A joy you wished could be bottled like jam, saving its sweetness for another day.'

Louis's hands desperately tried to find the opening of her dress; she raked his hair, pressed her body into his. *Why was it not enough?* He lured her, leg against leg, stepping backwards, until her back was flush to the tree's trunk.

'You are beautiful in this gown but it is ostentatious.'

Mervat feared her mother's dress might be ruined, but her need for him was more intense. She whipped her hands out from beneath his suit jacket. She unfurled the shirt tucked in to his trousers and clutched the flesh of his waist, pulling him closer still. She ran her hands to the line of navel hair she'd seen on the beach in Alexandrian, slid her index finger along it. She loved watching his reaction, how he closed his eyes in anticipation. When she'd delved a bit too far down, he shook his head, grasped her hand to pull it up to his lips. Took each finger in turn between them in a move that had her melting from within.

She caressed the veins on the back of his hands and up his wrists as they bulged like tributaries of a swollen river. Or the brook in Allenborough he used to dream beside.

'We should not have started what we cannot finish,' he managed.

'I love you, Louis.'

There it was. Mervat, caught up in the moment, had let it slip from her tongue. It wasn't the grand declaration he had made. There was no genealogy behind it, no speeches about the angles of love.

Only the simple truth of it.

Louis must have sensed, known what it had taken for Mervat to say it. Because he stopped. Looked at her, and despite the dark, it was as if he could see deep within her and everything about her. Now and the future. Even if the latter had not been decided or the former named.

He kissed her again, this time with a hunger she could barely keep pace with. Whatever sense of propriety or fear had held him back was gone.

He crouched to his knees. He lifted her dress, higher and higher until his palms flattened on the back of her thighs to hold it up. He felt the smooth flesh there as if she were some sort of artifact he was examining closely. His lips circled the terrain of her lower body, an exploration without a trail, his tongue leaving wetness and heat in its wake.

A moan gathered in her being so that when more fireworks boomed, Mervat thought it had come from her own chest.

What was between them then wasn't the formality, the hesitancy, of a fastidious viscount and a demure princess in a garden near the shores of the Nile. What was between them was ancestral, a passion buried beneath sand, the kind to shift wildly in heavy winds, to reveal treasure. A cave of wonders.

Mervat looked down on Louis, behind him the halo from the lantern made him devilishly handsome. He tempted her in all ways, despite the thing inside her that warned her off. The voice of her conscience that said that it was not too late to stop. That what she was doing was wrong. She was a virgin. Muslim. Egyptian. Louis was not her husband.

Them being together was not *halal*.

It was as if her heart and mind that had this thought, but her body rebelled and Mervat found herself jutting forward so that the mouth of her womanhood was at the tip of Louis's tongue.

Chapter Twenty-Five

Louis

Mervat had bathed in jasmine-scented bath water.

If he sampled her there, tasted her want, her need for him, Louis would not be able to stop himself from finishing and answering his own.

They were not married. Or even engaged to be.

And though both of them were lost in the moment, that pestering voice of propensity once again blared a warning. *You will ruin her.* It was a warning he might have ignored—if they had not been interrupted.

Before he realised it was happening, Louis was dragged up and away from Mervat.

Hussam had him by the shoulders, blocked him from advancing. But at the same time, didn't turn around to look at her, respecting her privacy.

'You shouldn't be here, Hussam,' Mervat said to her cousin's back as she adjusted her dress, and gathered her hair. The dim light couldn't hide the flush in her face. Her glorious beauty.

Or Louis's shame for letting it get so far.

'I know you, cousin,' Hussam answered. 'You would regret this. And I know Louis, he is an honourable man. I understand that you both were taken in by the moment. Allah knows it has happened to me.'

How was it that Hussam had become the voice of reason? Louis thought as he took calming breaths, brushed down his hair, adjusted his clothes too.

There was a question in his friend's face, one that asked if Mervat had finished adjusting her dress. If she was decent. If he could talk to her. If Louis trusted him too. He nodded.

'Emotions are heighted all around—the khedive is angry.' Hussam turned to his cousin slowly and with his hands up said, 'Mervat, he thought you were meek like your father or controllable like your mother, and you have proven you are neither. I fear what he will do.'

'What can he do?'

Louis saw something in Hussam's face he couldn't remember seeing ever before. *Fear.*

'Hussam, at one point, you seemed to think this plan of yours for defiant love would convince the khedive to let you marry Nadine,' Louis argued. 'What changed? Why is your father now a tyrant from whom we need to be scared rather than someone who is trying to modernise his country?'

But if Hussam felt reprimanded, he did not look it. He looked as if he were really trying to figure out the answer to the question. 'His paranoia has been heightened of late, even before tonight. I thought it had something to do with Louis's article, but I'm not sure. Last week I heard him wanting to put a guard on Mervat's father Abbas again.'

Louis recalled how the khedive had theorised about the Cleopatra Cerulean article. It was that day when the consul had offered him the job at the embassy. He'd felt it strange then, and then he'd been sent to the Suez Canal immediately thereafter so he'd not had a chance to discuss it with Hussam.

Mervat said, 'Mustafa is my father's guard. He was missing when we went there after al-Azhar. I thought it odd. They used to be friends. He was kind to Baba.'

'That is what the khedive does,' Hussam said with a huff. 'Allows freedoms, friendships—they are a rope he extends to test you with. You are supposed to appreciate them, appreciate *him* for allowing them. When you don't, he snatches them away. When you challenge him, he punishes. Quietly. Ruthlessly.'

'What happened to Mustafa?' she asked, her voice shaking.

Hussam's voice shook a little too when he answered. 'I do not know, Mervat. All I know is that my father is looking at our foursome and planning *something*. Not to punish me—I am his son and heir after all. But I worry for the rest of you. And I hate that it was me who initiated this plan in the first. I thought his love for me would be enough to protect the rest of you.'

Mervat protested, 'Surely us not marrying has nothing to do with Louis and Nadine? Why would he punish them?'

Louis's skin crawled with foreboding. He didn't want Mervat to hear what more Hussam had to say.

He stepped forward to take her by the shoulders. He loved Mervat and would do *anything* to protect her. 'Find Nadine. Make sure she is all right. Meet me in the study later? When the party dwindles and things settle.'

She didn't look up at him then, did not meet his gaze when she nodded. He could feel her sadness. The image of her praying in the mosque came to him. Her tears then. She would feel guilty about what they did just then. What they would have done if they had not been interrupted.

'We will only talk,' he stressed. 'I let myself be swept in the moment earlier. You are not to blame, Mervat.' He tilted her chin up so she could see he was teasing her lovingly when he added, 'Well, perhaps you are a little bit to blame.'

She smiled, but it was a sad one. She shrugged off his dinner jacket, giving it back to him.

He took the flower from his lapel, folded it into her hands. Mervat buried her face in it, inhaling deeply. He would do anything to keep her safe.

When she looked up from the flower, Mervat was composed. She smiled at Hussam. 'I will find Nadine, check on her.' She patted Louis's cheek, 'Then I'll wait for you in the study.'

He did not know if it would be a goodbye, but it was the second time in the span of one—albeit heated—encounter that he felt like it might be.

When he was sure she was gone, Louis faced Hussam. 'I stopped you from answering Mervat's question.'

Hussam nodded. 'The one about what my father's plan has to do with you and Nadine?'

'Yes. I don't care about myself. I don't want any of this to be her burden. She has too much already to deal with. Her guilt over disappointing her mother, over what's happened between us.' Louis sighed, '*My* question is—what will the khedive do to Mervat?'

Hussam scrubbed his face, stroked his beard before answering, 'Thankfully I was the one to catch you instead of one of his men. It wouldn't be adultery since Mervat is not married, but she'd be accused of fornication. One hundred lashes. My father could make it public. She would never live down the shame, be denied entry in holy places. Never marry, never—' The horror he must have seen in Louis's face made Hussam stop. 'But that's not going to happen because no one saw you, remember? I'm not worried about Mervat now, you're the immediate concern. Maybe a bit concerned for myself because my cousin would never forgive me if anything happened to you.'

Hussam smirked, shook his shoulder consolingly. The gesture made Louis feel bad about his anger towards him, the jealousy that had him believing he was saving Mervat for himself.

'I love her, Hussam.'

'I know. It's strange for me. She's like my sister and you're my best mate and a few minutes ago the two of you seemed like you were having a *very* good time.'

Louis raked his hands through his hair out of frustration. All manner of frustrations. But when he looked back at his friend who was jostling him, he knew they needed to be serious. 'Too bad we're not still boys at Eton fumbling in the dark to earn a woman's admiration. We have to understand what your father might do so we can stop it. The article I wrote. He asked me about it and I might have mentioned that she helped with it. I only meant to show gratitude but…'

Hussam sobered. 'But he fathomed that its message was about Mervat. Then you chose to dance with her in front of everyone. Gulnur Hanem warned the khedive about you, about Nadine. She told the khedive to keep you both away from me and Mervat. He will see you as part of the insult to him. He will want to punish you immediately.'

'How? By taking away my post at the embassy or cutting me off from his contact with the *Telegraph*? Those two I can handle, but if he we were to banish me from the country before I figured things out with Mervat…'

Hussam shook his head. 'Your writing has benefited Egypt, your name would carry you to other contacts at other newspapers. He wouldn't do that. And you have to be in the country to write about it so he would not banish you yet. The embassy post, maybe, but… I don't think so. It would draw too much attention. Maybe he will minimise the duties associated with the post.'

'There haven't been any of those thus far anyway,' Louis said.

'If I know my father at all, he will want to test you again. And it will likely have to do with Nadine.'

Louis searched his friend's face. 'Your previous plan? You think I should stress my admiration for her?'

Hussam cocked a brow. 'Her father *is* here.'

'But you love her still, do you not?'

'I ended it, for…reasons. I believe Nadine would accept a proposal from you.'

'A proposal?' Louis spluttered. 'Did you not see me being in love with your cousin right now? I would not hurt Mervat for anything in the world.'

'You do not have to marry Nadine or actually propose. Just prove your "interest in proposing", feign it to buy us time. Time to let this whole incident with Mervat simmer down, perhaps if she goes back to the quiet life her father leads, the khedive will forget in time. It is a risk, I know. But it will save you both now. And I will do my part, marry the next woman he chooses for me. He wants a wedding by summer's end, I will give him one.'

'And what would I do in the meantime? Plan a wedding with Nadine?' Louis wondered at the rattling in his mind. Was this how his father and grandfather had felt when refusing the sort of arranged marriages that would have benefited the Allenborough estate? He had always been against marrying solely for love, but, after Mervat, he could not imagine marrying for anything other than it. He hoped Hussam would find a semblance of it in his father's next choice.

'I dare say you will use the time to prepare to be a husband to my cousin. But I only ask that you let down Nadine gently after tonight. Make it so your "interest" does not harm her. She is beautiful and rich and if it be known that an English viscount wished to make her a viscountess then she will have no shortage of high-ranking suitors from which to choose. All right?'

They might have shaken hands, indicating their mutual resignation to the ploy, but they were interrupted by a group of men. Amongst them was the khedive.

'Here are the Banyan trees come to us from India via the Suez Canal.'

Chapter Twenty-Six

Mervat

Mervat was still tingling with Louis's touch, his kisses, the way she'd opened herself to him in every way and had wanted him in *that* way. She wanted to believe she'd have stopped it before they went too far, but the truth was that if it hadn't been for Hussam's interruption, she might not still be a virgin. And if she'd had sexual relations outside of marriage, the sin of it, her guilt, would have been impossible for Mervat to bear.

She determined to be stronger and moved now through the palace searching for Nadine whilst trying to avoid the khedive and her mother. The play was done, the young actors, mingling amongst the guests like the sprites they'd acted as. Servants were circling with platters of savoury foods, individual star-shaped English chicken pot pies and crescent moon–shaped Egyptian *hawawshi* bread baked with onioned ground beef. Mervat ate one of each and was still not satiated after them. She flushed to think her *activities* with Louis had made her ravenous.

Mervat caught sight of Nadine near the fountain, sitting sullenly apart from her harem friends. It looked as if she'd been forced to spend time in their company and would rather be anywhere else. When Mervat approached, the group dispersed like dry beans from a sack.

Most had been fawning over her after Anne's praise in the hammam a short while ago.

Nadine, thankfully, did not budge when Mervat took the seat beside her. 'They know I have refused the marriage?'

Nadine's eyes were swollen. She'd been crying. 'The harem gossips thrive on scandals. They were my friends because they wanted to hear about me and Hussam. You? They fear you because you have defied the khedive and anyone seen in your presence could face his wrath, as well. They are cowards too.'

'And you? Are you not scared to be seen with me?'

'My father is taking me away. I doubt I will be back here anytime soon.'

'Hussam sent me to check on you.'

Nadine scoffed, 'Because he will not ask for my hand, he thinks I will kill myself?'

It had actually been Louis who asked Mervat to check on Nadine. Rather than say it, she tried to console her, 'Hussam will talk to the khedive. Find a solution for you.'

'Can he do it in the next hour?' she spit out. 'Baba says my time in court has been a waste, that I can't do anything on my own so now he'll have to do it. He's entertaining proposals from other men now and says I will be engaged before night's end.'

Mervat put a hand on Nadine's knee. 'Can you not plead with your father to give him more time? Hussam loves you, Nadine.'

'He likes my body. He *loves* little else besides it. It is a good thing I kept my virtue intact. He would have taken it otherwise!'

Mervat had very recent experience as to how easily one

might be swept up in the heat of passion. She defended her cousin, saying, 'The very purpose of his plan for defiant love was to be in your company.'

Nadine moved her knee away from Mervat. 'Those outings? They were all Hussam boring me with talk of how much he admires you. Your goodness, your spirituality. He thinks Allah loves only you on this earth, and any you love Allah would love, as well. If you *had* agreed to marry Hussam from the start, no doubt he would not have come up with any plan at all.'

Maybe Nadine had been drinking, otherwise she was making no sense at all! 'You're hurt, needing someone to blame.'

'And you, good Princess Mervat, must be blameless?' Nadine stood and looked down on Mervat. 'Baba says my beauty and wealth will secure me someone better than the Prince. I should be close on hand for any arrangements he makes.'

She started to walk away, but then turned back to Mervat, a smug grin playing on her lips. 'Did I mention that the man he arranges for me is much handsomer than your cousin?'

What could Nadine possibly mean by that?

Trepidation prompted Mervat's steps back to the Banyan tree where she'd left Hussam and Louis. Maybe they were gone now, left to attend some other event. Louis had asked her to meet him in the study, perhaps she should go there.

But then she heard voices. Hussam's. The khedive's. Another man's. *Louis's.*

The khedive was asking, 'And my cousin's daughter, the princess Mervat, she would not lament this decision?'

'You know my cousin, Khedewy,' Hussam said. 'Recall her petition for a museum project? Her goals are noble, would serve all of Egypt.'

Nadine's words hit Mervat. It couldn't be true that Hussam loved her? He was her friend. *And friends should not eavesdrop on private conversations.* She made to retreat and wait for Louis in the study as he'd asked, but then she heard his voice.

'Further, Your Highness,' Louis said, 'the princess is a smart young lady, no doubt lovely, but I fear she would be wholly ill suited for England.'

He was working on saving her.

Her heart clenched with love for him, so much so that it felt like it would explode. But what came next made her heart drop.

'Our area of England may, unfortunately,' Louis said, 'be unwelcoming to women who look like the princess Mervat. Too *foreign*, they would call her. Miss Nadine, on the other hand, would make for the loveliest of viscountesses.'

'Then we must discuss the dowry that will shore up your estate for my daughter,' came the voice of the man who must be Nadine's father. In Arabic, he mumbled something about it being strange that the idiot Englishmen took dowries from their brides unlike the Egyptian women who took them from their husbands but luckily he could afford it.

Even amidst her pain, in the insult he'd doled on her, Mervat was afraid Louis would understand the Arabic and be insulted himself.

She ran from the Banyan tree. He'd said he loved her there. Would have made love to her there. How could he have turned on her so? Maybe it was just as Nadine had said about Hussam, that he'd only wanted what was on the outside, her body. But even in that, Mervat wasn't sure for hadn't Louis said the people of Allenborough would think Nadine the lovelier?

Maybe Louis was showing he cared for Mervat, sparing her feelings that he didn't believe she belonged in England with him. She herself had imagined it, hadn't she? His future of blond, blue-eyed children that could never have been Mervat's. But they could be Nadine's.

Louis hadn't made any promises to her, hadn't asked Mervat to make any to him. And love without commitment or promise? Well, that was but raw clay, unmoulded.

It took all Mervat's might to hold back her tears until she had run through the palace and found her way into the harem. In the sanctuary of its mosque, she collapsed and let them free.

Mervat was unceremoniously met the next morning by Amu Taha at the top of the stairs, near where she had first met him all those months ago.

'Are you here to help me down?' she smiled sadly. Even Anne had refused to open her door when Mervat had knocked now to bid her farewell. And though she thought there were no tears left, the way Amu Taha looked at her just then nearly brought them on again. He liked her, truly. Pitied her, perhaps.

'I am here as part of the duty to my new job,' he said. 'Late last night the missive came from the khedive that the princess Mervat and her father require a guard.'

Did the khedive know of her friendship with the elderly man before her and was using him as a reminder for her to behave? A threat. Or maybe Hussam had influenced his father, made it so that if a guard was *necessary*, it would be another kind one, like Mustafa had been. Either way, she was grateful and now had no reason to defy the khedive.

'It will likely require spying.' Amu Taha smiled. 'Not that I had a choice, but have I made a mistake in taking it?'

Mervat determined to return to the ways of the past; she had chosen a life away from court in all aspects and she would honour that. 'Baba and I are simple. There will be nothing to report.'

He relieved her of the single bag she'd first come to court with. '*Allah yikrimum*, because I am tired of living in a house with so many stories.'

The grand foyer of Sesostris was still littered with remnants of the previous night as they passed. Odd, for it seemed like a lifetime ago.

Odder still was coming home and finding that her house, even though she'd been there with Louis not long ago, seemed smaller than she remembered. Not that Mervat wished for the grander scale of Sesostris, for when she left there, she felt it too was smaller.

She realised that she was the one who had changed. Been broken and hurt, yes, but she'd also experienced things she had not before. Mervat had felt love, true love, for her part, at least, and friendship too. Of course, she would be changed by it. Melancholy might set in with the readjustment in the absence of what she had had with Louis, but she would take her time, return to the contentment she had before.

For Baba's sake and for her own.

Mervat and Amu Taha found her father in his herb patch, harvesting arugula and radishes. He barely looked up at her, when she introduced their new guard, but when she had changed her clothes and joined him there, he was happier.

'Have you come to help?' he asked.

'It is midsummer, Baba, and all farmers need help during the harvest.'

In the weeks that followed, they fell into a routine. Baba didn't enquire as to life at court; he did not reference Anne or Louis. He did not comment when he would catch Mervat crying at random moments, but he would stop what he was doing, give her a pat on the hand or a hug and wait patiently for the tears to cease.

One time when the cat, Mishmish, paid them a visit, she

found one of her great-grandmother's paintings Baba had neglected to store back in the box they'd come from.

A crumbling cave.

'Someday,' Mervat said to him, 'I will tell you of the *Aida* opera.'

Someday, but not yet. Louis was lost to her, and it hurt too much still.

Perhaps she'd have felt better if she were able to return to her love and pursuit of artifact genealogies. But even in this, Mervat's well had run dry. The interests which used to propel her, the hope she had of one day curating an Egyptian museum collection—felt, sadly, spent.

Fateema's housekeeping days were quite sporadic so it was Amu Taha's weekly excursions to the palace which marked Mervat's new routine. She'd walk to pray *Jumuah* with her father at a nearby mosque on Fridays, and on Thursdays, when Amu Taha took the hansom cab sent for him to Sesostris, she would accompany him—not all the way—he'd let her down in the market for their weekly groceries and retrieve her when he was done.

After a few Thursdays, she stopped asking about her mother because Mervat knew he was only being kind in answering, 'I am the lowest of servants, the others don't share harem gossip with me.'

The truth was that Anne didn't care about her now that Mervat had acted on her persistent refusal to marry Hussam. But that didn't mean that she wasn't worried about her mother or what Anne might have done to ensure her place at court despite her daughter's defiance of the khedive.

On one such Thursday, three weeks after she had left the palace and Amu Taha had picked her up from the marketplace, he asked her for the first time, 'You do not enquire about the viscount?'

Her heart pounded in her chest. She was eager to, every week she held her tongue, every waking minute of every day, she thought of Louis, wondered where he was and what he was doing, until she thought it would drive her mad, like her grandmother had been driven mad.

But she also knew that asking about him would open up the door to those desperate feelings of hers. If he had married Nadine already, it might be the end of Mervat. It was best to leave the sentiment she had for Louis contained behind a wall in her heart and mind.

Buried under a Banyan tree.

'I am sure he is well.'

Amu Taha did not look at her when he said, 'Mr Louis talked to me today in Arabic, claims he is intent on learning it for his future wife. He is studying Islam apparently too so he may convert for her. He asked I pass along his heartfelt *salaams* to you and your father.'

Louis's engagement to Nadine was confirmed then? He spoke of her to Amu Taha knowing it would reach Mervat? Proudly? He was converting for her? If he had suggested it to Mervat, done it for her, maybe things could have been different between them now. A *halal* marriage would have sanctified their relationship, their desire for each other— because she was quite sure that the physical desire between them could not have been only on her side.

Then again, she rationalised, some books said a man might desire any woman's body were his appetite for physical intimacy voracious. No matter if he loved her or not. After all, Mervat was not as beautiful as Nadine, who would fit in and make for the loveliest of viscountesses. As his own words throbbed in her ears, she wondered if Louis had wanted Nadine from the start but altered the object of his affections because of his past comradery with Hussam. Out of respect for Hussam's feelings for Nadine.

Hadn't Mervat herself at one time questioned Louis's lack of disclosure about his feelings for her to Hussam? Louis had dismissed her concern on that matter, but perhaps she should have listened to her own misgivings before she had overheard him that night.

A scream amassed in Mervat's chest. She knew Amu Taha was being kind to her, gentle, and she wanted to spare him her ire. She caught sight of a newspaper and bookstand and she knocked on the roof, asking the driver to stop.

'Do not wait for me, Amu Taha. There is a book I wish to find and will walk the rest of the way home.'

The scream came out in short gasps when she was alone.

She should hate Louis.

Forget Louis.

Yet, when she'd calmed enough to finally speak to the seller, it was the *Telegraph* she asked for. Mervat did not find Louis's paper there that day, but the seller told her on Sundays he received a few of whatever international papers had not sold from his distributor in the city's centre.

And that is how Mervat's lone strolls on Sundays became a part of her schedule. It was not every week an article from Louis appeared, but the ones that did were brilliant.

She could even imagine that his piece on the Banyan fig tree, which the khedive had arranged to be brought in from India for it was not native to Cairo, was somehow a coded message for Mervat.

That he was thinking of her.

That he missed her.

That his sentiments about loving her had not been ephemeral, passing amidst a burst of passion, that they were lasting and worthy of being immortalised in ink.

Mervat could imagine all of it but know as well that she was wrong. Because the truth was that Louis knew where she was, he had his own apartment and wasn't restricted to comings or goings under the gaze of anyone at Sesostris. He could have visited her. Enquired as to her well-being in person.

Had Mervat been that foolish, that besotted by his handsomeness and charm to not fathom that he'd been using her? That it was Nadine whom he had wanted all along.

'Is it not time you visited the library?' Baba wondered that evening, plopping the last of the *dawood basha* kofta meatballs in his mouth. The garlicky tomato sauce they were cooked in made for a pungent smell in their small house, but she'd nearly perfected Fateema's more Egyptian take on the dish, an originally Turkish one that Anne should have taught her as mothers are wont to teach their daughters. 'I miss hearing your genealogies.'

Mervat collected Baba's empty plate and her own and rose from the table where they'd once shared a meal with Louis.

She had let her sadness get the better of her, she decided then. She and Baba had been happy before him, not needing Anne—Mervat's genealogy projects had always been something Baba and she shared. He didn't need them, maybe didn't actually miss them for their content, but he knew they made her happy. That they filled the silences between them. The loneliness.

She had thought that researching the Cleopatra Cerulean would bring her closer to her mother. Mervat should have known that her father was only ever the one she'd begun them for.

'*Insh'Allah* tomorrow, Baba. I will decide on a new artifact tomorrow.'

Chapter Twenty-Seven

Louis

It had been nearly a month, but every time Louis had come back to Sesostris, his first thought was that Mervat had not waited for him in the study. She must have felt guilty for what had nearly transpired between them, and he had patiently worked towards making things right. But it tore at him, nonetheless. Because he hated to be the cause of her tears.

Hussam said to give it time before reaching out to her, that the khedive was watching, especially since Louis's engagement to Nadine had 'not come to fruition.' And because his friend had managed to get him out of that one, Louis was willing to heed Hussam's advice. He had found a replacement for Nadine, an Iranian prince, older yes but with more money and influence than Louis, Viscount of Allenborough, could possibly compete with. Hussam had considered it from the khedive's perspective since his father had been looking for a lasting connection to Iran and facilitating this marriage would be a boon. And Nadine's father was happy, Louis suspected, because he wouldn't have to waste his money on his daughter's dowry.

Funny how the richer some people were, the more miserly. Louis was getting impatient for news of Mervat. He'd managed a brief message to Amu Taha, hoped it would be enough to tide her over. Make her see that she should wait for him. That he was doing everything he could to make himself worthy, in her eyes, of that wait.

Today, he had been summoned to Sesostris with Sir Stuart for a meeting with Hanem Gulnur, Mervat's mother, and the matter was with regard to the Cleopatra Cerulean. Usually Louis would be summoned alone to field articles with the khedive or to see Hussam, but the inclusion of the consul was strange. It brought into relief how much had changed, how *he* had changed. Was it so long ago that Louis had wanted a place in this court and sought a post in the embassy so his siblings would have increased opportunities to better themselves in the world? Walking in step with Sir Stuart now, Louis could not help but think he'd gone about it wrong.

Now that he was part of an inner circle at court, he could see the shallowness of those within it, the utter disregard for those outside it, those they deemed 'lesser than' and it was quite depressing. When he'd tried to talk to Sir Stuart about it, the British consul preached some nonsense about the combined eagerness and shallowness of youth without experience.

'Keep writing those pretty words of yours and know you are serving Her Majesty.'

Indeed, Louis's duties besides composing his articles were decidedly scant; the consul did not yet trust him with more serious work. Once, when Louis had casually questioned the speculation expense on a cotton trade agreement, Sir Stuart had sneered that Louis should stay on his side of the fence.

And while his side of the fence *was* compensated handsomely enough, increasingly, Louis found himself working less in the embassy offices and spending more time writing pieces for submission to other newspapers beyond the *Tele-*

graph and the khedive's contact there. A venture that was proving profitable in its own right.

Sir Stuart bowed to the khedive and Louis followed.

'Gulnur Hanem,' he greeted the mother of the woman he loved. He wished he could ask her if she were being kind to Mervat. Demand it from her. Gulnur Hanem clutched the crown atop her head with both hands as though it were a raft and she a drowning woman.

The khedive cut to the purpose of the meeting, without ceremony: 'Gulnur Hanem has heard that your Queen Victoria collects jewels from countries her empire has had a hand in. She wishes to offer it as a gift and only asks that she be allowed to give it up herself. She would like the Queen to pay a visit to Egypt or Turkey upon which she can meet her. If none of these options work, a ceremony, in London, at Buckingham Palace, would be acceptable, as well.'

Next to Louis, the consul perked up, saying, 'That is very generous! Her Majesty would be most pleased. I am sure one of those options can be arranged.'

Louis's mind raced. The Cleopatra Cerulean Crown was a special one, no doubt, but having researched its origins with Mervat, knowing that it was a family heirloom and understanding its connection with Egyptian culture, it seemed sad to him that it would be given up in such a manner. And though it might cost him dearly, Louis had to speak up.

'I wonder why Gulnur Hanem wishes to do this? Does she not wish for the crown to pass to her daughter?'

The khedive lifted an eyebrow at this, but he translated the question in Turkish. Sir Stuart groaned beneath his breath, an expression of his exasperation towards Louis.

Gulnur Hanem stared icily at him whilst answering and waiting for the khedive to translate.

'She says her daughter cares little for the trappings of royalty. She would sooner donate the crown to a museum and have the common people enjoy it for free, then ever wear it herself. And why, she asks of Viscount Wesley, did he not go through with his marriage to Nadine. Was her wealth not required for his estate in England?'

The khedive watched Louis closely as he made the translation. Was that suspicion against him still there? And Hussam was nowhere in sight to help him along in fighting it.

Louis smiled, tried to muster as much charm in it as he could. 'Alas, Allenborough is still without a viscountess, but the Arabs have a beautiful saying that I must trust in, as well. *Kism wa naseeb*. One's destiny and share in life will be realised. Sometimes we do not know from whence or how things will turn out but we trust that they *will* turn out the way they were supposed to.'

'Indeed,' the khedive said with a scoff.

Louis focused on Mervat's mother. Gulnur Hanem must know he cared for her daughter and that her daughter would have done anything except for marrying a man she did not love in order to make her mother happy. He had once scorned Mervat for wanting to please her, but he wondered at the older woman before him now, clinging to the trappings of court. Gulnur Hanem wanted to stay at Sesostris, earn her place. She was even willing to give up her crown to do it.

Was there a way Louis could change her mind? Bring her closer to Mervat's side, for Mervat's sake?

Perhaps Gulnur Hanem thought Queen Victoria would appreciate the gift, make her a dear friend, but the truth was that the crown jewels were easily forgotten, pulled out on special occasions only. Were it not for the controversy around the koh-i-noor and how it had come to be, it too would have been merely one jewel in a court of many of them. Special mostly because of its carat count, its financial value. Louis's grandfather had believed that.

The Cleopatra Cerulean, on the other hand, was more a boon for archaeologists, historians.

Louis said, 'I am afraid Her Majesty has much more comelier pieces in her collection, that this one is worthless in the grand scheme of it.'

'Viscount, you mustn't be impertinent towards a gift freely given.' Sir Stuart widened his eyes, reprimanding him as one would a misbehaving child.

'I only mean to say as someone who has written on the crown's origins,' Louis said, gesturing towards it enthusiastically and moving towards the khedive with the express intent to convince him first, 'that it is a brilliant idea to put the crown in a museum. Indeed, it would be a boon to the country. Visitors would come from England and everywhere else my writings on it have reached. I would even suggest putting it in a museum in Tanta where the jewel initially came from so that tourism would spread to every corner of the country. People come to Cairo for the pyramids and travel to Upper Egypt for the Valley of the Kings. What if they could make a stop through the Nile Delta, Rosetta where the French found the Rosetta Stone and—'

'Which has come to the British Museum in England,' Sir Stuart interrupted. 'I must insist we talk about the options, so generously presented by Gulnur Hanem, with the Queen's office *before* entertaining talk of a museum.'

There was a warning there, but Louis would not stop. Here was an opportunity he must seize. A chance to show Mervat how very much he cared for her. That he valued what they'd worked on and saw now that it wasn't about one project, that he hoped theirs could be a partnership that involved *many* projects and a few of a very personal and intimate nature.

'We have not yet taken any options to the Queen's office. And surely, Her Majesty would love a gesture of goodwill—she is all grace.' Sir Stuart gestured towards the khedive, asking him to translate to Gulnur Hanem. 'Surely an option where her presence is requested to inaugurate a museum in Egypt would be appreciated.'

'Indeed,' the khedive said and translated for Mervat's mother. She didn't look as convinced, but then Louis countered, 'Obviously, this option would give Gulnur Hanem the meeting she wishes for *and* be a way to show her devotion, *Turkish* devotion, to the nation in which she now belongs.'

Louis stepped away, satisfied he'd made a successful argument. He knew it by the way the woman's hands fell to her side and how pleased the khedive was when he said, 'Hussam did say you had good ideas. I will call you to write about the museum opening in Tanta when we are ready.'

'As always, it will be my pleasure, Your Highness.'

Louis bowed before rushing from the khedive's office, but he could not avoid Sir Stuart who caught him by the sleeve and stopped him near the carriage. 'You put Turkey and the Ottomans ahead of British interests.'

'I only meant to honour the artifact. The people and cultures who brought it into being. Surely, understanding the sovereignty of all would bring about goodwill between all. Were I to speak to our Queen, I dare say she too would agree.'

'You will never speak with her,' Sir Stuart spat. And then he went on to announce in no uncertain terms, 'And, I am afraid, that the British Embassy in Cairo will no longer require your services, Viscount.'

Louis should have been upset, disappointed that he had lost the post he'd yearned for since his arrival in Egypt. But all he could muster was relief.

He was free.

Chapter Twenty-Eight

Mervat

It was Monday and Mervat had not been able to stop thinking about Louis's latest article in the *Telegraph*. Her mother's crown as the highlight of a new museum in Tanta? She only wanted to ponder it, go to her room and analyse it again and again, each word he had chosen and what it might mean to know his state of mind, his feelings towards her now he was set to marry Nadine. But Baba had insisted she spend the day finding a new project. He had even gone out of his way to speak to Mr Ali at the Al-Azhar Library on the previous Friday.

'Maybe it is better if I do not go with you to *Jumuah*,' she said, 'so you can meet other people.'

Mervat's melancholy must have been concerning because Baba acted very strangely that morning, going so far as to pick out her fanciest kaftan—a pink damask so pale it was nearly white, with gold thread–patterned embroidery along the front and clusters of pearls that looked like cotton blossoms.

And though she said it was fine enough for a wedding, that she couldn't go out with it in the middle of the day, Baba said Mr Ali, knowing now that she was an Egyptian princess, would have to clear the library. 'You must wear your *milaya* over top of it.'

He insisted too on getting her a *hantoor*. 'You cannot walk dressed like this.'

Mervat agreed because she hadn't the heart to tell Baba that, in truth, she had no idea what she would research. Her mind was too occupied with one thought. Or rather, one man.

'Why not delay until the carriage comes for Amu Taha on Thursday then? Instead of the marketplace, I will go to the library,' she protested. She was eager to hear of news from the palace. And doubted she would be able to focus on a new project until she learned anything she could from him. Amu Taha was from Tanta, his knowledge of the city might be more valuable to the khedive in establishing a museum rather than his position guarding their house, where the most eventful occurrences were getting chickens for their new coop or deciding what to do with the abundance of their garden's zucchinis.

'Mr Ali has reserved the time, says he must close off the library so you will have free rein, as you did the last time you were there.'

She would not dwell on how Louis had been there that last time.

Mervat once again wished she could get out of the trip, but Baba, sensing her reluctance, insisted on accompanying her. Was he that desperate to see her occupied he had to make sure of it? She'd been surprised enough when he'd returned late but happy on Friday, saying he'd spoken to many at the Azhar and one Mr Ali who, when he realised who Baba was, said Mervat was one of the smartest women he'd ever seen in his library.

Mervat wondered how the librarian knew Baba was her father. She hated thinking that Mr Ali might only have approached him because he now knew she was a princess and therefore her father might be influential and benefit him in some way. Such was the lingering repercussions of life at court: where before Mervat had not suspected people of having ulterior motives, now she was aware that they often did.

Baba was never friendly with people, but Amu Taha's presence had altered him this past while. Mustafa had been a kindly guard, ensuring he was taken care of, but not like Amu Taha who he played backgammon with and sipped his afternoon tea next to. They'd become almost like brothers and if Mr Ali took advantage somehow, Baba could be set back.

Her father needed friends in his life as did Mervat. Ones to curb the loneliness. Ones with similar interests. She'd have liked it to be Nadine—but that did not work out. And while she realised that Louis had been a friend to her, that did not work out either.

In the end, that was the main reason Mervat decided to dress like a princess and humour Baba. She had no topic in mind to research, she would go to gauge Mr Ali's intentions and tell him plainly that *if* she were to return to al-Azhar on a regular basis, it would be only on the days when the library was open to women and she would be dressed in her regular garb.

Not as a princess of the harem, but as a daughter of Egypt.

Al-Azhar was nearly empty when she and Baba arrived, much like that day when she and Nadine had gone there. Then, Louis had been in the courtyard and her heart had clenched in excitement at the sight of him. Now the corridor was empty and her heart clenched with melancholy.

Mervat could not help but question her deep sadness. Would she end up like her great-grandmother, a talented woman who, having been ripped from the man she loved and forced into a life she abhorred, could only see death around her?

Mervat still had Baba to take care of. She had to do better for him at least.

If Louis were here, he might tell her to experience the moment, to see the beauty in it.

Even as she thought it, a butterfly fluttered before Mervat. It was a commonly coloured one, brown and black with white dots, not particularly breathtaking in its beauty, but it was a variety that was rare in Egypt, nearly impossible this time of year and so far from the banks of the Nile or any flower patches.

Mervat followed its trajectory, lifting her veil to do so properly, her vision blurred slightly, until it landed on the library doors.

Mr Ali stood there, but he wasn't alone.

Louis.

She perceived her father squeezing her hand, the smile in his words when he said, 'Your viscount arranged this meeting. He has something important to ask you.'

'*Ahlan wa sahlan*, Princess Mervat,' Mr Ali said, greeting her first.

Louis might have been speaking to her next, but if he said anything she did not hear it for her gaze was fixed on her father giving the hand he held of hers—her right—up to him.

She nearly shivered at Louis's touch. Yet, the heat in her body, the flush rising from her very core to her cheeks, deigned to tell a different story.

'*Shukran.*' He thanked her father in Arabic, not meeting her gaze until Mr Ali and Baba had left them alone. Louis pulled her into the surprising brightness of the library.

All the windows were open and there were flowers, pots of them where books and parchments might have been. As if the place had been decorated for a party.

'Mervat,' he heaved her name. He took her other hand,

held her gaze intently, his pupils sweeping back and forth to be sure she continued to look at him.

She wished she could utter his name, tell him how much she missed him. How she had ached in his absence, how her life had felt meaningless. But he had chosen Nadine as his viscountess. Hadn't he?

'Your father mentioned I had something to ask you, he's quite confident what your answer will be but I confess that despite my efforts to prepare for today's surprise, I wonder if it was ill-advised to not acquaint you with my intent earlier than now. I have missed you terribly. From the moment under the Banyan tree when you slid out of my life, I have sought a path and…you did not return to the study to meet me. I waited for you there as long as I could. Perhaps you came after or perhaps the whole turmoil with what happened before Hussam found us or with the khedive changed your mind?'

He chuckled nervously, shook his head as if he couldn't find the right words, 'I am become a rambler.'

Mervat smiled despite wondering what he was trying to say, 'I cannot be one to accuse a person of rambling.'

He shook his head, pulled her hands to his lips, peppered her knuckles with small kisses. 'I have missed your talks. With my entire being, I have anguished over them, played them in my head and felt bereft.'

'You knew where my father's house was,' she said, drawing enough strength to pull her hands away, clasp them behind her back. Pretend to be angrier than she was for his sentiments rang true of her experiences? And then there was the matter of Nadine. The things she had heard him say that night. 'You might have visited.'

'Hussam warned me to wait it out until there was no longer a threat to you from the khedive…and for my part, I wished to make myself worthy of your acceptance. Rather than be a man who would only be *visiting*. I am greedy, Mervat, a man in love with you who did not want to come until I could have you completely.'

She focused on Hussam's warning, rather than the declaration embedded in Louis's words. 'Did you lose your post with the British consul?'

'I did, indeed.' He looked happy despite this answer.

Confused, she offered, 'I can talk to Hussam, make it right.'

'No, I don't want that. The consul didn't like my idea of starting a museum with the crown.' Louis marched to one of the tables, picked up a newspaper left there. He flipped through the pages. 'I wrote about it last week, the decision to open a museum in Tanta.'

Mervat surprised him when she said, 'I've read it.'

'You have?' Louis set down the paper and returned to where she stood.

'Yes.'

'And were you pleased?'

'It is a fine idea.'

'It was yours initially, and when your mother reminded me of it, I knew it was the best thing to do to prove to you how very much I wish to be a part of your life.'

Mervat's heart pounded, but even if what he said now was true... 'You were engaged to Nadine. I heard you say she would make a lovely viscountess.' She watched carefully for his reaction, registered the confusion in Louis's face, the widening of his eyes in realisation.

'I meant none of it, I promise. It was Hussam's ploy and a brilliant one really. I used to bail him out when he'd get in trouble at Eton. And he came through for me, for us, with that one. Nadine, you will happily know, is to be married to an Iranian prince and Hussam has some news which I will let him share with you.'

She barely heard the last bit. 'You don't think I wouldn't fit into life at Allenborough?'

'I never thought that! But I fretted that you would not feel at ease there. You are a princess in her own right, but more than that, you are the princess of my heart and soul.' He looked shy for having said it, but quickly moved on, 'Did you know that my family already loves you? For two reasons. First, from my letters extolling your virtues and second because—'

Mervat cut him off with a gasp of relief. She clasped both hands over her mouth to stymie the tears of joy that would have fallen.

'Sweet, darling Mervat.' Louis closed the distance between them and gently lifted her hands away from her mouth to hold them in his own. 'And second,' he continued, 'they love you for the opportunities you have brought to Allenborough. My father says that he and my stepmother argue about who is most responsible for the monies being invested in the land. He says it is I, for I am his son and a "father must be proud", whilst she takes your side not only because "women must stick together", but because she knows that I could not have written so successfully about the Cleopatra Cerulean without you as a muse. And my stepmother is right.'

'Opportunities? So Allenborough prospers?'

'It begins too, yes. Change is slow—they have hired a few people to help with the main house, but say if we would rather stay alone when we visit, they will build a cottage. I told them my grandfather's rectory would suffice. That you are a humble princess.'

What could he mean? Why did Louis speak of them as a couple?

'I too should like to visit them one day,' she said, hesitation in her words. 'Although I would have to travel there with Baba or Anne.'

He could not possibly mean that he and she would be married. They were different. Their backgrounds in particular. Was this very building not proof of it? She would come to al-Azhar to read or pray; he would come to write an article as a foreigner experiencing the unfamiliar.

Louis said, 'Actually, they would not need to come. Mervat, earlier your father said I had a question to ask you and you must know, that I have considered the angles of it thoroughly.'

He took a deep breath before continuing, 'Egyptian and Islamic law requires a Muslim woman to marry a Muslim man. I have been taking lessons here with a *shaykh* recommended by Mr Ali. I have converted to Islam of my own accord and would remain a Muslim no matter your answer to my question. I should admit that I once observed you praying in the mosque at Sesostris and it had guilted me to witness it but am grateful for it now. At the time, it hurt to know that you would not be content with the differences in our faiths. You would never ask me to convert for you, but you could not be content with a future in which our beliefs, our values were at odds. Trust, my darling Mervat, that that will not be a factor.'

Louis exhaled and smiled. 'I dare say that with the practice of Islam I have come to know a kind of peace in my heart that has been a surprise. I believe my grandfather would approve. He once spoke of watching a group of Afghans praying on a battlefield, how their frame of mind seemingly without fear prompted feelings of...' He let the sentence falter.

Perhaps he could see her struggling to make sense of what

was happening. Mervat understood what Louis was saying but try as she might to guess the question he wished to ask, she could not.

Even before their first meeting at the Louvre, she'd never really allowed herself to think of a future. And even since, she'd only known what she did *not* want.

She did not want to marry Hussam.

She did not want to disappoint her mother.

She did not want to live at court.

Her genealogy projects had been fun, time-consuming explorations, but she'd never really thought about her own place in them. Maybe that was why Mervat had struggled to find something new since she had known Louis.

Behind him now, the butterfly she'd seen in the courtyard, fluttered around a vase of flowers.

Louis seeing where her gaze had gone, said, 'The flowers are for us. Your father is just outside, waiting for your answer. He has given his blessing. Said he would ensure you wore a lovely dress, but I told him you could come in the plainest of frocks and still be the most beautiful woman in the world and only your answer would make me the happiest man alive.'

Mervat removed her *milaya* so he could see the dress Baba had chosen.

He swallowed deeply and when he looked into her eyes, he didn't have to say the words.

She felt like the most beautiful woman in the world when he looked at her like that. She had never seen Louis look at another woman like that. It seemed foolish now that she'd ever believed he wished to marry Nadine.

'Your mother will be here by now too,' Louis stressed. 'She said she would bring a platter of Turkish delight despite Amu Taha insisting on going to Tanta specifically for the sweets you like.'

'Anne is here?' Mervat still was not sure what exactly she was here for, but if it meant that she could be reconciled with her mother in some way, then she would not question it. Only be grateful to the man before her for Louis had arranged it. He had honoured her mother and her family via the museum. It would be her lasting legacy; she could invite Anne's sister from Turkey. Go and visit the country again, her head held high.

'Yes.'

She hugged him so suddenly, Louis was nearly knocked back but his arms came around her and he laughed.

'Hussam too. He helped me arrange it all,' he said. 'Though we should probably not delay much longer for his father has him courting all the daughters whose fathers he hopes to utilise in some way. I dare say that having Egypt's most eligible bachelor working his charms is serving the khedive well.'

Mervat pulled away from his embrace. She circled the table behind him, rejoiced as he followed her path. Looking over her shoulder at Louis, she asked, 'Why are we here, Louis? I have queried the different angles, but cannot guess what the question you wish to ask me is.'

'Can you not?' He grabbed her hand, made her stop to face him. Then he led her to the cabinet with Egypt's royal family tree. From it, he took a box, the one that had once held the Cleopatra Cerulean Crown, but when he opened it now, it was a jewellery set: a gold necklace, earrings, three bangle bracelets and a ring.

The ring he lifted and slipped onto her middle finger. It fit perfectly.

He swallowed when he looked at Mervat. 'Your mother helped me choose the *shabka* set from a jeweller who supplies the royal family. She has fine taste, clearly, but I especially liked the symbolism infused in the filigree and inlaid enamel cloisonné. The jeweller said the design and process emerged from the Fatimid period in Egypt. The Fatimids built this complex, the world's first university, and they were the ones to find and name this city Al Qahira. Cairo, the Victorious. And I am hoping that on this day, your *katb el-kitab* marriage ceremony, that I will also will be victorious in obtaining a *yes*.'

With a furtive glance towards the door behind them, Louis bent until his perfect nose nearly touched hers. 'I fear they have waited for my bumbling self too long and may intrude on us, demanding your answer to a question I have not yet asked.'

'Then ask it!' She teased, 'You really have turned into a rambler.'

The left half of his mouth lifted in a charming grin. 'Will you be my wife, Mervat Abbas?'

Her *katb el-kitab* day? Louis was asking her to marry him? All his talk had come down to one simple question with a very easy answer.

'Yes.'

Almost as soon as she said it, the library was flooded with those who'd been waiting. The high-pitched *zarghoota* sound her mother made trilled joy in her whole being.

Anne hugged her while Baba kissed her cheek. Amu Taha shook hands with her and so did Hussam, who'd brought his aunt to the ceremony, as well. It was a small, intimate occasion and Louis said something about having them all to Allenborough for a grander one in future.

The rest of the day passed in a blur. The ceremony itself was quick, during which the al-Azhar imam ensured that she consented to the marriage and that the bridegroom had made sufficient promises to care for her and treat her kindly in all matters. Louis's *mahr*, or dowry gift, was the jewellery set, and after Anne put the rest of it on her, the imam asked for both their signatures on a marriage certificate. He then opened his palms to read the opening *surah* of the Quran, Al-Fatiha, and all put together their palms, following along. He offered the new couple a *dua*, a small prayer that theirs be a companionship filled with love and children who would be a balm to their souls.

'*Ameen!*' the room chorused in unison, rubbing their hands across their faces. Mervat looked at them, the people she loved most in this world and though they were not many, she knew that they were enough. That, with them, she should never be lonely.

She caught Louis's eye when he lowered his hands to his sides and Mervat was sure she'd never seen him more handsome, if that were possible. And more than that, he looked as happy as he had made her.

Mervat wouldn't remember all the words spoken during her *katb el-kitab*, but Louis would record them in his notebook later. As for her, she would always remember the experience of blissful contentment. She might not have planned for her future nor ambitiously sought out opportunities to seize one of her making, but Mervat had been blessed all the same.

Chapter Twenty-Nine

Louis

Louis watched his new bride as Mervat gazed at the street below from the balcony of his flat. It was dusk on an evening very much like the one when he had first arrived in Cairo. He found his notebook, read the details he'd jotted back then. Everything had changed for him in the span of a few months and all because of the woman he loved in front of him, the pyramids silhouetted behind her.

Tonight was their wedding night and he wondered if Mervat was nervous or if it was something else? Earlier, she'd said little as he tried to make a case for her agreeing to marry him. And then, even during the marriage ceremony, she had mostly been quiet. Contemplative. Shyer than her usual self.

Louis set down his notebook and joined her on the balcony. He inhaled the breezy Cairo night. It had been hot when he'd first arrived; now winter was in the air, the clouds above heavy with the scent and promise of rain.

Mervat's hand gripped the railing, and as he took his place beside her, he set his own next to hers. She stared down at where their hands met. 'Will it ever stop feeling like this? The butterfly in my stomach when you are near?'

'I hope not. I endeavour to spend my life making you want me as I you.'

She lifted her hands away and brushed her fingers through her curls. 'You were writing?'

He nodded. 'Capturing the experience as I am wont to do. Yet, for the life of me, I could not understand the Quranic verse the imam cited. Did you happen to catch it? The word he used sounded like *mawada.*'

The melody of Mervat's voice as she recited the entire verse in Arabic brought on Louis's own butterflies.

'It is a common verse noted in weddings. It translates to, *"And of God's signs is that He has created mates for you from your own kind that you may find peace in them and He has set between you love and mercy."* The word *mawada* means love, but it is more than love, it is a kind of friendship. A love built on friendship.'

Louis asked, 'Like ours?'

Mervat smiled. 'Like ours.'

'I fear I threw too much at you today, all at once. That I didn't even give you a chance to think, to say no. That you feel I might have swindled you into agreeing to become my wife.'

She shook her head. 'You thought of all the details. I know that. It wasn't a chance opportunity that you seized and were depending on luck for. You took the time and effort to know me, *befriend* me.' Mervat laughed and it was glorious. 'The very feat it must have taken to get Anne to send over my bridal trousseau from Sesostris! I don't even know all that's in it, what she ordered from Paris when she thought I was going to marry Hussam.'

'It wasn't a feat, Mervat. She loves you, she is just a scared woman—thinking her life would be one thing and finding something else. Once I figured out that she wasn't very different than my grandfather, she was easy to charm.'

'Ahh, the famous Viscount Louis Wesley charm.' She kissed the palm he put to her cheek.

He lifted a brow and teased, 'Or maybe it was the promise I'd send an invitation to the Queen for our wedding party in Allenborough. Your mother *may* be disappointed when she does not accept—it will be too late then.'

'Perhaps I should search said trousseau for a...*sleeping* gown? Only, I've been wearing this all day and...'

'Sure. Yes. Certainly.' He led her inside the apartment, closed the balcony door and drew the curtain. While Mervat had gone to the bedroom chamber where the clothing chest was put, Louis lit candles, and brewed a pot of tea. He hadn't thought of supper but he put out *feteer meshaltit*, the croissant-like but crispier flat bread he'd purchased the day before with a bowl of olives and a creamy cheese blend he kept in the icebox. He loaded a small bowl with chopped cucumber and spooned apricot preserves into another.

It was hardly dinner, but this was the heart of Cairo and he could find a food stand open at all hours of the night, if his wife got hungry.

My wife. Even as Louis thought it such a glorious title, Mervat slid behind him. She clasped his waist, the only material between them his shirt and the transparent layer of silk she wore, which he saw when he turned to face her. He took her hands in his own and stepped back to take her in.

His gaze paused on the straps holding up the gown, thinner than ribbons. The soft brown skin of her neck, shoulders, clavicle beckoned to him. Nectar he had to sample.

'I do not have to ask any more.' She arched to him, tilted her head, knowing what and where he sought, granting his lips permission. Louis dipped, found a landing spot in the valley below the lobe of her right ear. He kissed, soft and gentle at first, then sucked with more pressure until she groaned with pleasure and he had to fight himself not to have her then and there.

'Your tea is cold,' he whispered against her ear, proud of his forbearance. 'A small supper.'

'And what if I do not want food nor drink?'

'I would not force you to do anything you do not want,' he said, 'but humbly suggest you might want to keep your strength. Also, I cannot abide being a husband who does not fulfil his wife's every need.'

Mervat grabbed his head and surprised him with a quick, happy kiss on his lips. 'Very well, *husband*. Feed me.'

She took the seat he offered, let him tuck her into it even though it wasn't a grand dining table and this wasn't a formal setting. 'There might be parties at Allenborough, not the Queen mind you, but with your approval and support, I hope to use some of my earnings to nurture the land. Make strong the title, uplift the surrounding areas.' Louis tore off a piece of the *feteer*, dipped it in the cheese and brought the bite to her lips.

Her eyes twinkled in the candlelight as she plucked it between her teeth and drew back to chew it out of his reach. 'What earnings? You said you lost your position at the embassy?'

'Are you worried about being poor, Princess?' he teased, then made himself a bite. He caught her staring at his mouth and he lifted his chin, licked the back of his thumb as if to say it could have been her thumb. He stretched his foot slowly beneath the table, letting his toe brush hers and knowing he'd succeeded in the desired effect when she closed her eyes and brought her feet together.

Louis would enjoy testing how often and in what ways he could make those butterflies in Mervat's belly somersault. 'Hmm?' he prompted.

'No.'

Was that frustration he detected?

'Tell me then, why?'

She fixed him with a knowing gaze. 'You are determined to make me talk.'

'When have you ever known me *not* to be a determined man who seizes opportunities?' He pitted an olive for her but rather than bringing it to her mouth, he placed it in the palm of his hand like a gift, gestured as if to say she should eat it herself.

Mervat caught on to his game, and before she took it to her mouth, she said, 'Tell me how then you will keep me not poor.'

Her mouth stayed open as she held the olive there, her eyes wide. Anticipating.

'Although I suspect Sir Stuart would gladly take me back, I have been offered a position as international correspondent with a New York newspaper. My pieces will be syndicated across Europe and the world. And it comes with a book agreement, a memoir of my travels. I will need to retain the services of a researcher, of course. An educated, smart young woman who fancies genealogies and spending time in museums and libraries.'

Louis quite enjoyed watching her eyes widen with unbridled joy, he even feared she would choke on the olive she was playing wanton with. She leapt from her chair to hug him, falling into his lap and his embrace as she did. 'Truly?'

He clutched her waist, brought her as close to him as possible. 'Unless you don't want the position? I *could* retain the services of a secretary.'

'Stop teasing me.'

'I'm charming you.'

'You are. You have. You always will charm me. My viscount. I love you, Louis.'

He swallowed at the playfulness and then sudden seriousness in her voice. The tears which swelled in her eyes.

He pushed her curls behind her head, cupped her beautiful heart-shaped face in his hands and stared into her eyes for a long moment.

'And I love you, Mervat. Everything I am and will ever be is yours. You have made me the happiest man alive and I will gladly spend my lifetime ensuring you too are happy, fulfilled.'

She bit her lower lip before speaking again. 'My mother's grandmother…sometimes I feel like I will be her. I have these depths of emotion. A brokenness because of the separation of my parents perhaps. I believe my incessant talking was to fill the silences, but what if it drives you mad? What if I push you away? I am weak.'

'You could never do that. Silly girl, do you not know that by now?' he scolded. 'I will always listen to your talks, Mervat. My dear, it is as if my ears have been imprisoned in your absence, how I have longed to hear them. As for your great-grandmother, she was taken from her home against her will. Forced to marry a man she did not love. Have you ever considered that those paintings were not her madness, but an abundance of talent which needed an outlet in a world that called her cursed? Even if I am wrong about her, I see you, Mervat. Know you. You stood against everyone, the khedive of Egypt himself, to ensure that your fate would not be the same as hers. My sweet, beautiful wife, you are authentic and honest, but most importantly—you are strong.'

His hands were wet with her tears, but even as Louis wiped them away, they had ceased. She wrapped her arms around his neck, lifted her lips to his. 'Love me,' she whispered.

Louis carried her to their marital bed, set her down in

front of it. He let her unbutton his shirt and trousers, stood patiently as her hands roamed and her gaze was filled with all of him.

Then she slipped off her dress, let his hands roam and his gaze fill with all of her.

Louis had wanted Mervat for so long. He would show her the rudimentary sketches he'd done of her after their first meeting in the Louvre. He'd tell her how woefully he'd fallen short of capturing her beauty or understanding then just how much she would come to mean to his life. How she had become everything.

But that would come tomorrow.

Tonight, there would be no words. There would only be deeds.

* * * * *

*If you enjoyed this story, be sure to read
Heba Helmy's debut Historical romance*

The Earl's Egyptian Heiress

HARLEQUIN
Reader Service

Enjoyed your book?

Try the perfect subscription for Romance readers and get more great books like this delivered right to your door.

See why over 10+ million readers have tried Harlequin Reader Service.

Start with a Free Welcome Collection with free books and a gift—valued over $20.

Choose any series in print or ebook.
See website for details and order today:

TryReaderService.com/subscriptions